PRAISE FOR SARIAH WILSON

The Friend Zone

"Wilson scores a touchdown with this engaging contemporary romance that delivers plenty of electric sexual chemistry and zingy banter while still being romantically sweet at its core."

—*Booklist*

"Snappy banter, palpable sexual tension, and a lively sense of fun combine with deeply felt emotional issues in a sweet, upbeat romance that will appeal to both the YA and new adult markets."

—*Library Journal*

The #Lovestruck Novels

"Wilson has mastered the art of creating a romance that manages to be both sexy and sweet, and her novel's skillfully drawn characters, deliciously snarky sense of humor, and vividly evoked music-business settings add up to a supremely satisfying love story that will be music to romance readers' ears."

—*Booklist*, starred review, *#Moonstruck*

"Making excellent use of sassy banter, hilarious texts, and a breezy style, Wilson's energetic story brims with sexual tension and takes readers on a musical road trip that will leave them smiling. Perfect as well for YA and new-adult collections."

—*Library Journal*, *#Moonstruck*

Roommaid

Roommaid

a Novel

SARIAH WILSON

Published by Montlake, Seattle

www.apub.com

Amazon, the Amazon logo, and Montlake are trademarks of Amazon.com, Inc., or its affiliates.

ISBN-13: 9781542023801
ISBN-10: 1542023807

Cover design by Philip Pascuzzo

Printed in the United States of America

For my aunt Pixie and her Pigeon

CHAPTER ONE

"Do you know what this apartment has?" Frederica asked me as she threw her arms wide, like she was the ringmaster about to introduce the clowns.

Which felt like an appropriate gesture, given how my life was going.

"Madison." She said my name, trying to get me to pay attention. "Do you know what this apartment has?"

She was obviously expecting a response equal to her level of theatrics. "A staph infection? Flesh-eating bacteria? A hantavirus?"

My real estate agent / aunt glared at me. "Wrong. The correct answer is it has nine-foot ceilings. Do you have any idea how hard it is to find this ceiling height in an apartment in the city at this price?"

The city was Houston, Texas. And I chalked up not noticing how tall the ceilings were to my upbringing. Because I'd grown up in one of the largest mansions in the state, nice things felt normal. Comfortable. But given my decision to become a teacher (a career choice my family heartily disagreed with by cutting me off, kicking me out of the house, and rescinding my trust fund), I was quickly finding out that on my salary I couldn't afford said nice things. Or even semilivable things.

I knew Frederica was getting frustrated with me. She had shown me dozens of apartments that were either too far away from my job as a second-grade teacher at Millstone Academy, or else they'd been completely terrible. Like they sported their own special petting zoos that consisted of cockroaches, ants, and bedbugs. Or they'd been little more than a dumping ground for cinder blocks, old magazines, and used tires.

But I couldn't afford better. When I'd opened my first paycheck, I had audibly gasped. The total net amount (after some jerk named FICA took most of my money) was for less than what I used to spend in hair maintenance every month. I didn't know how anyone was supposed to live on such a tiny amount.

Or how I was supposed to save up enough money for first and last month's rent as well as a deposit. I also needed to get a car to get to and from work and run errands. Apparently I needed to put a deposit down for that, too.

No matter how hard I tried, it felt impossible to set aside money. I had been crashing on my best friend Shay's couch for the last three months.

After I'd told her I'd be living with her for only two weeks.

It was way past time for me to move out.

This apartment seemed decent and was only a half hour away from work. I'd really wanted to be closer to the school but at this point I was going to have to take what I could get. I could make this tiny apartment work. I knew Frederica had grown tired of dragging me all over the city. Especially since she wasn't earning a commission and was running the risk of incurring my mother's wrath by helping me.

I figured she was doing it because, secretly, I'd always been her favorite niece.

Which was not a hard contest to win. My older twin sisters were terrible. The oldest, Violet, had been groomed to take over my dad's finance company. She was cutthroat and ambitious and did the Huntington name proud. Vanessa, since she hadn't gone into the family business, went the other acceptable route—she was married to a vice president at Daddy's company, had three children with a fourth on the way, and rubbed her Perfect Life in my face every chance she got. Both of my sisters were snobby, self-centered suck-ups who had always made my life miserable.

Frederica's voice pierced my thoughts, interrupting them. "This is a nice one, right?"

It was. I had opened my mouth to say as much when I caught the expression on her face. There was something she wasn't telling me. "Yes, it's nice. But what aren't you saying?"

"Oh." She waved one hand in the air, as if to suggest that I was being silly. "Nothing. It's got these great ceilings and laminate wood floors. It should work for you."

She was fine with laminate wood floors? Now I knew something was up. "Tell me."

"Fine." She turned the word into four syllables. "If you must know, the previous tenant was slightly . . . murdered here a year ago."

"Murdered?" I repeated. "As in, somebody came in and killed the person who lived here? The police found the body in this very apartment? This was a crime scene?" I folded my arms across my chest, suddenly afraid to touch anything.

"I mean, it was just the one person. It's not like some serial, ongoing situation. A crime of passion, apparently, and the man is good and locked up. So no need to worry. I only told you because the law requires me to. And it shouldn't really matter because lots of people die in houses."

That was probably true enough, but there was no way I would live here. I could almost see the police tape and chalk outline. "This is a definite no."

I would take the cockroaches over this. I was not up for being haunted.

She sighed, ever so slightly and dramatically, and opened the front door for me. I went out into the hallway while she locked up. Even though I knew it was all in my head, the hallway suddenly seemed dark and foreboding. As if crime-passioned murderers were waiting in every shadow. I felt a rush of relief when we exited the building, grateful for the setting sun.

We didn't say much as I followed her back down to her beloved car, a Ferrari she had named J. Lo. The color of the Ferrari was what Frederica called *Louboutin red*. It was her signature color. Right now, it was the shade of lipstick she wore, the color of her silk blouse, and the soles on the bottom of her high heels. Her expensive taste reminded me how much money she usually made finding homes for Houston's elite, and I felt instantly guilty that I had been wasting so much of her time.

"She's a beauty," I said, trying to get back on her good side by complimenting the Ferrari.

Her broad smile indicated that I'd accomplished my task as we slid onto the soft-as-butter leather seats. "She is. Are you still planning on buying a car of your own?"

"I am." I'd only recently acquired my license. It hadn't been necessary growing up since my family's drivers had always taken me everywhere I needed to go. My mother had often wondered aloud why Huntington women would even need a driver's license. It made "no rational sense" to her.

Not surprisingly, neither one of my sisters had a license.

And neither one of them had their own personal car, either.

I felt great pride that I'd be the first in my immediate family. "I'm even thinking about getting a used car." If that didn't send my mom into a fit of vapors, I didn't know if anything ever would. My mother refused to touch anything that had been used by someone else, which included such things as hotel sheets and duvets, towels at the gym, and bathrobes at her favorite spa. It gave me a small, rebellious thrill to plan on buying a car that had been previously owned.

"You should try the Ares dealership."

"Ares?" I echoed her recommendation. "Isn't that the car rental company?"

"Yes, but once their cars hit a certain mileage they sell them. So you can get an, er, *used* car that's been reasonably looked after and presumably kept up well." She said the word *used* the same way my mother did: as if it were an unsightly and invasive mole that should be beaten over the head with a tack hammer for daring to disturb her prizewinning roses.

"I'll check it out." We reached the outskirts of the downtown area and I realized I didn't know if our apartment-hunting tour was over. "Did you have any place else to show me or are we calling it a day?"

Frederica drummed her red-lacquered fingernails against her steering wheel. "There is one more possibility I've been considering. But it's really unorthodox."

More unorthodox than murder apartments and bug paradises? "How so?"

We came to a red light and she reached inside her Prada purse to pull out her cell phone. She quickly thumbed through a couple of screens, mumbling something about Instagram before the light changed. She handed me her phone and then pulled forward.

On the screen was the most handsome man I'd ever seen in my entire life. And that included all the men in movies, magazine ads, and TV shows. He was . . . stunning. Golden-brown hair with piercing blue eyes, a jawline that was so killer it was begging for its own Lifetime movie, and a brilliant, warm smile that could melt the coldest, frostiest heart.

"He's . . . he's . . . he's . . . wow," was all I could come up with. I zoomed in a little on his face. This had to be some filter, or angle or trick of the light. Nobody was actually this gorgeous.

As if she could read my mind, Frederica announced, "He's even better looking in real life."

My mouth gaped. That was just . . . not possible. How could it be? I was sitting here assuming he was just one of those people the camera loved. To be fair, the camera didn't just love him; it also brought him flowers every day for a month, sang him ballads, and wanted to meet his parents.

I kind of wanted to do that, too.

"Who is this?" I finally choked the words out. I mean, if I was going to be introduced to his family, I should probably find out what his name was first.

"Tyler Roth. I met him at the Wesleys' charity ball. Something about underprivileged iguanas. Anyway, he was standing in a corner all by himself and my heart just went out to him. Nobody that delicious should ever be alone."

I nodded, fervently. In total agreement. The still-functioning part of my brain that hadn't been rendered a drooling mess by his photo wondered what Frederica's unorthodox plan concerning Tyler was. Maybe she wanted me to marry him and then I'd have someplace to live. If her plan involved me eloping with him to Vegas, I had the sneaking suspicion I was probably going to agree.

"And he told me that he travels quite a bit for his job and that he's been looking to find someone to live in his apartment and look after his dog, Pigeon. She has some anxiety issues and he doesn't want her to be alone. Isn't she a beautiful dog?"

She pointed at her phone and it was only then that I realized that there was also a dog in the picture. A golden retriever. "Yes. The dog. Beautiful." Not that I could really tell as my gaze quickly drifted back to Tyler.

"Tyler also needs someone to clean up the apartment. He's had some bad luck with housekeepers lately. And in exchange for looking after Pigeon and cleaning, he's willing to offer a rent-free room. I told him I'd keep an eye out for a good candidate."

While I had zero experience with caring for dogs, I had even less with housekeeping. "I would have to clean?"

Frederica seemed to have either forgotten how spoiled I'd been or didn't consider it to be an obstacle. "Mm-hmm. You'd be his roommate who cleans. Oh! His roommaid!" She eased her Ferrari over to the side of the road and grabbed her phone back. I felt a little bereft at losing it. "I'm going to text my attorney and see if I can trademark that word. *Roommaid*." She let out a little laugh at her own cleverness.

Her fingers kept flying over her keyboard while she announced, "And now I'm texting Tyler to see if we can stop by and see his place." She paused. "If you're interested."

It would make sense that she would ask. Excepting Shay, the potential roommate situation had been somewhat terrifying. I'd explored that on my own, and either I had the world's worst luck or there were a scary number of disturbing people out there looking for someone to share their apartment and their crazy. It was why my aunt had been focusing on places I could afford on my own.

But anybody who looked like Tyler did and loved his dog and was that handsome and that gorgeous couldn't be a bad guy, could he? Plus, Frederica was sort of vouching for him after speaking to him for ten minutes at a party.

That should definitely count for something. Right?

It was then that I realized my aunt was waiting for my response. "Yes, I'm interested." Holy crap was I interested.

She smiled and pushed the send button. As we waited, it suddenly occurred to me that his apartment might be terrible. And just as quickly I decided I didn't care. I would seriously consider moving into the murder apartment for this guy.

That might have made me shallow, but given that I'd made such a big noble sacrifice lately, I felt like I was owed some tiny bit of cosmic justice.

And possibly some exquisite eye candy.

I didn't realize that I'd been holding my breath until I heard the ding of a reply message.

Frederica grinned at me. "He says to head over and he'll meet us there as soon as he can. He said his doorman will let us into the apartment."

A doorman? I thought of Shay's fourth-floor walk-up and what a relief it would be to live in a building where there was someone who could help me carry my groceries upstairs. Who would get my packages before they were stolen. That there might be an actual elevator involved was enough to make me giddy.

On our drive over, Frederica told me more about her conversation with Tyler, which consisted mostly of them exchanging information about their dogs, while I resisted the urge to reach for her phone and get another happy eyeful. Then she said something that pulled me out of imagining Tyler and me as the stars of a music video, where we fell in love to the swelling of a poignant love song.

"He said he'd prefer a male roommate because in college he shared an apartment with a platonic female friend who ended up falling in love with him and made his home life miserable. He had to take out a restraining order."

I'd seen a picture of him. I could kind of see where she'd been coming from.

"But that won't be a problem for you because you're in a serious relationship," she said in a self-satisfied tone.

I was? Oh, she meant Brad. More accurately, Bradford Beauregard Branson IV. My high school sweetheart who hadn't spoken to me since my parents had cut me off.

Something nobody in my family knew, and I certainly wasn't in any hurry to tell them.

Because the Bransons were the very heart of Houston society. Pedigreed and wealthy and super connected. Being permanently tied to the Bransons was my mother's fondest wish. If telling her I wasn't going into the family business had thrown a hand grenade into the middle of our relationship, breaking up with Brad would be the equivalent of going nuclear.

I'd been quietly rebellious in a serious way, but it was something my parents could ignore while waiting for me to see the light and come around. Despite my recent bravery, I was not ready for the fallout of a rebellion that loud and major. There would be no forgiveness in this world or in the world to come.

So I ignored whatever our current relationship status actually was and pretended like we were fine. My mother and Frederica feuded on a regular basis (and it was another part of the reason I suspected Frederica was helping me find an apartment: to annoy my mom), but sometimes they were the best of friends. I couldn't risk the truth getting back to my mom. So I said, "Right. I have Brad and so I won't be romantically pursuing Tyler."

Technically it wasn't a lie. Because Brad and I hadn't officially broken up. Although I was taking his ghosting me as confirmation that our on-again, off-again relationship was finally dead and buried.

We arrived at the apartment building and Frederica parked right in front of it. "There's a parking garage," she told me. "But we're just running in and out today. I don't know if you're familiar with this part of town, but we're only ten minutes away from your school."

I was glad to hear it was so close. We got out of the car and headed for the front door.

Once we entered the building, I realized that Tyler had money. Not just doctor or lawyer money, but a lot of money.

A fact that was reconfirmed when the doorman took us up to the penthouse. I let out a sigh of comfort when we stepped inside. This felt familiar. A few months ago this place wouldn't have impressed me. I probably would have thought of it as being cozy or cute. But now it seemed practically palatial. The entire living area was surrounded by windows that looked out over the city. I guessed it would be stunning at night. There was a large balcony, where I could see myself having my morning coffee, watching the sun rise. I turned to see the kitchen, and even though it had top-of-the-line stainless steel appliances and quartz countertops, it looked very lived in. The sink was full of dirty dishes and there were a dozen different things scattered over the various countertops. It didn't seem like Tyler was a neat freak.

Clearly no one had died here recently, and it had not been invaded by any kind of insect. That was enough to make it the winner.

"What do you think?" Frederica asked once the doorman had left us alone.

"It's fantastic."

"Let's go see the rest of it," she said. We found the guest bedroom and I sat on the edge of the queen-size bed, bouncing up and down a little to test the comfort level. Definitely better than Shay's couch.

The room had been decorated in a mixture of blues and grays that I found soothing. I could easily live in this room. My aunt was saying something about hand-scraped hardwoods and Italian marble, but I ran over to check out the large walk-in closet. I practically wept with joy at the thought of not having to live out of my suitcases any longer.

It was in that moment that I realized I would do whatever I had to do to become Tyler's roommate. He wanted me to take care of his dog? I'd turn into Dr. Dolittle. He needed a clean home? Then I'd be . . . Marie Kondo? No, that was organizational stuff. Mary Poppins? She was the kid expert. Martha Stewart? More on the entertaining side of things.

An image and a name flashed in my mind. Mr. Clean! I would be Mr. / Dr. Clean-Dolittle. Practically perfect in every way.

"Isn't this wonderful?" Frederica asked me, clearly sensing how much I'd been won over, given her victorious and smug smile.

"I have to live here. I love it."

The elevator doors opened and closed and I heard a man say, "Pidge! I'm home! Where are you, girl?"

That had to be Tyler. And of course his voice was sexy, too. All deep and masculine and shiver inducing. I heard the skittering of claws on the floors and caught a glimpse of a golden, furry blur go racing by. I half wanted to run and jump into his arms, too.

Frederica grabbed my arm. "Come on, I can't wait to introduce you to Tyler."

The last time my heart had beaten this hard and my stomach fluttered this hard had been the first day of school with my very own class. When I was at the beginning of something special and important, knowing my life was never going to be the same again.

I just knew that the same was true here. Standing at a precipice, everything was about to change.

Time to meet Tyler Roth.

CHAPTER TWO

I stepped out into the hallway and made eye contact with him. The thumping and fluttering increased. Frederica had not lied. Tyler was a hundred times better looking in real life and I still didn't understand how that was possible. It also allowed me to notice some things that the picture hadn't revealed. Like how tall and broad he was. Lean and athletic, like a professional swimmer.

Yum.

"Close your mouth, sweetheart, before you catch some flies," my aunt murmured as she brushed past me. I obediently snapped my jaw shut.

"Hellooo!" she called out, waving her arm as she walked toward Tyler. "So good to see you again!" She reached up and planted a kiss on his left cheek and I'd never been so deeply jealous of her, ever.

"Hello again, Mrs. Johnson."

She slapped him gently on his upper arm. "Oh, stop that. I told you to call me Frederica." She was shamelessly flirting with him while I stood in the hallway like a mannequin. I cleared my throat, intending to speak but not quite able to.

As if that reminded my aunt that I was in the room, she turned toward me. "This is Madison. Like I said in my text, I think she'd be the perfect person to live in your spare room."

Part of me was irritated that I hadn't been allowed to even introduce myself. Once again, someone in my family was speaking for me. To be fair, my throat felt like it was stopped up by a big ice block and speech seemed highly improbable.

He came over, hand extended. "Nice to meet you, Madison. I'm Tyler."

When he said my name, every nerve ending inside me sparked to life. The picture also hadn't prepared me for how good he smelled. With all my senses in overload, I briefly wondered what would happen when I touched him. I reached for his proffered hand, and when my hand made contact with his, those same nerve endings exploded into roaring fireworks. My knees might have buckled slightly.

I nodded silently at him, wanting to say it was nice to meet him, too. Talking would be good but what I needed to do in that moment was let go of his hand before I seemed creepy.

It was harder than I would have thought, but I finally managed it.

"Madison is a second-grade teacher," Frederica said, interrupting my awkward moment. My annoyance was gone, and I was just thankful that she could talk for me. Or I was, up until the moment she said, "She's very responsible and tidy and she just loves animals."

I raised my eyebrows at her. Two of those things were untrue. I might have been responsible, but since moving out of my parents' home I had quickly discovered that I was kind of a slob. I'd never noticed it earlier because there was always someone picking up after me.

Animals had not been allowed in my home growing up. I'd begged for a kitten, but my father had said animals were for working. Our ranch had all sorts of horses and goats and chickens, but we were always too busy to go there.

"Good to know." He nodded.

"She also loves your apartment. How could she not? It is divine," Frederica added, running her hands along the books on one of his bookshelves. She stopped at one and pulled it out. "Is this a photo album? Do you mind?"

"Uh, no. Go ahead."

Well, what else could he say? *No, creepy older woman with an inappropriate crush on me, put that back?*

"Aw, look at you as a baby. So sweet," she said. Lacking the strength to intervene and not wanting to participate in her invasiveness, I stayed put. Even though I desperately wanted to stand next to her and see all the pictures of him. I bet he was adorable.

She went on: "Oh, what happened here?"

Now I got to feel jealous as he stood close to her, in order to look over her shoulder. "The brace? One of my legs was shorter than the other and they had to lengthen it. Bunch of surgeries throughout my childhood. I still have some metal parts in my leg that set off metal detectors, but on the positive side, it's aiding me in my quest to become a modern-day Frankenstein."

The humor in his voice melted something inside me and I found myself saying, "No way. You should aim higher. Bionic Man. Cyborg. RoboCop."

His attention was on me, his eyes sparkling with delight, and it was like all the air had been sucked out of the room. I couldn't breathe. "I could have used that kind of optimism when I was a kid. Back then I was just mad about always being picked last for PE."

I'd pick him first for PE. "They didn't let you join in any reindeer games?"

He grinned. "Nope."

Maybe this penthouse was deceiving and Tyler was more of an underdog than I'd thought. Having never been an underdog until recently, I felt an unexpected kinship for him.

Frederica put the photo book back on the shelf. If I moved in here, it was going to be the very first thing I'd be borrowing. Just for . . . informational purposes.

Tyler gestured toward the couches. "Should we sit? And can I get you something to drink?"

"Aren't you sweet and so well mannered," Frederica cooed as we sat down. "Your mama raised you right."

A strange, haunted look flittered across Tyler's face, then was gone just as quickly as it had appeared. "At the moment I have water and some kefir. Maybe some orange juice."

"We're fine," she assured him. He sat down across from us and I tried to tell myself to look away from his face, because it was like staring into the sun. Like how every time there's an eclipse scientists are constantly warning the public not to stare at it so as to not go blind, and everybody stares at it anyway.

Or how that woman in the Bible got turned into a pillar of salt because she couldn't stop looking back.

That was me. About to be blinded and salinated.

"So I should probably tell you a little about me. I'm twenty-six years old, work in finance, am relatively neat, enjoy making lists, and travel more than I'd like. Because it takes me away from this good girl. This is Pigeon." The dog was lying on the floor next to his feet, intermittently whimpering but stopping when Tyler petted her head.

I wondered why she hadn't challenged us when we came into the penthouse. Didn't dogs usually bark at strangers?

Tyler smiled at me and it was then I realized that if I didn't say something soon, he was going to throw me out for being a quiet weirdo and I'd lose this apartment. I needed to speak. I cleared my throat and settled on, "Is she okay?"

"Pidge is just anxious around people she doesn't know. The shelter I adopted her from thinks she was abused in her last home. It takes a while for her to warm up, but when she does, she'll be the best buddy you could ask for."

Why did the idea of him rescuing and loving an abused dog make my heart heat up and glow like a five-hundred-degree oven?

"That's one of the reasons why I wanted a roommate. So that Pigeon isn't left alone for four or five days at a time. I've tried taking her to a kennel or a doggy day care, but she's terrified of the other people and the other dogs. She needs someone here in her home, where she feels safe."

"You wouldn't have to worry about that," Frederica said. "Madison is not the kind of girl who will be out all the time. She has a serious boyfriend, Brad. They're high school sweethearts."

I tried not to flinch when she said that. It was sort of technically true, I reminded myself. Brad and I were high school sweethearts, and for all I knew, he might think we were together and he was still my boyfriend. Even though we hadn't spoken in months.

"In fact," she continued, "we're all expecting an announcement from these two any day now."

Again, still true. My mother had decided that once I graduated from college, Brad and I should get engaged. From what I'd heard last, she was still waiting for that to happen.

I couldn't miss the relief that was evident on Tyler's face. "That's great!" I wondered if it was great because it meant I wasn't going to throw myself at him, like that girl from college. Although now that I'd met him, I felt very empathetic toward her. I wondered how many women he had to fend off on a regular basis.

Probably thousands.

Then, as if to answer my unasked question, he said, "It's important that I have that boundary established with whomever I share an apartment with. That we agree to be roommates and friends and nothing more. I was in a bad situation when I was younger that got worse and worse, and I don't want to go through that again."

From what he was saying, the last thing he needed was another woman throwing herself at him. I decided then and there that I would put my shallow, massive, and recent crush aside so that I could live in this apartment. It was close to my school, and an actual penthouse with no vermin and still-living people in it. I could control my starved hormones that, given the weird and limbo state of my last relationship, seemed to be desperate for affection and attention.

Tyler would not be the guy to fix things.

"I'm on board for that." Even though my agreeing to keep my distance was stabbing tiny little knives into my heart.

"Good. I know this situation is a little unusual," he said. "And I hope you don't think I'm trying to take advantage of you or anything. You won't be my employee. We'll just be roommates with you picking up the slack while I'm gone."

I nodded. It all sounded perfect, but yes, a little unusual. I was concerned about the total absence of cleaning anything ever in my life and wanted to know more about what he expected. "Frederica mentioned that you've had to let housekeepers go in the past. Can I ask why? Were they not cleaning up to your standards?"

"What?" he asked with a laugh. "Oh, I'm not a neat freak or anything. I don't have to be able to eat off my kitchen floor." He swung one of his arms toward the kitchen to the mess in there. "As you can see. I'm not looking for it to be pristine, just kept up. And I do clean up after myself; I need someone who can help me out with that and get to the deeper cleaning I don't have time for. I could make you up a list, if that would be okay."

"Yeah, that would be great." Having his expectations laid out would definitely help me. I also loved a good list. I used them all the time in my classroom.

"I'll do that. And to answer your earlier question, the last few people I employed to clean have stolen from me. When you grow up poor, you pay attention to everything you own. I'm sure they thought I wouldn't miss the things they'd taken."

At that Frederica let out a little laugh, letting me know that Tyler's "poor" was probably like when my sorority sisters in college complained about being broke because they could afford only a new Kate Spade bag instead of a new Prada.

I filed this new information in my brain under something I now knew about Tyler Roth. He considered himself "poor" growing up, had done well for himself, had pieces of metal in his leg, and loved his dog. It felt good to have some new additions in there besides the one folder labeled *Insanely Hot*.

"Madison is from an *excellent* family," Frederica said after she finished laughing. "Her people don't steal."

Ha. Rich people stole all the time. Just ask my great-aunt Ida, who never failed to collect an expensive "souvenir" from every home she visited. Whenever Ida planned to come over, my mother used to have her staff spend hours clearing out anything small that Ida might try to pilfer.

"I hope you don't think I was suggesting . . ." Tyler's voice trailed off and he looked so uncomfortable I wanted to fix things.

"No one thought you were suggesting anything." My tone was firm, mostly as a warning to my aunt, who seemed ready to defend Huntington honor, even though she wasn't one herself.

"Good." He again sounded relieved. "Because you seem nice and you come so highly recommended that I think this could work. Do you think it could? I never asked you what you're looking for in an apartment."

"Mostly I'm looking for a place to live where I have my own bed, I don't have to worry about catching the bubonic plague or becoming the victim of a deranged killer."

He laughed, and his laughter was like a thousand perfect sunsets combined with the happiness of a hundred seven-year-olds' surprise birthday parties. It was warmth and joy and exuberance all rolled into one, and it lit up the butterflies in my stomach, making them dance and swirl.

"That's . . . oddly specific," he said when he finished. "I definitely think I can promise you those things here. It's also important to me that we have an equitable situation. Like I love to cook, so I'll be happy to do the cooking for us when I'm home. I want us to have a good quid pro quo arrangement."

I would quid his pro quo any day of the week. But instead of saying so, I settled on, "That works for me."

"Fantastic!" He got up, walked over to a dark wood credenza, and pulled open one of the drawers. He came back with a key. "In my personal life I'm a handshake-and-keep-my-word kind of guy, but I'm happy to have the legal department at work draw something up if you'd prefer. That is, if you're in."

Tyler gave me the key. He wanted me to move in!

And have his babies, my inappropriate inner vixen whispered. I told her to be quiet.

Then my rational brain had its own thoughts—about whether I should be so quick to agree to become his roommate. There was something inherently trustworthy and honest about him. He seemed to be exactly who he presented himself to be. Maybe that was my deprived hormones taking over again, and all drooling at his attractiveness aside, this was the first apartment besides Shay's that I had felt comfortable in since I'd started house hunting. Not to mention that he had Frederica's mark of approval—which might have been due to her own hormones, but I decided that I'd count it.

"A handshake works for me. And I am in." I knew to never sign anything without having a lawyer look at it first, and since I couldn't afford a lawyer, a handshake and his word were good enough.

I stood up when he held out his hand again, presumably for the handshake portion of the deal. I figured that since I'd already touched him, this second time would be no big deal.

Wrong. Tremors racked my insides at the warmth and strength of his grip and I held on for probably a second or so longer than what would be considered normal.

He gave me that grin that lit up my nerves like the Fourth of July. "I have a good feeling about this."

Oh baby, me too. I internally hushed her again. He told me I could move in whenever I liked and that he'd be sure to let the doorman know to expect me.

"I'm looking forward to being your roommate," I replied. It was a good thing he had no idea how much.

"Roommaid," I heard Frederica quietly correct behind me. Fortunately, Tyler didn't seem to notice.

Roommate, roommaid, whatever. I was so in.

He walked us to the door and pushed the button for the elevator. Frederica made small talk with him about any real estate needs that he might have and made sure to pass him her card. I stared straight ahead, ignoring them both because one, I was embarrassed by my aunt using this opportunity to try and grab a new client, and two, I needed to stop staring at him creepily.

I knew I shouldn't be frustrated with Frederica trying to drum up business. According to my mother, Frederica had made a play for my father, who had instead chosen to marry my mom. Then it was love at first sight when my aunt met Thurston Cottonwood, a man forty years her senior. (My father liked to say it was love at first sight of Thurston's medical history.) He had a heart condition, more money than even the Bransons, and Frederica expected him to not last long.

Good old Uncle Thurston was now in his nineties, and thanks to his ironclad prenup, when he traded Frederica in for a new twenty-four-year-old model, she walked away with only $1 million. Which she blew through in the first six months.

The prospect of poverty had awoken a savvy and determined businesswoman. She'd become a real estate agent to the wealthy in an attempt to keep something of her former lifestyle intact.

I admired her hustle even if it could be potentially embarrassing.

The doors finally opened and I hurried inside. Frederica was lingering, saying she'd keep in touch with Tyler, and I grabbed her forearm and gently tugged—or, more accurately, forcibly yanked—her into the elevator.

"See you soon!" he said with that smile that made my knees turn into melted butter.

"Yep!" was my clever reply. I forced a smile in return and jabbed repeatedly at the lobby button until the doors closed. When they finally did, I exhaled heavily, leaning over to try and get blood rushing back into my brain.

"Didn't I tell you? Gorgeous, right?"

I didn't respond because I wasn't sure whether she was talking about the man or his penthouse.

"This isn't a long-term solution," was what I said instead. "I can't stay here forever pretending I know how to clean or how to care for his poor traumatized dog."

"Of course this is temporary. You can save up money and get a decent place of your own. Or Brad could finally pop the question and then you move in with him. And that's when you call your favorite aunt and let me find you the best home his money can buy. Because I'm sure your boyfriend is not going to be happy about you living with that fine specimen of a man. Jealousy is often a powerful motivator when it comes to engagements."

Brad's "jealousy" was the absolute least of my concerns at the moment. Especially since I would never want a man to propose to me solely because I'd managed to make him envious. I wasn't into the same games my mother and aunt had played when they'd set about getting husbands.

I wanted a man who would love and accept me. Someone who didn't care about money or who my family was. I knew a guy like that was out there. I also knew that he wasn't Brad Branson and never would be.

It was time to start a new life with a new roommate, new apartment, and new responsibilities. I was up for the challenge.

At least, I hoped I was.

CHAPTER THREE

The one place I already felt settled in was at my job. My first recess corresponded with Shay's free period, and I was headed to the teachers' lounge so that we could catch up. Millstone Academy was a private school that specialized in STEM education and ran from kindergarten all the way up to twelfth grade. I taught the second grade and Shay taught upper-level advanced mathematics. She was also the adviser of the Mathlete team.

I'd met Shay Simmons my freshman year of college. It was the first night of rush week and I was standing on the grass outside the Delta Alpha Gamma house. Their opening party had begun and my family expected that I would join this sorority. This was the "right" house. Brad belonged to their brother fraternity, as had both of our fathers. All I had to do was cross the lawn, go up the porch steps, and enter the house.

I couldn't do it. I could not get my feet to move.

"Hey, are you okay? You look a little lost." The first thing I noticed about the girl speaking to me was her concerned expression. The second was her bright-purple hair and how she'd shaved one side of her head.

"You have no idea how right you are," I said to her. I was lost in a way I hadn't realized until this very moment. "I'm supposed to go inside and I . . . can't."

She glanced over her shoulder. "I can't blame you for that. Those girls are terrible."

"It's not that. If I go in there, then I'm saying I agree to it. That I'll end up being my mother and the things I want for myself don't matter and I'll never make my own decisions ever again. That I'll marry the boy they picked out for me and spend my days at the country club and lunching with the other bored housewives. I'll be saying that I accept it, and I'm not sure I can accept it."

"That sounds heavy."

"They've chosen everything for me. Including the two majors I'm allowed to decide between."

She made a sound. "You aren't allowed to pick your own major? You're the one going to school. Not them."

"I can major in economics or be prelaw. But I don't want to be a lawyer."

"What do you want to be?"

Her question hit me hard, slamming against my chest so that it was difficult to catch my breath. It was such a simple question, but it suddenly felt cosmic and profound. "Do you know that you're the first person in my life who has ever asked me that?"

"That's . . . sad."

It was. It was ridiculously sad. And I had a secret wish, one I'd never admitted aloud, something I wanted to be. A career that mattered, where I could change lives. I decided to say it, to see how it made me feel. "I want to be a teacher."

"Really?" She smiled. "Me too. I'm majoring in math with an emphasis on teaching. I'm hoping to teach at the high school level." She studied me carefully, as if forming an opinion. "A bunch of the girls in my sorority are majoring in elementary and secondary education. You should come over and meet with them."

I'd always been grateful for whatever fates conspired for us to meet that night. I joined her sorority, and even though she was two years older than me, Shay became my best friend and closest confidant. She changed my life in so many ways, mainly by showing me that the things I wanted did matter and that I was strong enough to make my own choices. That it wasn't normal for your parents to map out your entire life, not allowing you to have any say in it. She was always there for me, and I was grateful that her job kept her in Houston, nearby. It allowed us to stay close.

When I was applying to all the schools in the area after I'd completed my year of student teaching, she was the one who recommended me to the headmistress and helped me get my position. And she'd been kindly letting me sleep on her couch for the last three months.

Shay was the first person I wanted to tell about Tyler and the penthouse, but when I got back to her place, she'd left me a note saying she had a date. I tried to wait up for her, but I passed out before she got home and she had already left before I woke up the next day, which wasn't surprising. She had her Mathletes practicing and drilling both before and after school. She intended for them to win nationals this year.

I probably could have texted her, but this was an in-person conversation. And I needed to have it soon. Talking things out with Shay made it so I could let them go and move on.

Delia Hawthorne was the other member of our triumvirate friendship. She and Shay had been first-year teachers together at Millstone and they'd instantly bonded. There had been a short period of time when I had been a little envious of their friendship, but once I started working at the academy as well, we became an inseparable trio.

Because of Shay's early-morning plans, Delia picked me up to drive me to school. I'd attempted taking public transportation on a few occasions but it turned out that having zero sense of direction was a problem. I kept ending up in different cities. Not even Google Maps helped; I had no idea how far six hundred feet or a quarter mile actually was. Delia and Shay informed me that for purely selfish reasons they were going to arrange to drive me to and from school. "I mostly don't want to drive to Oklahoma to pick you up the next time this happens," Shay said.

It was their way of being my friends without making me feel like I was relying too heavily on their charitable hearts. Which was something I struggled with every day. How it was so important to me to be independent and able to strike out on my own without my family paying my way and here I was letting my friends pick up the slack. It was one of the many reasons I was looking forward to moving into Tyler's place and getting my own car. I would start picking up my own slack.

Caught up in my own thoughts, it took me a minute to realize that Delia was doing her daily rant and I'd missed the first part. But since they were always the same, I knew I hadn't missed much. "And then I told *Mr. Ramon* that studies have proved that scientists with artistic skill were more likely to win awards than those without. Einstein himself said that imagination was more important than knowledge when it comes to science. And where do these students get imagination? From art!"

Pretty much every car ride to school involved Delia getting upset about the advanced sciences teacher, Mr. Tristan Ramon, shading the art classes she taught. She was our resident flower child, a bohemian artist who had been born in the wrong era. Usually she was all about inner peace and tranquility and artistic expression, but something about the way the very cute Mr. Ramon teased her made her more than a little crazy.

Fortunately, not much was required from me during these diatribes. My job was to nod and to periodically comment about what a jerk and/ or how stupid Mr. Ramon was (even though both Shay and I agreed he obviously had a crush on Delia and didn't seem to understand that teasing her was not the way to her heart). Which left me with time to think about Tyler and moving in to his apartment.

Thoughts of Tyler and second-guessing whether I'd made the right choice had led to me being so distracted this morning during class that I hadn't been able to focus properly on my kids. I finally gave in and showed them an educational movie. Which they were neither entertained nor, I suspected, educated by. I was pretty sure that a quarter of them had just fallen asleep.

I also had to put one of my students, Denny, in a chair next to my desk since he wouldn't stop throwing wads of paper at the other students. The past two weeks he had been acting out behaviorally, which wasn't like him. I wasn't sure what I could do to help him get back on track since this was the first time I'd had to deal with a situation like this. I made a note on my desk to get in touch with his parents and to discuss it with Delia and Shay when I got the chance.

I practically sprinted to the teachers' lounge when the bell rang, anxious to talk things over with my best friend.

"There you are!" I exclaimed when I saw her. Shay was standing by the coffee machine and gave me a confused look.

Her purple hair was long gone, as was her half-shaved head. Now she had her dark-brown hair styled in a pixie cut that emphasized her large brown eyes. Where Delia wore gauzy skirts and peasant blouses, Shay always looked like she was about to walk into a law office. Pencil skirt, berry-colored satin blouse, blazer. "Here's where I always am during my break. What's going on with you?"

I came over and grabbed her arm, pulling her to an empty table. "I have so, so much to tell you. So my aunt—"

"Frederica? I love that crazy broad. I have to admire anyone with such naked ambition."

"What? That's not the point. Anyway, she took me to more horrible places—"

"And you have to keep sleeping on my couch." She said it with a smile, but I could hear the weariness in her voice. We loved each other, but I knew I was starting to get on her nerves. Shay had her limits and

I'd stretched each and every one. I knew how to be a good guest, making sure I wasn't messy as was apparently my natural inclination, but her place was tiny and even best friends could get sick of each other. I also kept hearing my mother's voice in my head reminding me that houseguests, like fish, go bad after three days.

And it had been three months.

"No, I am officially moving out!"

"Finally!" A mortified look covered Shay's face. "I mean, yay for you! You found a place!"

I couldn't help but laugh. "It's okay. It is long overdue. But Frederica is the one who found me the most amazing apartment and I won't even have to pay rent. I'm going to do the cleaning and take care of his dog while he's out of town in exchange for living there."

"He?" she echoed. "You're going to live with some random guy and clean up after him? So you can live rent-free? Let me guess, do you have to sleep with him, too?"

"What? No!" I was outraged that she'd even suggest I'd stoop that low. Then I saw her real smile, letting me know she'd been teasing me. "This guy—his name is Tyler, by the way—had a bad situation years ago where his roommate fell in love with him and I think the only reason he's letting me move in is that he thinks I'm in a relationship."

"With who? The leprechaun from Lucky Charms?"

My mother hadn't allowed any sugary cereals and I may or may not have gone a little crazy when I moved into Shay's and was no longer following any of my mother's rules. Plus, cold cereal was the easiest thing to make for myself and it was inexpensive. "Oh, ha-ha. No, he thinks I'm in a relationship with an actual person. You should have seen his face when Frederica told him I was with Brad."

"Was it a look of disgust?"

"Why would it be? He doesn't even know Brad."

"You don't have to know Brad to be disgusted."

"No, Tyler looked like a prisoner on death row who had just been pardoned. He is unnaturally happy that I'm with someone else."

She studied me skeptically. "Is this Tyler dude blind? Because you are gorgeous. Why wouldn't he want to get with you?"

I was much vainer than I would have ever admitted out loud. I suspected this was because I had been raised by a self-centered woman whose entire identity was based on her outward appearance. Even though I tried telling myself that my outer shell didn't matter, I still spent a lot of time trying to make mine pretty.

Although I was limited in my new financial situation. I now had to use a grocery store brand to dye my hair blonde and was trying out drugstore makeup products to go along with my hazel eyes and fair skin.

I didn't know how well it was actually working.

"You're a very good friend," I told her. "But I get the feeling he doesn't care how I look. He made it pretty clear he'd prefer to have his female roommate involved in a relationship so that she wouldn't become his personal in-home stalker."

"So this Tyler guy wants someone to live in his apartment who will clean up after him, look after his dog, and not have sex with him. Don't they usually call those people wives?"

"You're hilarious," I said, while rolling my eyes.

"I just can't believe you've been reduced to this. The other apartments couldn't possibly have been as bad as you described."

"Then I haven't been explaining it thoroughly enough. Those other places . . . it was like the plagues-of-the-apocalypse type of stuff. I went in with the absolute lowest expectations and I still managed to come back disappointed. This Tyler thing fell out of the sky like manna from heaven. I'm not passing it up." Defending my position restored my faith in the choice I'd made and I felt easier about it. "Not to mention that I get to come home to this."

Frederica had sent me a link to an old listing of Tyler's penthouse that had pictures of all the rooms. She had included a link to Tyler's

Instagram account, too, which I had clicked on quite a bit since she'd sent it. My hope was that I could somehow inoculate myself to his pretty, make myself immune to his charms.

So far it wasn't working.

"Here." I handed her my phone. She needed to see for herself how nice the apartment was. "Just click on that link and you'll see what I'm talking about."

Shay let out a strangled sound. "Are you kidding me with this? Way to bury the lede! Great googly moogly! Someday, when I tell this tale to my grandchildren, I will tell them my ovaries grew three sizes that day."

"What are you talking about . ." It was then that I realized that she'd clicked on the second link instead of the first and was now ogling Tyler.

"Suddenly you wanting to move in with him makes so much more sense."

"That's a tall drink of wow." I looked up to see Delia standing behind Shay, peering over her shoulder.

"Madison's going to live with him," Shay gleefully informed her. The last time I'd seen her this giddy was when one of our fellow teachers, Owen James, poured coffee on himself before the first bell.

"Good for you!" Delia grinned at me as she took the empty chair next to Shay. "I'm really out of the loop. I didn't even know you were dating anyone."

I detected the slightest note of hurt in her voice. "No, we're not dating or anything. I'm his new roommate."

"And his maid," Shay couldn't help but add.

At Delia's shocked expression, I hurried to fill her in on everything I'd told Shay so far, adding, "I thought you had recess duty today or else I would have waited for you."

"I switched with Amanda. I have to help Jayden with one of his perspective art projects after school and so I'm going to stay late."

"You are like a human granola bar," Shay told her. "You're too nice."

"That's kind of a weird insult," she replied. "But my niceness is not what we're discussing. Like shouldn't we talk about the problematic implications of what Madison's doing?"

"What do you mean?" I asked.

She shrugged. "You cleaning up his apartment is really playing into those traditional gender and economic roles."

"Except for the fact that I can't be conforming to a gender role because I have no idea how to clean."

"Good point," she said, lifting up her cup of peppermint tea to take a quick sip.

And during all this, Shay had continued to stare at Tyler's picture on my phone with a goofy grin on her face. An inclination I understood, but it was starting to make me a little uneasy. Possibly jealous as well.

Shay turned the phone screen toward Delia. "Did you see his dog, too? Men are a hundred times hotter when they love dogs. That's legit math. From a math teacher."

I couldn't help but brag about him a little, because it was one of the facts I knew from my Tyler brain file. "He rescued that dog, Pigeon, from an abusive home. I mean, I guess it was actually the shelter who rescued her and then Tyler adopted her, but still."

Shay nodded. "I was wrong in my calculations. He is now ten thousand times hotter."

"He's like a real-life Captain America," Delia agreed. "He should have his own ticker-tape parade."

"I'll be grand marshal," Shay said.

"I think the fact that we're all so gaga over him means we should probably be dating more," I said.

Shay shook her head, disagreeing with me. "I date plenty."

"I mean guys you go out on more than one date with."

She rolled her eyes at me and in apparent retaliation announced, "I feel like Tyler Roth is in need of a deep dive."

I said, "No," and reached for my phone, but she ignored me. Delia grabbed her own phone and started tapping on it. "He hasn't posted anything on Facebook in years. No account on Twitter that I can find."

Shay showed her my phone. "But look at the stuff he's posted on Insta. He not only adopted his dog from that shelter, but he volunteers there, too. Speaking of volunteering, he's involved with this coffee company that donates its profits to building homes in Guatemala. He actually flew out there and helped build them. He really is Captain America." She hesitated slightly to suck in a deep breath of appreciation. "Oh, look, he does the cutest thing. He takes pictures with his dog and Photoshops famous sites behind them. Like the Eiffel Tower, Colosseum, the Statue of Liberty. He says she's too nervous to fly but he wishes he could show her the world. That is the cutest thing ever. And he hashtags them all with #ohtheplacesyoullgo."

"That's enough," I said, reaching for my phone.

Shay tapped the screen thoughtfully, ignoring my hand. "Maybe he's too kind."

"Too kind?" I repeated. Was that even possible?

"Yeah. You know the type that's so nice and helpful that he winds up being taken advantage of."

I didn't know him well enough to know whether or not that was true. It could be. But he seemed so strong and confident and sure of himself that I had a hard time imagining it.

"Personally, I think you should marry this guy immediately," Delia announced. "Now on to LinkedIn to check out his employment prospects."

That was enough. "This feels too much like invading his privacy. You guys should stop."

There was loud male laughter from the other side of the room, which put an end to the search as we turned to see Tristan Ramon and Owen James laughing loudly. Tristan waved slightly at Delia, who pretended not to notice. While both men were tall, Tristan had dark-black hair and dark eyes and Owen was his polar opposite, with dirty-blond hair and light-brown eyes. The two men had both started five years ago and had become best friends. Because the academy had only been open for about ten years, Millstone had a disproportionate number of young teachers. Which wasn't an issue until it was.

Like with Owen and Shay's rivalry. Where Tristan just seemed emotionally stunted in how he went about wooing women by teasing them, Owen was not like that. He and Shay legitimately despised one another.

Owen nodded his chin at Shay and asked, "Why are you smiling so much? Did your huntsman finally bring you your stepdaughter's heart?"

That got Shay to put my phone down and I snatched it back before she realized what she had done. "Look who decided to grace us with his douchedom."

"Eloquent and charming as ever, Ms. Simmons. But I think I'll head out because, thanks to your predictability, I already know where this is going."

"Maybe grab a handbasket on your way out and see where it takes you," she invited, her arms crossed over her chest. I wondered how long it would take him to figure that one out. He was a smart guy. I was betting he'd get it eventually.

With a shake of his head, Owen left. Tristan followed behind him, sporting a sheepish and apologetic smile.

"Assault should be legal against people like him," Shay muttered under her breath, adding a word that sounded suspiciously like "pass goal."

I figured my best bet was to distract her, so I waved my phone back and forth in front of her. "I was planning on trying to move in today."

It did the trick and she leaned forward and said, "I have two questions. One, can I help you move in?"

"Of course." I was hoping she'd offer because I had a lot of clothing.

"Great. And my second question—does Tyler have another extra room?"

CHAPTER FOUR

Shay was suitably impressed by everything at Tyler's place—the doorman (Gerald) who greeted us, the swanky elevator, the view from the balcony, the state-of-the-art kitchen, my large and luxurious bedroom. "Your room is the same size as my whole apartment!"

I didn't say anything, but trust me, I knew.

She stuck her head in Tyler's room and I caught a glimpse of Pigeon's tail before she hid under the bed. "Come on. We need to get me moved in." I tugged on Shay's arm and closed his door. While I was just as curious, I didn't want to infringe on his personal space and stress Pigeon out any further.

Bringing up all my junk, even with Gerald's help, was a slow and tedious process. I tried to tell myself I was getting a great workout, given that I could no longer afford to see my personal trainer.

We were close to being done when I heard Tyler's voice call out, "Madison?"

The sound of my name on his lips sent weird shivers up my spine. Shay and I were still in my room, dropping off boxes. We exchanged glances and before I could mouth the word *behave* to her, Tyler rapped on my open door and stuck his head in.

"Oh, hi! I didn't realize you had company. I'm Tyler."

Shay stood there, motionless.

"This is Shay, my best friend."

"Great to meet you." He smiled at her and then focused his gaze on me. "Hey, I'm going to go change and then I'll come help you with the rest of the boxes."

"Sounds good!"

When I heard his door shut, I said to Shay, "I'll give you the same advice Frederica gave me. Close your mouth, sweetheart."

She recovered much more quickly than I had. "Are you kidding me right now? I mean, you told me he was better looking in real life but . . . how much is a soul going for these days?"

Not able to follow her line of thinking, I asked, "What?"

"I'm assuming you had to have sold yours, given that beautiful man." She paused, tapping one fingertip against her mouth. "You do realize that he's half-naked in a room across the hall from yours *right now*."

Unbidden imagery filled my brain and I had to blink several times in an attempt to get it to stop. "And?"

She looked at me like I was insane. "And if I were you I would kick down that door and have my way with him."

"That's what he's trying to avoid, remember?"

"Then he should stop walking around looking like that. Good grief. I bet every woman in a three-block radius is in constant heat just from the proximity." She shook her head as if this were beyond her comprehension. "Explain this situation to me again, like I'm stupid. You're living with that man and you're not allowed to be attracted to him?"

"I think it's okay if I'm attracted to him." I hoped it was, because I totally was. "Just that we both understand nobody will be acting on it. And by nobody, I mean me."

Her eyes lit up. "Does that mean he's allowed to make a move?"

I wish. "That won't be happening. Frederica made him think that I'm with Brad."

"Ugh. Right. And Tyler seems like a good guy, which means he won't do anything." She said this with so much disappointment that I couldn't help but laugh.

Then she added, "You are the only person I know that this could happen to. You lose all your money, can't afford your own place, and wind up in a penthouse with a man hotter than the surface of the sun. If I didn't love you so much, I would totally hate you. Also, are you sure there isn't another room here? Your closet is pretty big. I could live there."

We heard Tyler's door open and he stuck his head back through my doorframe. "Is your car parked out front?"

"My car is," Shay said, all but batting her eyelashes at him as honey dripped from her voice. "Let me show you where we have the rest of the boxes."

I started to follow them, but Shay turned and hissed at me, "Stay." So I fought off my slight flare of jealousy and went out and watched as she trailed behind him to the elevator. She turned at the last minute to mouth the letters *O*, *M*, and *G* at me.

I held my laughter in until the elevator doors shut. I knew she'd only been joking about moving in with me but part of me was thinking how nice it would be to have her here as my own personal security blanket. A buffer to keep me away from Tyler so that I could respect his boundaries. Because that might be the only way this could possibly work.

But Shay needed her own personal space back. Time to be the adult I kept claiming I was.

When they returned they were both laughing, and I unnecessarily directed them into my room. Shay had had her chance to do some one-on-one flirting, so this time I went down to help with the few boxes that remained. In a matter of minutes we'd cleared out the rest and had it all moved into my room. I was going to be unpacking for a long time.

Tyler put his hands on his hips, which made him look like an actual superhero. "Seems like that's it. If you'll excuse me, I'm off to take a shower. It was nice to meet you, Shay."

"Likewise," she said, and we both watched him walk into his room.

"Say nothing about him in the shower," I told her when his door shut. My hormone-addled brain could take only so much. She gave me a wink and reached for her purse.

My phone buzzed. There was a text. From my mother.

It said:

> Family dinner. Driver will pick
> you up at 7:30. Text address.

"What is it?" Shay asked. I showed her my phone.

There was no ignoring a text or a summoning of this level. My parents had made it clear they weren't speaking to me, so to send a message instructing me to come to dinner was something I couldn't ignore or else this would escalate to telenovela levels of drama. Everything was always on my mother's terms.

Well, almost everything.

"Do you want to come with me?" I asked Shay, hopeful for a moment after I texted Tyler's address back.

"Oh, I would but I have this thing where I don't want to go."

I sighed. "Fine. Abandon me to the wolves."

"You'll be fine. Tell Satan and her husband I say what's up."

I was in the middle of picturing my mother's reaction to Shay's message when she said, "Come walk me out to the car."

"What, you don't want to hang around in case he comes out here in a towel?" I teased.

"Don't tempt me. Let's go." We headed for the elevator and waited for it to travel up to the top floor.

"Just so you know," Shay said, "I think he's dating someone."

Why did that make my heart drop from my chest down to my feet? "What makes you say that?"

"I just full-court pressed him on our trip down to my car and nothing. Not even a tiny nibble. And I put out a lot of bait."

The doors opened and we got in. "I think you're mixing some of your metaphors."

"Regardless, I'm glad you're the one living here and not me. You're a much better woman than I."

I doubted that. I just had more reason to keep my lips and grubby paws to myself.

She went on: "I think Tyler is proof that the universe is patently unfair. How is a guy that good looking, rich, helpful, charming, and rescues abused dogs? It's like when they were making people they just poured the entire bag of human bonuses on his head."

The doors to the lobby opened while I was laughing at her remark. She wasn't wrong. It didn't seem quite fair for Tyler to be so perfect. Shay and I both waved to Gerald and I thanked him for his help.

We reached Shay's car and I said, "And thank you for your help, too. For everything. I never would have gotten through all this without you."

To my surprise, she hugged me. Shay was not really the hugging type. "Have fun in your new place. And just know that if you pretend to sleepwalk and accidentally climb into his bed in the middle of the night, no one will blame you."

I hugged her even tighter while laughing again. She had no idea how much our friendship meant to me, how much I relied on it. I told her I would call her soon.

"You better," she replied. "I want to hear what the queen of the underworld wants. Also, remember when dealing with your family that we live in Texas, so please don't do anything that will get you the death penalty."

"I can't make that kind of promise."

"Okay, okay. But if Tyler asks about me, I am single and ready to mingle!" She smiled and shook her head. She waved one last time and got into her car, then drove off. I headed back inside, eager to start my new life. When I got to the apartment, Tyler's door was still closed and I went into my room and opened the closest box.

There were sweaters I had forgotten I even owned. At Shay's place I had been basically living out of a few suitcases and had left most of my wardrobe in boxes. After I'd pulled out the sweaters, I found a bunch of underwear next. Cute underwear! I had so much of it!

Too bad there was no one else to see it.

I went through a bunch more boxes and found skirts and dresses and jeans and blouses and so many things that I was excited to wear again. In the fourth box I opened I found my kitchen mug, the one Shay had got me at graduation that said WORLD'S BEST TEACHER. I brought it into the kitchen and was surprised to find Tyler at the stove, humming to himself as he cooked.

Little shivers of awareness shot through me at the sight of him. His shoulders were so broad and he was so deliciously tall and his arms were just perfectly formed and . . . I forced myself to clear my throat and said, "Hi."

I wanted to roll my eyes at myself because that was so stupid. We were roommates. I couldn't say hi to him every time I saw him.

Fortunately, he didn't call me out on my dumbness. "Hey, I'm making some fettuccine Alfredo. Would you like some?"

He was going to feed me? Did he not understand the possible fallout from that? He was obviously going to make me fall in love with him. *Be an adult who respects rules,* I told myself as I put my mug down on the counter. I sat on the barstool in front of the island. "I would love some."

Nodding at my mug, he said, "Do you need help unpacking?"

Oh. He assumed that I was a normal person and had more things to put in the kitchen besides one single mug. "No, I'm good. It kind of feels like Christmas, only for stuff you already own. I'd forgotten half of the things in there. Like the Birkin bag my grandmother gave me for graduation. It's one of my favorite things in the whole world." My mother had been livid when I opened it. It was one of the bags from the first Birkin line and my mom had been certain she would add this particular heirloom to her stash.

She had been pretty shocked, too, when I'd refused to hand it over.

"It's a good thing you have such a great attitude about it. Most people would just see it as a chore. Oh, speaking of . . ." He turned around to grab a piece of paper off the fridge. "So, full disclosure, I copied this off one of those house-organizational websites. I thought it might be helpful. But if you don't want to do things this way, it's totally up to you."

He handed me the paper and it was a list of chores for the apartment. Dusting, vacuuming, washing the windows. Cleaning toilets. Ick. My stomach sank at the prospect. I hadn't even thought about that. I was going to need one of those full-on hazmat suits to do it.

"Don't worry about my room or my bathroom. Like I said, I'll clean up after myself. This is just some deeper cleaning in the general areas. Are you good with that?"

"Yes." I was going to have to be, wasn't I?

"While I'm thinking about it, I have my calendar hanging up on the fridge so that you know when I'll be here and when I won't. I'm flying out for New York first thing in the morning and I'll be gone for a few days."

"That's thoughtful, thank you."

Tyler nodded and grabbed two plates. He started dishing them up but I stopped him by saying, "Not very much for me. I have to go over to my parents' house later for dinner."

"Sure thing. You don't seem very happy about it. Having dinner with your parents. You kind of make it sound like you're going to a funeral."

"The night's still young, so it's too early to rule that out." Realizing Tyler might not get my sense of humor, I added, "Sorry, my family doesn't put me in the best mood."

"Oh, I get that all too well." He flashed me a bone-melting grin as he brought the plates over to the small dining room table between his kitchen and living room. "Would you grab some forks? They're in the drawer closest to the dishwasher."

I wasn't a hundred percent sure which appliance was the dishwasher, but thankfully I guessed correctly and found the silverware. I came over to the table and handed him a fork. I tried not to gasp when our fingers brushed together, the sensation of his skin on mine again rendering me mindless.

He, apparently, did not have the same kind of reaction. "Thanks. Dig in!"

Despite his disinterest, I found myself wanting to "accidentally" touch him again, so I focused on the dinner instead. I twirled the pasta around my fork, brought it up to my mouth, and tried not to groan in pleasure as I began to eat it. This was so much better than Lucky Charms. "This is amazing."

"I knew I liked you," he said with a wink that made my stomach flop over.

"As long as you keep feeding me this way, I'll give you whatever compliments you want."

He laughed, and his laughter still had that same magical quality to it that made my insides feel fizzy and light. There was something about him that I couldn't put my finger on. That I wasn't allowed to put my finger on.

It wasn't just that he was handsome and sexy, which he obviously was, but there was something magnetic about him. He was effortlessly charming. People were drawn to him and wanted to be close to him. Or at least that was true for my anecdotal evidence of having seen him in action with three different women. I had the feeling it would be true of almost every woman in his presence.

Hence the restraining order.

He spoke, interrupting my thoughts: "I forgot to say anything earlier, but I want you to be comfortable here. Please feel free to decorate however you want or put up pictures of your family or whatever."

"Oh no, they don't show up on film." Not to mention the last thing I needed was my mother's disapproving stare gazing out at me on a daily basis.

That made him chuckle and he said, "I am serious, though. The offer stands. This is your home now, too."

"Thanks." I couldn't see myself actually doing it, though. He'd obviously paid a decorator a lot of money to get a specific look and I wasn't going to mess with that. It was actually a little sad that he'd settled into this decor. As I looked around, I felt like the apartment lacked Tyler's personality. It was technically beautiful, but it didn't feel like a home. This was how he wanted to live his life and how he wanted to organize his space. Surrounded by showpieces meant to impress.

It was how my childhood home had been decorated, as well.

So regardless of how nice he was, and how gorgeous, I needed to remember that Tyler was like the people from my old life. I'd recently decided, mostly thanks to Brad and my parents, that I wasn't interested in dating a man with money. I'd seen that life. I'd grown up in it. It wasn't what I wanted. I didn't want appearances to matter more than anything else. Where it was fine if your marriage was falling apart as long as you put on a brave face and pretended like everything was normal. Where you ignored your children and let them be raised by nannies because you had to go to the spa and take multiple vacations a year because of how very stressful your life was. A life where you pitted your children against one another and made them compete for your time and affection.

To be fair, there were probably wealthy families that were normal and functioned well. I just hadn't met any of them yet.

Which meant that despite my daydreaming, I would never share a life or a home with Tyler. I wasn't going to stay here long term. I was going to save up enough to get a decent apartment and then I would move on.

"So how long have you and Shay been friends?" he asked.

That flare of jealousy was back, but I put it out. "Since my freshman year of college."

"What's her story?"

The jealousy flamed up again. Was he interested? Or just making conversation? It didn't matter, I reminded myself, and answered his question: "She's a teacher, like me. She teaches math to the secondary students. Really smart. She's a great person. She's also, um, single. If you were interested."

His food was halfway to his mouth and he froze for a second, as if I'd caught him off guard. It took him a moment to recover. "She seems nice, but she's not really my type."

What is your type? The words were on the very tip of my tongue and it was only with the greatest self-control imaginable that I managed to keep them inside me. As if I'd ask the question and then he'd turn slowly toward me and say, *Why, you, of course.* And then we'd kiss as the screen faded to black.

Nope. This was real life. Something I needed to remember.

I also needed to remember to keep my nose out of his private life. We were going to be roommates, not best friends.

"Message received."

Again, he seemed anxious about having possibly offended me. "I don't mean any disrespect to your friend. My life's not really set up for a relationship. I have a lot of obligations."

"Like what?" The words were out before I could stop them. Maybe I was the one being offensive, getting too personal. Even though I'd just told myself to stay out of it.

"That's a very long story. Maybe I'll share it with you another day."

Yep, too far. Because that was a way to close down a line of questioning you didn't want to answer.

It made me wonder about Shay's instinct that he was seeing someone. It sounded as if he wasn't, but I was not going to ask him anything further about it.

This conversation felt over and I was back to feeling stupid again.

"Well, I need to get some more unpacking done and then get ready to head over to my parents'. Thanks for dinner." I carried my plate over to the sink and made sure to rinse it off. I had learned how important that was living at Shay's. But she refused to let me help clean the kitchen because, as she said, I did everything wrong. That didn't bode well for my situation with Tyler, but I would figure it out.

"Before you go, would it be okay if I talked to you about Pigeon's schedule?"

"Sure."

He came over and rinsed his plate off as well. He leaned in close, his warmth beckoning me, and I closed my eyes, inhaling his scent before I forced myself to take a step back. He left his plate in the sink, which made me feel marginally better that I had done the same. Shay was one of those as-soon-as-it's-used-put-it-in-the-dishwasher kind of people. I'd done my best to remember but still routinely aggravated her.

Tyler then showed me Pigeon's dog food that he kept in the pantry, and where her food and water bowls were, and told me how often I should feed her while he was gone. He had a dog walker, a college student, who came and grabbed Pigeon in the morning and in the late afternoon, so I wouldn't have to walk her unless she needed to go outside to relieve herself.

It was then that I realized I had no idea how to walk a dog. Another thing for me to ask Google.

"Have you always had a dog?" I asked. I so wanted to know everything about him.

"No, Pigeon's my first pet."

"And you didn't consider getting any other kind? Like a cat?"

"A cat?" he scoffed. "Never. I'm not bringing home some sociopath intent on luring you into a false sense of security before they eat your face."

That made me laugh. "Some cats are nice and affectionate." Not that I had any firsthand knowledge, but it had to be true.

"Decoys. They've never forgotten that they used to be worshipped as gods. You'll never see dogs planning on destroying humankind. Which is one of the reasons I adopted Pigeon."

"She won't eat your face?"

He smiled. "I'm pretty sure she's not plotting my demise. And it's nice to love somebody who doesn't want anything in return."

Whoa, that sounded deep and like an area that was obviously none of my business but I still wanted to ask too many questions about.

Before I could figure out what to say in response, he said, "While we're on the topic of animals and their devious plans, something you should definitely know about Pidge is that she loves shoes. And by love, I mean she chews them into tiny pieces until they no longer resemble shoes. So you always want to keep your closet door shut."

"Got it. She won't come for my face, but she will for my shoes." Pigeon and I were going to have issues if she chewed up my shoes. I'd been forced to sell off most of my bags and footwear. The shoes I had now were very inexpensive and I wasn't emotionally attached to them, but I didn't have enough money to buy more cheap shoes.

He led me into the living room, where there was a giant dog bed. "Pidge is kind of funny when it comes to sleep. Sometimes she wants to sleep with me, and sometimes she prefers to be out here on her bed.

I'm assuming when I'm gone that she'll want to be out here. But she has . . ." He reached down and picked up a couple of toys shaped like pigeons. "These. The chew toy she's had since the shelter. It's why I named her Pigeon. She wouldn't leave without it. And then I bought her a stuffed pigeon to sleep with and she needs it to go to bed at night. And she also needs her favorite blanket pulled up over her."

I couldn't hide my smile at how cute he was about his dog.

"I know, I know," he said with a grin. "I spoil her."

"Maybe a little. And I thought I'd been spoiled growing up."

"When I love something, I don't do it halfway."

That made my heart twist painfully. No man had ever loved me the way he loved this dog.

I cleared my throat, surprised at how thick it suddenly felt. "I think I've got it. So don't worry about anything. It's all under control." I moved away from him but he put a hand out to stop me, lightly grasping my forearm.

I felt the zing of his touch everywhere.

"Wait a second. We should exchange phone numbers. Just in case you need to get in touch with me."

"Right. Good idea." I handed him my phone, hoping he didn't notice how my hands shook. I also tried to quiet my inner fourteen-year-old self, who was giddily jumping up and down at the idea that I had his phone number. Which was so stupid because I was already living in his apartment.

He used my phone to call his, and when his phone rang he handed mine back to me. When I added him as a contact, I was going to have to refrain from nicknaming him *Hot Tyler*. Just in case.

"There. I'll see you in a few days."

"Yep!" Then because I was still feeling awkward, I decided to go ahead and make things weirder. "So I have to go get ready for that dinner with my family. I would invite you, but you seem like a very nice

45

person and it would be very mean of me to introduce you to them. Personally I'd like to not go, either, but I don't really have a choice."

Shut up, I told myself. *Stop talking and just . . . shut up.*

He put both of his hands into his jean pockets. "I believe you always have a choice."

I shook my head. Not where my mother was concerned, I didn't. "Not really," was the answer I settled on.

"I actually get that."

What had happened in his life to make him feel like sometimes he didn't have a choice, either? I wondered if he'd ever tell me.

It wasn't a good thing that I wanted to know so much about Tyler.

I cleared my throat. "So have a good flight and I'll see you when you get back."

"Enjoy your evening. Or . . . don't."

I smiled at his joke and headed back to my room.

This was fine. Everything was fine. I would learn to clean, how to take care of a dog, keep my hormones in check, and I would go to my parents' home and see what fresh nightmare waited for me there.

And hope that dinner with my mother maybe wouldn't be as bad as I absolutely knew it would be.

CHAPTER FIVE

I was delighted to see that Julio was the driver who had been sent to fetch me. He was the one who had taught me how to drive and helped me get my license. I felt relieved that my parents hadn't fired him for it. He caught me up on how his three small boys (holy terrors, he affectionately called them) were doing, and talking to him distracted me from thinking about where we were headed.

Until we arrived at the house. I stood outside the front door, not sure if I should ring the bell or go in. The problem was resolved for me when the door was opened up by our butler, Coughlin. I wanted to throw my arms around him to say hello, but his reserved manner made me stop.

"Good evening, Miss Huntington." He let me inside and I followed him across our vast foyer.

"How are you, Coughlin?" I handed him my coat and he folded it over his forearm.

"As well as can be expected under the circumstances. Someone stole our sunshine." I saw the twinkle in his eye and felt a rush of relief that loyalty to my parents hadn't turned him against me. The staff had nicknamed me *Sunshine* when I was younger, something I didn't think anyone in my family knew. "Your family has gathered in the west parlor."

He stopped short of the door, and taking a risk, I leaned up to kiss his cheek. "I've missed you, too, Coughlin."

Then he turned slightly red, smiling, and nodded at me. As he walked away, I drew in a big breath. I could do this. And maybe it wouldn't be as bad as I was expecting it to be.

"Speaking of things Mother and Father did to try and save their marriage, Madison's here!"

My sister Vanessa's shrill voice shattered any illusions I had left about this evening. Ignoring them, I headed into the lion's den, passing by them to reach the wet bar so that I could pour myself a drink. Or twenty. Anything to get through this. I didn't know how accurate her statement actually was. I knew that my parents had me when the twins were ten years old in a last-ditch effort to give my father a son, a true heir. Everybody had been disappointed that I was a girl and had spent the last twenty-three years reminding me of that fact.

When I didn't respond to her barb, Vanessa turned back around to bark some command to her husband, Gilbert Washington Buchanan III. Gilbert was the grandson of a former US president and had his own political ambitions.

Or, more accurately, the ambitions came from all the people around him, because Gilbert was exceptionally stupid. But he had name recognition and people loved his grandpa. He currently had a "job" as a vice president at Daddy's company. He was waiting for my father to retire from the Senate and then Gilbert would take over his seat and Vanessa would morph into the perfect political wife, with her pink business suits and platinum-blonde bob, just like our mother.

My other sister, Violet, had her back turned on the couple, which seemed like an unwise move. You should never expose a vulnerable spot to a predator. But she was deep in conversation with a man I didn't recognize. My gaze didn't linger on him, either, because she drew all the attention to herself. She had dyed her hair a dark brown, almost black. She had on a black cocktail dress that was all severe lines and angles. She radiated wealth and power. And rightfully so—she was going to take over as CEO when my father stepped down.

It felt a little odd when I realized that there were people in this room who would get their dream jobs only when my father was either forced to quit (*retiring* wasn't in his vocabulary) or died.

I also realized that in my skirt, blouse, and cardigan I was severely underdressed but didn't actually care. I considered that a big step.

Instead of joining their void of suck, I wandered around the edge of the room. I'd never spent much time here as a kid since this was a place designed solely to impress and intimidate. Some small part of me was tempted to take a page out of Great-Aunt Ida's playbook and pick up something valuable that I could sell. I actually wrapped my fingers around a Fabergé egg sitting on a bookshelf. I hadn't been raised with much of a moral code—in fact, I'd been taught that anything went as long as my end goals were reached, that laws were merely suggestions. I credited my teachers and our servants for teaching me right from wrong. Which meant that I couldn't live with myself if I stole from my parents.

"Come and join us, Madison!" Vanessa invited. I wished her pregnancy didn't prevent her from drinking because my sister was one of those rare people who was meaner sober. "Tell us all about your little school and how you're enjoying being a glorified nanny."

I gritted my teeth together and counted to five, slowly. "No, thanks. I'm not in the mood for you and your particular shade of evil."

She let out a fake laugh, as if I were just the funniest person in the world. "Now, you know we just worry about you and your health! All those children and their diseases."

About to remind her that she was pregnant with her fourth child, I stopped myself. She understood only one kind of response. "You shouldn't be worried about me. Personally I'm a little concerned about all that sucking up you do to our parents and whether it might cause you to burst a lung while giving birth."

Now her laugh was genuine. "Aw, the kitten has her claws out! Isn't that adorable!"

I hated that they all made me feel this way. Like I was a mouse trying to roar. That I was too small and inconsequential for anyone to take seriously. It had been that way my whole life.

A soft bell rang, followed by the sound of heels clacking loudly against the floor outside the salon. Which meant my mother was nearly here. I gulped down a large amount of whiskey, letting it burn my throat as I grimaced.

"The icewoman cometh," Violet muttered loud enough for all of us to hear. Nobody responded.

A few seconds later, my parents made their grand entrance. My father had thick, salt-and-pepper hair, thanks to some expensive hair plugs. He was in a suit with a blue tie and made his way over to Gilbert's side, presumably to talk business. Although I wondered how something so one sided would actually go.

If Frederica's signature color was red, my mother's was pink. She wore a tight baby-pink sheath that she offset with a large diamond necklace and matching earrings. Her icy-blonde hair was in her signature updo. I couldn't recall ever seeing her with her hair down.

She headed straight for me and I squared my shoulders, lifting my chin. I could do this.

"Madison."

Uh-oh. I wasn't going to even get the barest veneer of civility? "Nice to see you, Mother." Or, more accurately, it was nice to see the latest version of her face.

I knew I shouldn't judge her. I had either inherited or absorbed her vanity, despite trying to not be so shallow. I'd probably wind up getting work done on my face when I was her age, too. Well, I would if I could afford it, which was looking very questionable.

"Do you know what I had to do today?" she demanded, and I drew in a large breath, discarding all my initial responses.

Overreact to a perceived slight?

Make a list of all the ways I've failed and disappointed you?

Be offended when someone failed to recognize you and how important you are?

Start a new diet?

I settled on, "What?" That seemed safe-ish.

My father joined us. "What did I miss?"

That was followed by an awkward silence—my mother annoyed at being interrupted, me not knowing what to say next, him not having anything else to add to the discussion beyond that question. As far back as I could remember, I'd never had an actual conversation with my father. Nothing beyond him asking me a single question. I could never understand how a man who could so easily schmooze the media and wealthy donors was so bad at interacting with his own family.

Coughlin then appeared in the doorway to announce that dinner was served. I wanted to kiss him again for saving me from temporarily having to find out what my mother had to do that day.

Everybody went into the dining room two by two with me acting like the caboose, bringing up the rear solo.

I pulled my own chair out and scooted it back in as two servers brought out the first course. I smoothed my linen napkin onto my lap before anyone could do it for me. My mother's eyes were on me, glaring.

My father was telling a tale of a particularly grueling round of golf he'd played that day and in the middle of it my mother interrupted him to say, "You were playing with Randall Ducksworth? I was at lunch with his wife Laura today. We were at Le Chateau and then to our surprise we found the Horvath sisters and . . ."

She continued talking but I tuned her out. My mother hated when the spotlight was off her for even a second and would often use someone else's story to turn it into something about her. During my twenty-first birthday celebration a couple of years ago, I'd decided to do a shot every time my mom made the conversation about her, but five minutes into it I had to stop because I was going to wind up in the hospital with an exploded liver.

And instead of my father being upset about getting cut off, he just sat there and calmly ate his soup. While my mother had never had a formal diagnosis (and never would, as she was never wrong for any reason ever), I'd come to suspect she did suffer from a narcissistic personality disorder. People liked to throw around that term a lot, but I was pretty sure she actually had it. I had read multiple diagnostic lists where the instructions would say something like *a person is a narcissist if they meet six of these twelve requirements*, and my mom would meet all twelve. Everything in our lives was about her, her feelings and wants; nobody else mattered. My parents had fought for my entire childhood. They had come close to divorce on several occasions. But in the end my father gave in and had learned to get along by going along. For the sake of their relationship, he deferred to my mom on everything. He was always on her side, no matter how wrong she might have been.

She'd also been careful in grooming my two older sisters. If she told them to jump, they would always ask how high and what else she wanted them to do right after. I was the only one who had ever defied her.

It had always seemed odd to me that the world regarded my father as a powerful and successful businessman and politician, because he had no control over his personal life. He always did whatever she wanted. She ruled our home with an iron fist.

To make sure that her children and grandchildren stayed in line, she had constructed a will with multiple conditions concerning levels of success and what behaviors were appropriate and not appropriate. Like we had to have a college degree to inherit, and my parents would contact their attorneys on a yearly basis to assess whether or not we had a "good" relationship. Church attendance and volunteering hours were mandatory. Inheriting would happen only if we met every single one of their conditions. It struck me as immeasurably sad that my mother was so desperate to control us that she planned on doing it from beyond the grave.

It made me slightly more sympathetic to think that she behaved the way she did because she was ill, even if she wouldn't acknowledge it. But it also infuriated me that I'd grown up the way I had, thinking it was normal for your parents to say things like *my love has to be earned*.

Mom's story about her shopping excursion with her boring friends continued on through the appetizers and on to our main meal. The vein in the top left of my forehead had started to throb and I wondered how much longer I was going to be subjected to this before somebody explained what I was doing there.

Because I hated sitting there all nervous, waiting for the other shoe to drop. Despite her talking about something inane, I could still feel her disapproval radiating toward me. It was agony. I would have preferred the lions being set loose into the arena at the beginning of dinner instead of anxiously anticipating their release.

Then, as if in direct response to my anxiety, Vanessa said, "So are we not going to talk about the black sheep in the room?"

I knew what the "right" thing to do here was. I was supposed to hang my head and feel ashamed of my choices. I wasn't supposed to respond and should just let them humiliate me for blemishing the precious Huntington name.

That didn't really work for me anymore. "Here we go. I don't know how I've managed to survive the last few months without your constant criticism."

Vanessa narrowed her eyes at me. "Criticism is just an unpleasant way of telling the truth. Something nobody else at this table seems to want to do."

"Whatever. Being a teacher doesn't qualify me for black-sheep status."

"No, it doesn't," Violet agreed. Part of me wanted to believe that she was sticking up for me, but I knew it was because she wanted to get the upper hand in an argument she and Vanessa had been having since, I suspected, they were forced to share a womb.

"Right." Vanessa nodded, her attention now focused on her twin. "I suppose that's reserved for someone who just got out of rehab for the fifth time."

"Or maybe it's for someone who has a husband with so many mistresses they could populate their own small country," Violet hissed back. Believe it or not, this was what passed for mostly civil in our family. I wondered whether I should go over and take away their knives.

"Helping people is not a bad thing." I wanted to stand up for myself and I wasn't going to let my sister belittle my career choice.

Vanessa decided to turn her venomous wrath on me. "You could take over the philanthropy division at Daddy's company. You could help a lot more people than you ever will in your little job."

I was about to explain the numerous issues with her suggestion when my mother imperiously told us to be quiet. While my father and brother-in-law were ignoring all of us and focusing on their steaks, Violet's date looked both horrified and concerned. I wanted to tell him to run far and run fast.

Coughlin appeared with an extra place setting and put it on the table next to me. What was happening?

"You're about to be really sad that you put that cheap garbage on your hair," Vanessa whispered at me, and I wondered what she knew that I didn't.

"What's wrong with my hair?"

"If your sister doesn't want to pay for life's necessities, it's not something we need to concern ourselves with," my mother sniffed. I decided not to tell her that visiting her hairstylist once a week was not an actual necessity.

Instead I was too caught up as to who would be joining us. A reporter? Was that why I was here? To sell my father's image as a loving family man? Or were Frederica and my mother back on good terms? Some new business partner who needed to be impressed?

"Constance! So good to see you. Ronald, how are you, sir?"

As my mother stood up to greet her guest, I realized that it was so much worse than anything else I had considered.

It was Brad. Here. Kissing my mother hello.

I only barely registered Vanessa smirking at me as blood rushed through my ears, making it impossible to hear.

What was happening?

My mother told Brad to have a seat. Next to me. And she was smiling.

Suddenly, I knew. I knew what was going on.

I saw him reach inside his coat pocket as he approached me, confirming my worst fear. The lion had finally been set loose.

Bradford Beauregard Branson IV was going to propose to me.

CHAPTER SIX

How had I not recognized that this was a trap? That my mother had lured me here so that Brad could ask me to marry him in front of my family? The two of them had put me in a position where I couldn't say no. Frederica had said they were all expecting an announcement any day now. Was it because she knew something I didn't?

Something that felt akin to hate bubbled up inside my chest, pouring into the rest of my body like angry molten lava. I was so furious with them both that I didn't know how to calm myself down.

Instead, I did the unthinkable. I was rude to a guest.

I stood up without excusing myself, throwing my napkin on the table. I headed toward the kitchen, the anger nipping at my heels with each step I took. How could they?

"Madison!" Brad calling my name only made me walk faster. I'd get someone on the staff to call Julio or I'd eat the cost of an Uber back to my apartment.

"Wait." His voice was right behind me and then his hand was on my arm. I jerked it away.

"What do you want?" I growled.

"Just to talk to you for a minute. Please."

My initial inclination was to tell him to go screw himself and walk away. But it warred with that teenage part of myself that had adored him. He stood there with that self-deprecating grin that I'd always loved and it was even harder to tell him no. It was like he knew exactly what to do to get me to agree.

I gave a curt nod and we walked into my father's study. Brad closed the door behind us and I folded my arms across my chest. He stood there a minute, flustered, as if he didn't know what to say. It was very unlike him.

Because Brad was his family's metaphorical and literal golden boy. Tall, blond, soft-brown eyes. Toothpaste-commercial smile. Girls had fallen all over themselves for years.

It had always made me feel special that I was the one he chose. I got the title of girlfriend. I was the one on his arm. I had loved all the envious stares.

What I hadn't loved was his inability to be faithful to me.

"So, uh, hi."

Really? We hadn't spoken in three months and he resorted to *hi*? I started for the door and he put both of his hands out.

"Wait. That was stupid. I'm sorry. It's just . . . we haven't talked in a while and I wasn't sure what to say."

When he stopped answering my texts, I had been so hurt and angry. I had wanted to pretend he didn't exist. To just . . . forget about him.

Which was harder to do than I thought it would be. He was my first boyfriend. My first kiss. My first everything. Some part of me wanted so badly to believe that he had loved me the way that I had loved him. It was what made me give him chance after chance. Like I believed that if I were just patient and waited for him to stop being a moron, we really could end up happily ever after.

He rubbed the back of his neck with his right hand, giving me a wry look. "I'm really messing this all up, aren't I?"

If he expected me to respond, or to make things better, he was mistaken.

I stayed silent.

"I guess it's just Brad timing," he said, probably thinking that his making puns of his name was adorable. It was actually one of the things about him that annoyed the living daylights out of me. To be fair, it was partly my fault for never telling him just how obnoxious it was.

"Uh-oh. You're not smiling. I guess you aren't Brad I came."

"Enough." I ground the word out. "What do you want?"

He looked taken aback, which wasn't too surprising given that I'd never snapped at him before. I was always so busy trying to make sure that he liked me that I never got angry at him.

Something else that needed to change.

"Okay . . . so I was in New York last night."

It probably didn't say much about the status of our relationship if my first thought after hearing those words was to think of Tyler. Who would soon be in New York.

"And I was thinking about you," Brad continued. "Thinking how much I've taken you for granted. How much I've missed you. You've always been the best thing that ever happened to me, Madison."

I blinked, slowly. There was a time when I would have done anything to hear him say these words.

But now? They were just that. Words. Empty, meaningless words.

When my parents kicked me out and cut me off, he was the person I'd reached out to. He had been my boyfriend and I expected his support. His love. But he never responded to my texts, never picked up my phone calls. Until I finally understood that in addition to losing my family I'd also lost the one person who was always supposed to be on my side.

I never knew if his silence meant that he agreed with my parents. Or if he just wasn't mature enough to be there for me. He hadn't even had the decency to break up with me. He just . . . disappeared.

Whatever his reasons were, his actions had been terrible.

Something on my face must have tipped him off as to how I was feeling because he rushed on. "And when I started thinking about my future, about what I want and who I want standing by my side, that person is always you. You're my girl."

I had to admit, a bit of me melted. I didn't want it to, but it still happened.

Then he reached into his pocket again, as if he sensed his small victory. He pulled out something that was from Tiffany's, but was most definitely not a ring box. The relief I felt was immediate and overwhelming.

He handed it to me and against my better judgment I took it. "It made me think of you," he said.

I opened it to find a diamond tennis bracelet. I caught my breath for a second because of the vast number of carats sitting in front of me. It was gorgeous.

"Do you like it?" he asked. He'd already known how much I would. I had such a weakness for big and sparkly gems. My parents had confiscated my jewelry, which was easy to do since most of it was in my mother's safe.

It was like the shiny diamonds were mesmerizing me, and it took a second to collect myself. To remember who I was and who I was talking to. "What do you think this earns you?"

"Nothing!" He held up both of his hands, as if surrendering. "I know how badly I've messed up. I know we have a lot to work through and talk about. So I wanted to ask you a favor. Don't close the door on us. Not permanently, anyway. I think we have a future. I want to show you how I've changed."

"I don't believe you."

He let out a sigh. "That's fair, I guess. I haven't really given you a reason to."

Some part of me wanted to believe so badly. That our time apart had changed Brad and he was going to be a totally different person. That things could work out.

The other part of me wanted to waltz back into the dining room and announce that there was not going to be a Branson/Huntington wedding. Not now, not ever. My mother would lose her ever-loving mind.

I regretfully ran my fingers across the bracelet one last time before I closed the box and tried handing it back to him. He refused.

"That's yours. No matter what happens. No strings attached."

It didn't feel string-free. There was a definite Pinocchio vibe going on here.

He pushed the box back toward me, and I wasn't sure what to do. If I just left it here, someone would find it, and that would open up a whole barrel of drama with my mother that I wasn't currently prepared for.

Or my great-aunt Ida might make a visit, and nobody would ever see the bracelet ever again.

I sighed. "I'll take it now, but only with the understanding that I will be giving it back to you when you realize that we are over. There's nothing for me to think about because that door is closed. I think we've run our course and it's time for both of us to move on. Find the person we're really meant to be with."

Why was Tyler's face flashing in my mind? So random. And ridiculous.

I knew I couldn't be with Tyler. But I deserved to find someone like him.

Brad frowned. "I don't know if I can accept that. I don't want to move on. I want us to be together. You should know that I'm committed to you. To us. Keep the bracelet. Even if the answer is no."

Unfortunately, it didn't take much to convince me to hang on to it.

He said, "I'll keep hoping that you'll change your mind and that your answer will be yes. If nothing else, think about how much emergency Botox our mothers would have to schedule to erase their laugh lines from all the grinning they'd be doing. Maybe you should say yes for the economy's sake."

I'll admit that made me smile. Just a little. But we needed some parameters. I didn't want to be harassed by him or by my family. "You may not want to accept it, but this is done. We don't have to tell our families right away." That was a bit selfish on my part, but I most definitely did not want my mother hounding me day and night over it while I was in the middle of figuring out my life. "But I think it would be better for both of us if we agree to no contact." It shouldn't have been too hard, considering he'd been silent for the last few months. "That means no texts, no phone calls, no emails. It will make it easier for us to move on."

Brad cleared his throat, as if unsure what to say next. It was so unlike him. He was always confident, his place in the world so sure and so secure that nothing ever threatened him. "Okay. I can do that. I would like to be able to plead my case, but I'll wait for you. I'm going to show you how much I've changed, how devoted I am to you."

He leaned forward, as if he meant to kiss me. I stepped out of reach and I saw a combination of hurt and something else—anger?—in his eyes.

With that, he left the room. I leaned against my dad's desk, taking in a couple of deep breaths to center myself. The most logical response would be to find him, give him back the bracelet, and tell him in front of everyone that things were definitely over.

But I held back because I knew if I did, if I told him it was over, my parents would never recover. This dinner would be the last time I'd see them. They'd called me here only so that Brad could talk to me and pass along his bribe.

So many of their plans and hopes to expand their business and launch themselves into a new social stratum were pinned on me marrying into the Branson empire. If I were being honest, I could admit that Brad had been a safety net for me. If I ever got tired of fending for myself and decided to be absorbed back into the collective, he was my ticket home. Marrying him would erase every rebellious choice I'd made to this point. He was my get-out-of-jail-free card.

But I had to let go of that possibility. Things were over between us and had been for a long time. Maybe I should have made that clearer to him. Let him know that there definitely wasn't any hope for us getting back together. Because I was done with him and our very toxic past.

While I debated whether or not I should find him and make sure he understood that we were done, I heard Vanessa say, "Did I hear wedding bells? When's the big day?"

"I'm not engaged," I told her.

She closed the study door behind her. "That's a shame." She cradled her stomach with her left hand. "You should hurry up and make that happen. It's your one job."

I resented the implication that my only purpose in life was to marry Brad. "What if I don't want to marry him?"

"Since when did anybody here care about that?" I heard the resentment in her tone. I wanted to feel bad for her, but marrying Gilbert had been her choice. "You and Brad would make a good team."

"I don't want to be part of a team. I want to be in love."

She let out a laugh, tinged with bitterness. "You are such a child. It's better to be with someone who understands you and your lifestyle. Who wants the same things out of life that you do."

That sounded lonely to me. "Why can't I have both?"

"Because that's not how real life works. It's time you grew up and realized that. Do your duty for this family and what's expected of you. Your rebellious little tantrum has gone on long enough."

"In case you didn't know," I said with a shake of my head, "you are turning into Mom. And I always thought you were better than that."

Vanessa gasped in outrage as Coughlin entered the room, carrying my coat. "Julio is waiting for you, Miss Madison." He handed me my coat and I again was struck with the urge to kiss his cheek for saving me.

I walked out of the study without looking back, heading directly for the black town car in front of the house. I climbed in before I could be accosted by another member of my family and as Julio headed down the long driveway I wondered what Vanessa had been up to.

What was her goal? Was she trying to trick me down the same miserable path her life had taken? If she suffered, so should everyone else?

Or was she using some kind of reverse psychology, hoping to push me into publicly breaking up with Brad? Knowing how angry it would make our parents? Ensuring the amount of her inheritance went from thirty-three percent to fifty?

Sighing, I leaned my head back against the seat. What I did know was two things—I didn't want to play any more Huntington games.

And despite his hopes that I'd keep an open mind, I really didn't want to get back together with Brad.

~

The next day, after school, Delia had to stop by the grocery store before she dropped me off at home. As we passed by a display of dog food, I felt proud of myself that I had successfully fed and watered Pigeon earlier that morning. Or, I assumed I had because she hadn't come out to eat when I called for her.

While I followed Delia through the aisles, a box of macaroni and cheese caught my attention. Another food that had been banned from my household that I'd always wanted to try thanks to commercials.

When she dropped me off, I was eager to make my own dinner. I checked Pigeon's food bowl and saw that she had eaten. I grabbed her some more kibble before taking my box of mac and cheese over to the counter to read the directions.

Because that's all cooking was, right? Following directions?

I had no idea what a saucepan was, or how it was different from a pot. But I found one that looked like the image on the box. It sounded easy: boiling water, putting in the pasta until it got soft.

Why hadn't I tried this years ago?

While I waited for the water to boil, I started wandering around the apartment. I had mostly kept to my room and hadn't had much of a chance to investigate. While I decided snooping in Tyler's room was off limits, I figured anything in our communal living space was fair game.

In the living room he had an eclectic mix of books. Some of them were about finance and looked like they were old college textbooks. Others looked like they were about computers and programming. But most of his books were spy novels. And they looked worn, as if he'd read them often.

I loved that.

I checked out his movies on the media stand just below the TV. I expected to see action thrillers about spies, given his reading tastes, but instead found a bunch of sci-fi DVDs with a couple of big-budget explosion fests thrown in. Along with a few romantic comedies. Hm. I frowned. Had he picked them out or had some previous (or current) girlfriend left them here?

When I put the DVDs back, I noticed a stack of what looked like ticket stubs on top of the stand. They were parking tickets and I wanted to laugh. Apparently Tyler wasn't great at reading the permitted parking hours on signs. He suddenly seemed so much more human to me.

And why did I find his illegal parking adorable?

I heard the sound of the water boiling on the stove. After I located a bowl with holes in it so that I could drain the pasta, I set the pan down. Then I read over the directions again. I needed butter and milk. I found the butter . . . but no milk. I didn't know how much of an issue this was going to be and I was concerned.

There was a quarter gallon of chocolate milk left in the fridge. I considered my options. How bad could it be? I'd eaten cheese and chocolate together for dessert many times. I poured in a quarter cup of the chocolate milk and added the "cheese" packet.

Maybe I'd just discovered a new side hobby and I could become a YouTube star. I'd make videos of me combining interesting flavors for basic foods.

And I held on to that notion that it could work right up until the moment when I put my concoction in my mouth.

It was like misery combined with regurgitated chocolate and wet, curdled cheese. Foul. I spit my bite back into the bowl.

Pigeon wandered into the kitchen, keeping distance between us as she went over to her food bowl.

"Don't mind me. Just over here committing food felonies," I told her. I stuck the pan back into the sink to rinse it out. I didn't know a lot about dogs, but I did remember reading they couldn't eat chocolate. I didn't know if that included chocolate milk, and while I couldn't imagine Pigeon would want a bite of this monstrosity, it was better to be safe than sorry.

My phone buzzed, and my heart fluttered when I saw who the text was from. Tyler.

> How are things?

How were things? I lacked the basic ability to even feed myself. But that was probably not something I should tell him considering that he believed I could do things. Like cook. And clean stuff.

And keep his dog alive.

Fine.

Wow, deep meaningful answer.

Good. Remind Pigeon to keep
her blood alcohol level below
the legal minimum and that
she has a curfew of midnight.

That made me smile and I considered whether or not I should work
on raising my own blood alcohol level a little, but my mess of a dinner
had ruined my whole night. I wasn't even hungry anymore. My war
crimes against food had effectively ruined my own appetite, something
I never would have thought possible. Since I'd failed so spectacularly at
cooking, I figured cleaning couldn't be much worse.

I retrieved the cleaning list Tyler had made up and hung on the
fridge. It was then that I noticed he'd doodled a bunch of stick figures
acting out the various chores and it made me smile again. First on the
list was filling up the dishwasher.

I'd seen Shay fill the dishwasher many times. I knew from her past
scoldings that I was supposed to rinse stuff out and then make sure the
water sprays could reach the whole surface of the dish when I put it in.
Easy enough. After I'd put in all the dishes I'd dirtied, I grabbed some
that Tyler must have left out from that morning. I'd smelled bacon
when I woke up, but he'd been long gone and so had the bacon.

I grabbed the heavy pan he'd used off the stove and put it in the
dishwasher. I knew I was supposed to add soap. Shay had a powder
she'd pour into the little drawer. I didn't see any powder. Just something
called Dawn that was blue. It said *dishwashing liquid* on the front of
the bottle. This must have been the brand that Tyler used. I wasn't sure
how much to put in, so I filled the slot full, closed it, and pushed start.

Feeling very accomplished, I headed off to the hall bathroom, which was basically mine. Although guests would probably use it, too. I wondered if Tyler had guests. And how often.

And how female.

I brushed my teeth, wanting to get rid of that choco-cheese taste that lingered on my tongue. Once I'd finished up, I went into my room to resume unpacking. I'd made a lot of headway, but I still needed to get the rest of the boxes emptied.

I quickly lost track of time, humming to myself as I worked.

Pigeon started barking. I didn't know what to make of that. Tyler had never mentioned what it meant if she barked. Did that mean she needed to go outside?

I came out to investigate. "Hey girl, what do you . . ." My voice trailed off as I took in the state of the kitchen. Massive white bubbles covered the entire floor, growing into a mountain that was already countertop height.

I gasped. Oh no! I'd turned Tyler's kitchen into a three-year-old's outdoor summer birthday party!

CHAPTER SEVEN

Pigeon stood in the dining room, yelping at the bubble mound.

Quickly realizing the dishwasher was the culprit, I ran over and opened the door. I was hit with a blast of hot steam and more bubbles poured out.

But at least they stopped reproducing.

I went to the linen closet and started grabbing towels. I didn't know how else to clean up that many bubbles.

"Pigeon! Please keep out of the kitchen!" I knew she wouldn't understand me, but I needed her to not go in there and add to the mess. I had zero idea how to wash a bubble-covered dog.

Fortunately, she stayed put and watched me as I laid down a barrier of towels between the kitchen and the dining room. While I thought the tile in the kitchen would survive the bubbles, I was afraid the hardwoods in the rest of the penthouse might not.

It took some problem-solving, but I figured out to wet the towels to mop up the bubbles. After I'd cleaned the floor, I piled the wet and dry towels on the counter. I was going to have to wash them. Fortunately, laundry was one of the things I actually knew how to do. While living with Shay I'd figured it out through trial and error and had lost /

permanently damaged only a handful of items. (Apparently the ones with tags marked "dry cleaning only" were not just suggestions.)

Pigeon observed me silently as I took my pile to the stackable washer and dryer located next to my bathroom. I decided to do a rinse cycle and then wash them. I then grabbed my phone to figure out where I'd gone wrong. Turned out only dishwasher soap should go in the dishwasher. Which was different from dishwashing liquid. And there were also handy directions on how to clean soap out of a dishwasher when you used the wrong kind.

Feeling reassured that I wasn't the only one who'd ever done this, I pulled all the dishes out of the dishwasher. When I got to the bottom rack, I noticed that the heavy pan I'd placed in there looked . . . rusted.

I finally gave in and called Shay. I explained what had happened, and after she stopped laughing she told me to send her a picture of the pan in question.

"You put his cast-iron pan in the dishwasher?" she shrieked when my text arrived.

"Is that bad?"

"So bad! I mean, there's things you can do to try and fix it once you've rusted it up like that, but if you don't want him to know . . ."

"I definitely don't want him to know." I'd been at his place for twenty-four hours and I was already destroying his property. This did not bode well.

"Then I think you're better off buying him a new one. When you do, watch a video on how to take care of it. They're not like regular pans."

"Why would someone buy something you couldn't put in a dishwasher?" I asked.

"Because it cooks certain foods so much better. It's one of those things where if I have to explain it to you, you're not going to get it. But time to replace that sucker. And make sure you season it."

She hung up before I could ask her what seasoning it meant. Time to do more research.

I looked his pan up on Amazon. I gasped when I saw how much it cost. "Why would anyone spend this much on a pan that, I repeat, you cannot put in a dishwasher?"

Pigeon cocked her head at me.

I'd put a self-ban on online shopping mainly because American Express had invited me to stop using their card.

But desperate times and all that . . . I put the pan in my shopping cart and then entered my new address and my debit card information. The new pan was going to arrive in two days, which was plenty of time before Tyler was due back.

Pigeon had continued to study me, keeping her distance. Was it an improvement that she was choosing to hang around me?

"We just had our first adventure together," I told her.

She gave me a disdainful look and trotted off.

I went back into the kitchen to finish properly cleaning out the dishwasher. I'd have to clean the floor next. My first night alone had been an unmitigated disaster, and instead of being able to save money, now I was going to have to spend what little I'd managed to save up to fix my mistake.

Things had to get better from here on out.

~

The next morning I took my aunt's suggestion and checked out the local Ares dealership online. They had several cars that had (according to the internet) low miles for being only a year old. I went to my bank during lunch to see what I could afford. It was the same bank my parents used for both their personal and business needs, and when the manager offered me what sounded like a good car loan, I supposed he did so in order to make my parents happy. The payments sounded doable as long as I stopped ordering food in and actually learned how to cook and shop for groceries, but that was a compromise I was willing to make for more independence.

When Delia dropped me off at my apartment, I gave her gas money, as I typically did at the end of the week.

"This will be the last time," I told her. "Come tomorrow, I'm going to be a proud car owner."

"Good for you," was what she said, but she had that I'll-believe-it-when-I-see-it look in her eyes. "Do you need a ride to the dealership?"

"No, Shay is going to take me and make sure I don't get ripped off." It was something I hadn't thought much about until the internet repeatedly warned me that all car salesmen were looking to scam unsuspecting female buyers.

We waved goodbye, and as I headed inside, I checked my phone to make sure the car I wanted was still on the lot. It was a cute little black Honda. I figured my best defense would be a good offense, so I learned everything I could about the car. The blue book value, how much the dealership had marked it up, what I should offer them. Shay would be there to support me, but I was determined that I would be the one making the deal.

Owning a car had become an important symbol for me, maybe even more so than the apartment. It was proof that I could make my own way in the real world, something my mother had accused me of being unable to do, and that I had the ability to provide for myself. A car meant freedom and total independence. I could load it up and go anywhere I wanted. Not that I would, because I had to keep my job to pay for said car, but it was the principle of the thing. In knowing I could.

Not only was it Buying My Own Car Eve, it was also the day Tyler got back from New York. I was excited to see him again. Once I got inside the lobby, Gerald called me over to give me a package. It was the replacement pan, a day late. I was relieved it had finally arrived, and since I'd watched two videos on how to take care of a new cast-iron pan, I was set.

Hopefully Tyler wouldn't notice.

I mentally reviewed the list of what I had to do that evening. What I wanted to do was to not have to clean or cook at all but to have a hot bath with a glass of wine and then maybe the whole bottle of wine while I binge-watched some television and ate chocolate ice cream.

TV and books had always been my refuge. I suspected that I watched more TV than what other people would consider normal. I mean, if Netflix were a person, I would totally invite it to my wedding. When I discovered that Tyler had a DVR, I nearly shrieked with joy. I left a blue Post-it note on his door asking if I could record my shows. As long as they didn't interfere with his.

I sighed as the elevator doors shut behind me. Working all day was hard. I felt like somebody in my life should have told me this. It wouldn't have changed my choices, but at least I would have been more prepared.

Pigeon had started greeting me when I came into the apartment. She still kept her distance, but I figured this was good progress because I needed her to love me so that I could stay.

But today, she wasn't there. I dropped the package off in the kitchen and headed into my room. To my surprise I found Pigeon there, lying on the foot of my bed. This was new. I said hello to her and then kicked off my shoes, making sure that I immediately closed the closet door after to keep her out. I changed into some yoga pants and a T-shirt and went back to the kitchen to try and cover my tracks. Pigeon decided to accompany me, just out of arm's reach.

I was unpacking the pan when I heard a loud thumping noise. It had come from Tyler's bedroom.

My first panicked thought was, *Oh no! He'll know what I've done to his pan!*

The second excited one was, *Tyler's home!*

Not knowing how much time I had, I rubbed the pan with oil and put it on the stove, heating it up until the oil soaked in. I found myself holding my breath, hoping he didn't catch me before I finished. I willed it to hurry up.

There was another loud sound, more like a crash. As if something heavy had fallen over.

"Tyler?" I called out. I waited a beat or two, no response.

Pigeon whimpered next to me.

Okay, now I was worried. This seemed strange. I called Tyler's name again. Still nothing.

What if we were being robbed? The likelihood seemed small, with Gerald downstairs. I went down the hall to Tyler's room, knocking on his door.

No answer.

What if he had fallen and hit his head? What if he was in dire need of mouth-to-mouth resuscitation and I was just standing on this side of the door like an idiot? I knocked, again saying his name. I tried the doorknob. It wasn't locked.

"Tyler?" I pushed the door open slowly.

The first thing I noticed was that there was an incredibly beautiful woman with thick black hair lying on his bed, studying a bridal magazine like it was a textbook.

The second thing I noticed was that she was wearing lingerie so revealing that I wondered if she'd accidentally mistaken Tyler's bedroom for her OB-GYN's office.

I realized why Shay wasn't Tyler's type. Because his type was an exotic model–looking creature who didn't resemble real human women in the least.

She wore earbuds, which explained why she hadn't heard me earlier. She was in the process of removing one while I said, "Sorry! I'm so sorry! I didn't mean to interrupt your . . . whatever this was."

I quickly closed his door and ran for the safety of my room. That would teach me to go into his bedroom without an invitation. I cursed the part of my brain that lit up at the words *invitation* and *bedroom*. I reminded myself I'd just gotten an eyeful of a half-naked woman who was living proof that nothing would ever happen between Tyler and me.

My door opened behind me and my heart jumped into my throat. It was the Other Woman, wearing one of Tyler's dress shirts and looking like she'd just stepped out of the pages of a magazine. She seemed to be about the same height as me, until I saw that she was wearing heels. She had high cheekbones and large, dark eyes. Perfect bee-stung lips.

While I'd always been confident in my appearance, I suddenly felt like the dowdy, ugly stepsister.

"You are the roommate?" she asked. Her low, husky voice surprised me. Her Russian-sounding accent was thick.

"Yes. Hi. I'm Madison. Sorry for busting in on you like that, but I heard a noise and . . . anyway. Hi. Nice to meet you." I held out my hand.

She stared at my hand with contempt and I wasn't sure if I'd done something to offend her. Other than bursting in on her in what we were agreeing to call *underwear*.

"I am Oksana. From what Tyler said I thought you would be . . . attractive." She dismissed my entire presence with a single glance. "I see that I have no reason to worry."

My mouth was wide open and I could only gape at her in response. I lowered my hand. Had that really just happened? Had she come into my room to call me ugly and say I wasn't a threat?

"Where is Tyler?" she asked, now bored with me and my inability to challenge her.

"I don't know." Which was true. I didn't know where he was at that particular moment in time. New York, the airport, on his way home. Too bad he wasn't here, protecting me from his she-devil of a girlfriend.

"You will tell him I was here." She gracefully turned and walked away. I heard his bedroom door close.

I could only imagine writing that Post-it note. Did our current roommate relationship extend to me informing him that mostly naked women lounged in his bed while he was away? Clearly, this was none of my business, and if she wanted him to know she was here, she could leave her own note.

I turned to Pigeon, like she might have some answers for me. But she was hiding under my bed and I understood the inclination. I kind of wanted to hide, too.

But I had chores to do. Mean Russian supermodels could show themselves out. I went into the kitchen and got the broom and dustpan from the pantry. I started attacking the corners like they were at fault.

Why would Tyler date someone like that? He seemed so nice. Maybe I had misjudged him.

I heard her heels and looked up to see her strut past the kitchen, like the hall was her own personal catwalk.

Just to be obnoxious I called out, "Bye, Oksana!"

She didn't respond and walked out.

I went back to my sweeping and tried to empty my brain out and forget the last five minutes had ever happened.

In large part because of how jealous I was currently feeling.

I finished the chores, watched an hour of TV while eating the spaghetti I'd made for myself, and then graded some tests. Feeling exhausted, I decided to turn in early.

As I got ready for bed, for reasons I didn't quite understand, Pigeon brought her stuffed animal and blanket into my room to sleep in my bed. After my earlier encounter with Oksana, I didn't mind having the company. It also made me feel good that Pigeon was starting to feel more comfortable with me. I needed that win. I did worry that when Tyler got home he might be looking for Pigeon, so I left another note on his door before climbing into my bed.

As I tried to fall asleep, I was still attempting to actively not think about my Oksana encounter and failing miserably when something she'd said came rushing back. Something not horrible or dismissive.

From what Tyler said, I thought you would be . . . attractive.

It was meant to be an insult, but that meant Tyler had told her about me. And that based on his description she thought I would be attractive.

And if I followed that through to its logical conclusion, that meant Tyler thought I was attractive.

The words flitted through me, leaving me feeling happy and light. He thought I was with Brad and he had an evil girlfriend and thanks to his rule we couldn't be together, but Tyler thought I was pretty.

I couldn't keep the smile off my face as I drifted off to sleep.

~

The next morning that smile was still there. I got up, showered, and got ready for my car-buying trip. I went out to the kitchen to grab some cereal. While I was sitting at the island eating, I heard Tyler greeting Pigeon and my heart skipped a beat.

He came into the kitchen with a "Good morning!" His hair was still wet; he must have just gotten out of the shower as well. He had on a dark-blue T-shirt that lovingly showed off his muscled arms and made me wonder about the muscles I wasn't seeing.

I so wanted to leap over this counter, tackle him, and make out with his face. I decided to use polite words instead. "Morning! Welcome back."

Then I almost choked on my cereal when he reached up for his coffee mug, exposing an expanse of skin that showed me exactly what the shirt covered. I was so glad I was already sitting down as I lost all feeling in my knees.

"So I have a question for you," he said, and every part of my body tensed in anticipation. *He knows. He knows I replaced the pan!* "Does the kitchen smell like, I don't know, dishwashing soap to you?"

Oh crap. It kind of did. I thought I'd done a better job of cleaning it. I grimaced slightly in response. "I hadn't noticed."

"Huh." Thankfully he didn't say anything about the cast-iron pan. Instead he asked, "Do you have any fun plans today?"

"I'm going to buy a car." I couldn't keep the glee out of my voice, and it made him smile. "I've never bought a car before. I'm really looking forward to it."

"That does sound . . . well, I don't know if *fun's* the word I would use. Having the car is fun. Buying it usually not so much."

"I've been adequately warned. And my friend Shay is supposed to be here in a few minutes. I'm hoping to get to the lot before it opens so I can get the car I want." This was the dealer's busiest day of the week and I was afraid the car would get sold. My phone buzzed with a text from Shay. "Speak of the devil."

> My mom needs my help; I have to cancel this morning. I'm so sorry!

"Oh no," I said.

"Everything okay?"

"Not really. Shay had to cancel. I'm going to try one of my other friends." I called Delia and she didn't pick up. Which was unlike her. I tried texting her and waited.

"No answer?" Tyler asked.

"She didn't reply," I confirmed, a sinking feeling settling in my stomach. "Which means I'm going to have to take an Uber to get to this dealership." It wouldn't be cheap.

"I can drive you."

"What?" Had I heard him correctly?

"I can drive you," he said, repeating his offer. "I don't have much going on until later on this evening, so if you want, I can go with you."

He's not interested in you. He has a girlfriend who looks like a Russian Barbie come to life. He is just being your friend. Stop being so excited.

My pounding heart didn't listen.

Something in my expression made him laugh. "Is that a yes?"

CHAPTER EIGHT

Um, obviously the answer was yes. Because I might have been a lot of things, but stupid was not one of them. It was, in fact, an overly enthusiastic "Yes!" It made him laugh again. So even if I was embarrassing myself, it was worth it to hear his reaction.

"From what I've read online, you'll be even better backup than Shay," I told him. "Because you're a man. And you're tall." And hot.

Thankfully, my lips refrained from uttering that last part.

"You don't know any other tall men?" he asked.

"We did discuss this as a friend group, and no, we didn't have anybody else to ask that we thought might do it. Delia did offer to send along her giant cardboard cutout of Edward from *Twilight*, but I passed."

"Good choice," he said with a grin. "Are you ready to go?"

"Let me grab my purse." *I'm spending the day with Tyler Roth!* I felt like a teenager again, giddy over her first crush. Not to mention that I hadn't forgotten what Oksana had inadvertently told me and not only did it add a spring to my step, but it filled me with a confidence that I hadn't felt in a long time.

Tyler was holding the elevator open and I grabbed my coat from the wall. It was sunny outside, but the weather had dipped down into the fifties.

We walked to the parking garage and Tyler showed me where my parking spot would be. It was right next to his, where his car, a classic red Mustang, sat. His choice surprised me. I thought he'd be more of a sleek-sports-car type of guy. "This doesn't seem like you," I said.

He opened the passenger door for me. "It doesn't?"

I shrugged one shoulder as I got in. To be fair, I didn't really know much about him. A guy who dated Oksana should be driving a Porsche or a Lamborghini. He seemed full of contradictions and I wanted to figure him out.

He got in on his side and put on his seat belt, then started up the car. "So, I was surprised that Pigeon slept in your room last night."

"Me too. I think she's coming around."

"I noticed this morning that she seemed calmer. I think having you there while I was gone was good for her."

"She's become my little shadow. She doesn't want me to pet her, but she watches everything I do." And I was very fortunate that she couldn't talk or else I'd be in trouble. While following his list and trying to get everything cleaned before he got back, I'd found out that I hadn't fully yet learned my lesson when I used Dawn to clean the windows in the living room. It made sense—if it could clean glass bowls, shouldn't it be able to clean regular glass, too? I'd also had a mishap of sucking up half a roll of floss in the vacuum. But the worst had been when I'd forgotten to return the lint screen to the dryer and a sock had gotten sucked in there, covering a vent and making the drum go off balance. I'd called a repair person to come out the same day to fix it and had emptied out the rest of the money I'd been setting aside for a deposit on my own apartment.

From that point I decided not to attempt any more cleaning until I had thoroughly researched it first. I had a college degree, and five days a week I was in charge of educating and keeping twenty-five tiny humans alive. I knew I could figure out my cleaning issues if I learned how to do my new chores correctly.

So far, so good.

Although, to be fair, I hadn't cleaned my bathroom yet and could only imagine that was going to be unfun.

"I had a feeling the two of you would get along. I'm glad I've been proven right," he said. "It will make traveling a little easier knowing you're there."

"Speaking of, how was your trip to New York?"

At some point he'd put on sunglasses, making it so I couldn't see his eyes. Boo. "Tiring. A bunch of boring meetings. I've actually been working toward a promotion so I don't have to travel so much."

"You don't like traveling?"

"I do. Or, I did. A few years ago I really enjoyed it but now . . . I guess I want to be around more. Be at home. Settle down a little. If I get that promotion, I'll still be working long hours, but at least I'll be here in Houston. I mean, I just got here and I have to turn around and leave tomorrow afternoon for Singapore."

"What? Now I feel bad that you're coming with me," I said. "Especially given that you're not going to be here for very long."

"Don't. I'm happy to be here with you. This should be fun. What about you? Do you travel?"

"Not anymore. But I used to." I told him about some of my family's vacations while we compared notes of places we'd both traveled to. I told him about a restaurant in Singapore that he should check out when he got there. "It has the most beautiful view. The city skyline looks amazing. You should see it at sunset. That view is one of my favorite things in the world. You have to stop by."

"I will," he said.

"It was always one of my favorite places. Mostly because around the corner they had this massive Hello Kitty shop. I was obsessed with Hello Kitty when I was younger. Like bedsheets, towels, stuffed animals, underwear, anything you could think of, I had it in Hello Kitty form." I hadn't ever told anyone about that particular obsession before. Mostly because my mother had dismissed it as silly. I wondered what it was about him that made him so easy to talk to.

"You're talking to a guy who went through a serious Pokémon phase, so I get it. You should have seen me when *Pokémon Go* came out. I was a grown man in a business suit catching Pokémon in the streets."

That made me laugh. I loved that he wasn't too macho to admit to something potentially embarrassing with that much kid-like enthusiasm.

Time passed so quickly that I was surprised when we pulled into the dealership. "Here we are," I said, hoping this would go the way I wanted it to.

"Are you ready for this?" he asked.

"In what way?"

"Since it is your first time, do you know your financial information? Like your credit score?"

"It's not great," I told him. "I may actually weigh more than my credit score."

At that he laughed and my heart warmed. "But I've already got my financing arranged. I wasn't raised with a lot of basic life skills, but I've researched this. I'm ready for whatever they throw at me."

"Then let's go," he said.

As soon as we got out of his car, a salesman immediately descended on us. "How are you folks doing? I'm Larry. What can I help you find today?"

"Hi, Larry. I'm Madison. And I know exactly what I'm looking for." I showed him the car on my phone. "I'd like to see this one."

"A lady who knows what she wants! Follow me." He headed over to the far end of the lot. There it was. My car.

"Would you like to take a test drive?" Larry asked.

I nodded.

"Well, then let me go in and grab the keys. Do you have your driver's license so I can make a copy?"

"Yeah, of course." I dug through my purse, found my wallet, and handed the license to him. When he left, I turned to ask Tyler, "Do you think I seem too eager?"

"This is your circus," he said. "I'm just here to watch the show."

That made my heart flutter. I really appreciated what he'd said. My parents would never have let me make my own choice here. They would have talked over me and selected a different car from what I actually wanted. My decisions wouldn't have mattered to them.

Larry ran back with the keys and gave them to me. He opened the driver's door. "You did say your name was Madison Huntington, right?"

Why was he checking? Did he think my ID was fake? "I did. That's me."

He nodded and handed me my license. "Great. Let's go so you can see what this car is capable of!"

I grabbed the keys and climbed in, adjusting the seat and mirrors. I caught a glimpse of Tyler sitting in the back seat and he shot me two thumbs-up. I smiled, shaking my head as I clicked my seat belt into place.

Once Larry was situated in the passenger seat, I pulled the car forward. I didn't know what I was supposed to be checking for, but the car went forward when I pushed the gas and stopped when I depressed the brake. The signal lights also seemed to be in order.

Larry carried on a one-sided conversation listing all the car's safety features and something about horsepower. I understood only about half of what he was saying.

I wanted to listen, but I kept getting distracted because Tyler, sitting in the back seat, was having very expressive responses to Larry's monologue. Whenever I checked my rearview mirror, I tried hard not to giggle as Tyler alternated between rolling his eyes, raising both eyebrows in mock surprise, and flashing me impish grins.

I didn't drive very far, as my answers as to whether the car ran had been answered. Everything else was just icing on the cake. When I got back to the parking lot, Larry asked, "So tell me, Madison, what can I do to get you to drive this car home today?"

It was nice that Larry didn't address himself to Tyler and talked solely to me. It was a heady experience to be treated like an actual adult capable of making a decision. "Here's the thing, Larry. I'm going to be blunt. I've done my research. I have a cashier's check in my purse that's for four thousand dollars less than your asking price. It's what I can afford. I can't go any higher. Do we have a deal?"

Larry seemed to consider this and then nodded. "Sounds good. Deal."

Wow, that had been much easier than I expected and went against everything I'd read online about how this exchange was supposed to go down. "Really? You don't want to go get your manager or something?"

"I am the manager and you caught me in a good mood. Let's go inside and fill out the paperwork."

Larry got out and I turned around and let out a squeal of excitement to Tyler. Why had all my friends complained about this process? Getting what you wanted was either much easier than I'd been led to believe or I had some secret ninja negotiating skills.

"You did it!" Tyler said. "High-five on that one. You handled that guy like a boss."

I slapped my hand against his. "I can't believe it worked."

"Yeah, I wish my business deals went that smoothly. Come on, let's go in and get this process started. This is going to take a long time."

"You don't have to stay," I told him. I mean, I was probably going to get lost several times on my way home, but I'd find it eventually. I hated the idea of taking up more of his Saturday by sitting in a car dealership.

"No way. You're stuck with me. I have to see how this ends."

"It ends with me having a car."

"Possibly. Let's go find out."

He made it seem like some kind of grand adventure, which in turn made me excited to see if things would actually turn out the way I thought they would. "Lead the way."

"Nope. You're the boss here. You go keep Larry in line. We can't leave the circus until the lions have been sufficiently tamed. You've got this."

Grinning, I headed off toward the dealership offices. I liked feeling as if I could conquer every obstacle around me and tame all the lions in my path. A girl could get used to a guy who made her feel like she could take over the world.

~

What should have been a mind-numbing and thoroughly boring afternoon spent at a car dealership turned out to be one of the most fun in recent memory. Tyler and I got on so well. Talking to him was easy, uncomplicated, and beyond enjoyable. We talked a lot more about traveling, then about Pigeon and the progress I'd made in our relationship, and about his job. There were no awkward silences or trying to decide what to say next. I loved how new it felt, how I wanted to know everything about him, but at the same time how it seemed comfortable and familiar, like we were good friends just continuing an old conversation. Finally the last paper had been signed, my ownership papers and temporary license had been handed to me, and it was finally (finally!) time to go home.

After I explained my inability to follow a GPS, Tyler carefully led the way home and when we got back to the apartment I pulled into the spot next to his in the parking garage. He was waiting for me when I climbed out of my car.

"So how does it feel to be driving your own car? A car that you own?"

"It feels fantastic! Like I want to celebrate." I realized a moment too late how that might have sounded. As if I were insinuating that I wanted to celebrate with him. I was about to correct myself when he pulled out his phone, checking something.

"I have this charity thing I have to go to tonight. Want to come with me and we can celebrate there?"

Two warring emotions struck me. The first, sheer excitement that while I logically understood it wasn't a date, it still felt like a date. The second put me on an anxiety high alert. "Charity things" were my parents' favorite way to spend their time. Other than belittling their children and trying to crush their dreams.

I had no desire to be in a ballroom with my mother, father, and Tyler. I was trying to be his friend. I didn't want to scare him off with the crazy that was my life.

"Who's hosting it?" I asked.

He looked confused. "I don't know. Let me pull up the invitation."

We walked back to our apartment as Tyler scrolled through his phone, finally finding what he'd been looking for. "Here it is. It's the Women's Texan League. It's to help fund some local homeless shelters. My boss wants me to go and network."

The Women's Texan League was chaired by my mother's mortal enemy, Bitsie Fernley. Which meant I didn't have to worry about running into my parents and was free to show up and enjoy myself.

"Bitsie is hosting so, yes, I can go hang out and celebrate," I told him. Thankfully, he didn't ask me to explain.

But when we got into the elevator, he did ask, "I can't believe you know who is hosting the event just based on the organization's name. Do you think this is the kind of stuff I should know? Who hosts events?"

"I only know who's in charge because I grew up with people that it mattered to. People with more money than they know what to do with. Didn't you?"

"No, I didn't grow up with money." His voice had a haunted quality to it and I immediately wondered what made him sound that way.

Then I immediately felt stupid because when we first met he said he'd grown up without money. "Right. You told me that. But I thought you meant 'poor' like your family had one yacht instead of three."

He laughed. "Not quite."

I think I'd forgotten about his upbringing because most guys that I'd met who worked in investing and finance usually had someone in their family to open a door for them. They'd grown up with wealth and felt comfortable in that world. My parents had some pretty strong prejudices against what they called "new money" and made it into a game to spot people at parties who "didn't belong." I'd seen Tyler's custom-tailored suits. I lived in his very expensive apartment. He seemed at ease in his environment. I never would have guessed that it was recently acquired.

"Oh," was my initial brilliant and insightful response. "You seem like you belong to all this."

We went into the apartment and he sat on the back of the couch, facing me. "Then I'm a better actor than I've given myself credit for. It's like I'm impersonating someone else. Maybe that's the reason I always feel so out of place at these things. I graduated from USC. It's not like I'm uneducated. But sometimes it seems like everyone there is speaking a language I don't quite understand."

He wasn't wrong. I hung my purse up and came over to stand in front of him. "My people are look-down-their-noses-at-you rich. So I am fluent in snob. I could teach you."

"Really? You'd do that?"

"For the guy who just spent his entire day helping me get a car? Absolutely."

"I didn't do anything to help."

There was no way I could explain to him that him standing aside, letting me get my car on my own, had been the absolute best thing he could have done. It was just what I'd needed. At the time I'd also understood that if I'd asked him for advice on any part of the process, he would have given it to me, which I'd also found very reassuring. "You may not think so, but you being there was helpful to me. I appreciated you having my back. Now I can have yours. What's the dress code for tonight and what time do we need to leave?"

He checked his phone again. "It says cocktail and it starts in about half an hour."

"Is there a dinner? Dancing?"

"It doesn't say anything about dinner, but yes to dancing."

"Okay. That means we want to show up late. You never want to be on time for an event like this. I'm going to go start getting ready. Meet you back here in about an hour so we can drive over together?" I held my breath, wanting a yes.

Probably because of how date-like it felt.

"Sounds like a plan."

I wanted to kick myself for not allotting enough time to get ready. I'd have to forgo a shower and get dressed. While all my formal gowns were in a closet at my parents' house, I still had most of my semi-formal and cocktail dresses, given all the mixers and events our sorority had done in college. I picked out a midi-length dark-blue dress with delicate beading across the neckline. It was my favorite; I'd picked it up in New York during Fashion Week three years ago. I had always loved that it was one of a kind.

Since I was the kind of person who was overly committed to staying in bed until the last possible moment every morning, it had forced me to learn how to apply my makeup quickly and yet still make it look good. Expensive products and brushes helped, and now I used them only for special occasions like this one. I tried not to think about the day when I was going to run out of everything completely.

I tugged my hair up into a messy bun, using hair spray to tame the flyaways. I went back into my room to go through my jewelry box to see what I had to wear. I had a pair of square sapphire earrings deemed not worth enough money to be put into the family vault.

The diamond tennis bracelet Brad had given to me glittered inside the box. For a moment I was tempted to pick it up and put it on. But only for a moment. I closed the jewelry box, leaving the bracelet behind.

I grabbed a pair of black heels and then gave myself a once-over in the mirror I'd hung up on the inside door of my closet.

Satisfied with what I saw, I dug through the top closet shelf to find a small black clutch. I headed out toward the foyer to transfer over my ID, debit card, cell phone, and lipstick from my purse.

Tyler had apparently been sitting on the couch, waiting for me. He stood up when he saw me and my breath caught as I skidded to a halt, dumbstruck by how handsome he looked.

At some point I was going to have to get used to the sight of him in a suit. It emphasized his broad shoulders and the darkness of it highlighted his light-blue eyes. I gulped.

"You look nice," he told me with a smile.

You look like I want to bear your children. Shaking off my gut response, I smiled back and said, "So do you." As far as compliments went, "nice" was on the bland side, but I'd take it. If I'd been entirely truthful in returning his compliment, what I would have said was that he looked choke-on-your-own-tongue good, but I didn't feel it was appropriate to say so.

"Should we go?"

I grabbed my purse and made the transfer of stuff I thought I'd need. "I'm ready," I told him, as I reached for my coat.

"Here, let me."

It had been a very long time since a man besides my butler had helped me put my coat on. And it was a totally different experience to be standing so close to Tyler, because he smelled like heaven and radiated a delicious heat that made me want to get even closer to him. The feel of him standing just behind me, so close that we were almost touching, made me tremble slightly. It took me two tries to get my left arm into the sleeve, but I finally managed it.

When he put his hands on my shoulders for a brief moment after I'd accomplished the apparently impossible task of dressing myself with assistance, it took all the willpower I possessed not to lean back into him.

Oblivious to my plight, he pushed the button to the elevator and I gave him a shaky smile, hoping he didn't sense how nervous and excited he made me.

Now if I could just remember that nothing was going to happen between us, everything would be fine.

CHAPTER NINE

The charity event was, as so many of them were, in the ballroom of a hotel downtown. There was a DJ playing innocuous music in the background, trees with white Christmas lights surrounding the room, tables and chairs set up on the outskirts of the dance floor. A few couples danced, but most of the people were congregated around either the open bar or what looked to be a silent auction.

There was a podium up front on the stage near the DJ and I wondered whether we had missed the speeches or if we'd be forced to sit through them while the Women's Texan League congratulated themselves on how amazing they were for what would feel like an actual eternity.

"Can I get you a drink?" Tyler offered.

I figured with how pretty he was I should probably keep my wits about me. "Just a club soda for me. Thank you."

"I'll be right back."

I tried to tamp down my jealousy when I noticed all the female gazes that followed him to the bar. I found an empty table and sat. My phone buzzed inside my purse and I took it out.

There was a text from Brad.

So much for not contacting me. He hadn't even made it an entire week.

Annoyed, I clicked on the text. It said:

> Just wanted to tell you I was thinking about you. Hope you're thinking about me.

It was hard to tell with Brad whether this was just a friendly but completely misguided text, him forgetting that I'd asked for no contact. Or if he was just ignoring the fact that I had ended things and was still holding out some hope that he could "win" me back.

He couldn't. I wanted more.

Speaking of more, my eyes were drawn to where Tyler stood. He had run into somebody he knew at the bar and I watched as he shook hands with the other man. The man must have said something funny, because Tyler laughed, and I wished I were closer so that I could hear him.

Brad got what he wanted because I was thinking about him and our relationship, but none of it was good. I remembered when I'd been talking to him at my parents' house and had told him that we should move on and find other people. At the time I had thought it was strange that Tyler had popped into my head. But I realized that it was because he was the first person I'd been this attracted to, ever. It was quickly becoming a more intense crush for me than the one I'd had on Brad when I was fifteen.

And if I were still that teenage girl, I'd probably be scheming to figure out a way to get Tyler away from Oksana and to fall in love with me. But Tyler had been beyond clear that all he wanted was a friendship and for boundaries not to be crossed. I could do that. Even if part of me (okay, nearly all of me) resisted. I could respect what he wanted and just enjoy what he did offer, his friendship. I'd just spent the whole day with him. He was a fun guy to hang out with. That could be enough.

I couldn't really control whether or not I was attracted to him. The constant flutter in my stomach when I looked at him testified that I was. And there was nothing wrong with that. It would only be wrong if I tried to push it to be something more.

If nothing else, at least I was going to get some amazing eye candy out of the deal.

Tyler got our drinks and I saw him looking for me, raising my heartbeat slightly. I waved so that he could see me and he made his way over.

"Thank you," I said when he gave me my drink.

"My pleasure."

His words sent little chills up and down my back. I took a sip of my drink, hoping it would cool off my heated skin. It was more than a little ridiculous to be getting so worked up over such an innocent statement.

"So, why a teacher?"

It took me a second to recognize that he had asked me a question. "What do you mean?" Didn't most people become teachers because they loved teaching? I wasn't sure exactly what he was trying to get at.

"Based on what you told me earlier, I'm assuming that you're an heiress." Well, that wasn't quite right, but I understood why he'd come to that conclusion. "You don't really hear about heiresses leaving it all behind to become an elementary school teacher."

"No, you usually don't," I agreed.

"Why did you make that choice?"

This was something I had thought a lot about, because my parents had wondered the same thing. "Growing up, my parents had very specific things they wanted me to focus on. I loved stories and reading and drawing, but they thought those were wastes of time. That I should focus on more serious academics. It was my teachers who encouraged me, made me feel supported. I usually felt unseen and unknown at home. My teachers made me feel seen and heard. I wanted to do the same for other kids."

He nodded. "I know what that feels like. It's cool that you wanted to do that for other kids."

"Nobody should have to feel that way. My family always made me feel like the odd one out. They thought television and movies were vulgar, and they only wanted me to associate with girls who were of our 'standing.' Which left me with a lot of time alone to read and daydream. From eight to ten years old, I was convinced that my parents were changeling trolls who had taken me away from my real parents." I'd never told anyone that before. How alienated and alone I'd always felt, unwanted for not being a boy and for not living up to my parents' expectations of me. Not wanting to dwell on it too much, I shifted gears. "But I just really love teaching. Seeing a kid's expression light up when they grasp a concept is amazing. Although sometimes I feel like they teach me more than I teach them."

"How so?"

"I love when they blow your mind with something you've never really considered. Like a couple of days ago we were talking about word pronunciation and letter sounds and this girl in my class, Brinley, came to ask me why all the *C*s in *Pacific Ocean* are pronounced differently. She's so smart."

"I can see the appeal." His gaze was intense and inquisitive, and it made me catch my breath.

Then I wondered if maybe I was painting too rosy a picture, so I said, "It's usually great. That doesn't mean it's not without some hardships. And sometimes I'm not sure what to do. There's a boy named Denny that I can't get to stop acting out. I've sent his parents a couple of emails and called, but there hasn't been any response. He's never had an issue before, and now it's like he just lives to find ways to get in trouble. I've been trying to discipline him, but it seems to make things worse.

But even when it's hard, my classroom is where I feel the most like me. Like I'm finally the person I was meant to be."

"That's a real gift," he said. "Not everyone gets that."

For some reason, his words hit me hard, sinking deep inside. It was a gift and I loved that he recognized it as such. But he said it like it wasn't something he had in his own life. "Do you feel that way in your job?"

He glanced down at his drink, looking sad. "I would like to. But my job is just a job. A means to an end."

Now I felt awful, like I'd been bragging about my life. "As to your earlier comment, I'm not an heiress anymore. My parents cut me off."

That got his attention back on me. "What? Why on earth would they do that?"

He looked appropriately shocked, which always made me feel better. When you grew up in Wonderland, and you kept trying to tell people that the painted red roses were actually white and no one believed you and/or cared, it was such a relief to have someone respond, "Yeah, of course they're white roses!" It made me not feel so alone.

"They had other plans for me and none of them included me becoming a teacher. They kicked me out when I told them that was what I'd chosen. Do you think I'd need to be your live-in maid if I still had money?"

I had meant it as a joke, but he just shook his head. "You're not my maid. We're roommates."

Right. As if I needed a reminder. I could practically hear Frederica's voice whispering *roommaid*.

He added, "I think what you did was really brave. You're an admirable person, do you know that?"

Flustered by his words and his gaze, I tried to shrug them off while forcing myself to try and breathe normally. "We're not here to talk about me. We're here for you and to help you navigate these shark-infested waters. And I'm your personal Jacques Cousteau."

He shot me a wry smile. "I appreciate the assist. Networking with potential clients is really important at my company. My boss repeatedly reminds us that it's the most important thing we can do besides being good with numbers and investments. And all my other responsibilities." He sounded so very tired that I wanted to soothe him and make things better. It strengthened my resolve to be a good friend to him.

I looked around the room and realized that I didn't recognize most of the people here. My mother would be cackling over her cauldron to see how the major movers and shakers of society hadn't shown up for Bitsie's fundraiser. If this was the level of event that Tyler was being invited to, and he needed to network with wealthy people, we had to get him into a better caliber of party. That meant making a name for him, starting here. Because everyone in this room knew someone higher up in the food chain and all it would take was a whisper in the right ear.

Walter and Patty Loveless were walking by our table and I stood up to get their attention. "Mr. and Mrs. Loveless! How nice to see you!"

"Oh, Madison. How are you, dear? And please call us Walter and Patty," she reminded me. They were an elderly couple who had dedicated their twilight years to donating as much of their large fortune as they could to charity, to the dismay of their children and grandchildren.

She hugged me gently, and I shook hands with Walter.

"May I introduce you to Tyler Roth?"

Tyler stood up and shook hands with both of them. "It is nice to meet you."

"Oh, any friend of Madison's is a friend of ours." Patty batted her eyelashes at him. Good grief, no one was immune to his handsomeness. "The two of you make a beautiful couple."

I flushed. "Oh, we're not—"

"Thank you," Tyler cut me off. And even though I knew he didn't mean anything by it, like, AT ALL, it was still thrilling and my flush deepened. I hoped nobody noticed. I raised my eyebrows at him and he shrugged, as if to say, *It's easier than trying to explain.*

"Madison, did you attend the Vermeer exhibit last month?" Walter asked me.

"I did." I totally hadn't.

"What did you think?"

"Oh, Vermeer is such a master. His attention to light and detail is just . . ." I let my voice trail off deliberately and as I'd expected, Walter jumped in to pick up the slack.

"Yes, I know exactly what you mean!"

"What is your favorite Vermeer work?" I asked before he could press me to expound on what else I thought about Vermeer's art.

Walter leaned in and said conspiratorially, "I'm afraid I'm rather pedestrian with my tastes and I just love *Girl with a Pearl Earring.* Even if it is his most popular piece."

"Who can blame you for choosing that one? It's popular for a reason," I said. "Will the two of you be going to the abstract expressionist exhibit?"

"We will!" Patty beamed.

"Have you heard whether they're going to include any work by Mark Rothko?"

"I haven't, but we'll keep an eye out and let you know," she replied.

"Excellent. It was so good to catch up with you, but I see someone that I must introduce Tyler to. If you'll please excuse us."

Tyler told them it was good to meet them and let me lead him over toward the bar. Once we'd gotten far enough away, he said, "You're so good at this. Mark Rothko?"

"My parents have two of his paintings. Some stuff you just absorb. I can take you out and show you what I mean. You do some cultural stuff and then you'll have a good baseline to work from. Museum exhibits, opera performances, that kind of thing. Back there with Walter and Patty, I had almost no idea what I was talking about. But rich people practically invented fear of missing out. So they pretend they went to things even if they didn't. I mean, I don't even know if those two actually went to the exhibit. The secret is to have some knowledge to operate from and then get them talking about themselves. Which makes them like you more because you're letting them do all the talking."

He let out a little laugh. "You're amazing. Go on, sensei."

Feeling heady from his approval, I looked around the room and found my target. "Now the next part is getting your name in circulation. I'm about to make every society mother with an eligible daughter fall in love with you."

His eyes danced with delight. "And just how do you plan on doing that?"

"By starting a rumor that you're an extremely successful and wealthy businessman looking to meet someone."

"But I'm not—"

I held up my hand, not letting him finish while my brain tried to figure out how he was going to end that sentence. Not successful? Not wealthy? Not looking for a relationship? None of them mattered. "Don't tell me. I need plausible deniability here. The actual facts are irrelevant. It helps our cause that you are easily the hottest guy here."

His smile was instant, flirtatious, and overwhelming. "Did you just say I was the hottest guy here?"

I rolled my eyes so hard I nearly gave myself a migraine. He knew how he looked. "Take the compliment and say thank you."

"Thank you."

A woman in a red dress came into view and I set my sights on her. She was perfect. "What is your job title?"

"I'm a mid-senior manager of investments and funds management."

That sounded impressive and would act like a particularly potent type of catnip. Fortunately, not everyone here was a complete snob like my parents—most didn't care whether his money was old or new just so long as it was green. They would be impressed, like I was, that he'd been so successful at such a young age. And hadn't had to rely on nepotism.

"Stay here and look busy. Get on your phone if you have to. There's someone I'm going to talk to. And if you thought I was good before, wait until you see what I do next," I told him.

As I walked away, I could feel his grin and his gaze following me. It gave me a boost to execute this part of my plan.

I was about to make Tyler the most sought-after guy in Houston.

Being so caught up in showing off to him, I didn't recognize how stupid my scheme was until it was too late.

CHAPTER TEN

My steps slowed as I wondered why I was throwing him at other women. Some selfish part of me was all *if I can't have him no one can,* but not in a lock-him-in-my-basement sort of way. I just liked the world better where Tyler didn't have a girlfriend. Then I reminded myself that he was dating the winner of the Miss Universe pageant. Not to mention that I'd already firmly told myself that Tyler and I were going to be only friends and nothing more.

Maybe doing this would drive that point home for me.

Standing in front of me was Erin Fernley, Bitsie's oldest daughter. It was well known that she'd been on the hunt for a man ever since her younger sister had gotten married and become pregnant. That Erin had battled her entire life with being "not quite"—not quite as pretty as her sister, not quite as witty, not quite as charming, not quite as popular.

She felt left behind and it made her the perfect target for the opening shot of my campaign.

"Erin! How are you?" I asked.

We exchanged empty air kisses, and Erin's keen sense of observation made it so that I didn't have to come up with a believable way to introduce Tyler. "Hello, Madison. Who is that delectable man you're here with? Are you together? Aw, did something happen with Brad?"

I kept my smile neutral while inwardly seething. Not at her unspoken implication that she was pleased Brad and I might be broken up, possibly paving the way for herself to pursue him. Because she was welcome to him. It was that she already knew that Brad and I were having issues and this was her way of twisting the knife. This was the problem with such a tight-knit and hateful group of people. They knew your secrets and enjoyed exploiting what they saw as a potential weakness.

It was another good reminder as to why it hadn't been hard to leave this life behind.

"Brad and I are taking a bit of a break. I'm here with my friend Tyler Roth. He's in finance." I put an emphasis on the last word so that Erin would pick up my obvious bait.

And she did. Her eyebrows lifted slightly, the corners of her mouth turning up. It was one thing to be gorgeous and quite another to be gorgeous, young, *and* rich. "Is he? And he's single?"

As far as I knew, thanks to my plausible deniability, he was. I had no idea what his actual status was with Oksana. "Yes. I met him recently and discovered that he doesn't socialize much. New in town and all that. Which is a shame, because he is so ambitious, so talented, so good humored. I thought a man like that didn't belong hidden on a shelf."

"You're right," she murmured. I knew my words were working because she was no longer looking me in the eye but watching whatever it was Tyler was doing behind me. "He should be getting to know all the right people."

And by "right people" she clearly meant herself.

"Absolutely. If you see your mother, please give her my best and let her know how much we've enjoyed this evening. I shouldn't leave him alone for too long, don't you agree?"

Another seed planted. Someone as competitive as Erin wouldn't let me win. If I knew anything about her, it was that I'd set her on a collision course with Tyler. Now it would be up to him to handle her and the small talk and turn it into something more.

I turned on my heel, satisfied with what I'd done. I found Tyler, who gave me a questioning look when I slipped my hand through the crook of his arm. While I loved touching him and being close, this was solely for Erin's benefit. I wasn't getting anything out of it.

Or, at least, that was what I told myself.

"Just keep walking," I told him, leading him toward the dance floor. More couples had joined in and were swaying to the jazz music being played. "If someone comes up to you, make sure that when you end the conversation you give them your business card."

"What is happening?" He sounded so amused.

"We're going to dance and let everyone get an eyeful of you."

But before he could agree, Erin interrupted us. "I'm so sorry. I'm Erin Fernley. Madison has told me so much about you." Her slight accent had now taken on a heavy southern twang.

She held her hand out weirdly, in that way where you couldn't tell whether she wanted you to kiss it or shake it. Tyler chose shaking it, which I thought was a good call. This wasn't *Gone with the Wind* and Erin was no Scarlett O'Hara.

"I'm Tyler."

"Oh, I know." She giggled. "Madison, you won't mind if I steal your date for a moment? Because I was wondering if he'd care to dance."

Man, I was good. I'd hardly expected things to work so quickly.

"Do you mind?" Tyler asked me, that amusement still evident in his voice.

For one second, I minded so hard my vision blurred. But I was helping him out and this was the best way I knew of to get his foot in the door.

"Of course not."

He nodded, smiling at me. "Only if you promise that we're going to finish our dance another time."

I swallowed, hard. I knew he didn't mean anything by it, even though it sounded like he did. As if he'd wanted to dance with me, hold me close, and was making sure that we'd get to do it again in the future. I could only nod back, silently agreeing.

It looked like he was going to walk away when he suddenly turned and leaned toward me, his mouth close to my ear. "By the way, I say yes to you teaching me culture." His words were hot against my skin, sending waves of tingles across my neck and scalp.

"I am going to culture you so hard," I whispered back, trying to joke but failing in the attempt.

"Perfect," he said. Was I imagining that twinkling in his eyes?

I'd forgotten that I'd offered to help him out with cultural stuff during our discussion about how to schmooze rich people. But I definitely wasn't going to turn down the chance to spend more time with him.

Not knowing of the plans we'd just made, Erin gave me a smug smirk before she slipped her own arm through Tyler's, leading him onto the floor. I found a chair nearby and sat down. This was better. Since this event was comprised of people Bitsie knew, they were far more likely to pay attention to the young man dancing with her daughter than they would have if I'd danced with him. I could already see the glances, hear their whispers.

Erin could dance with him. I was the one who was going to spend time with him. And I was the one who would be going home with him at the end of the night. Well, not going *home* home with him, but sleeping in the same place he slept. In a separate room. Because we were just friends and roommates, I reminded my hormones for the millionth time.

Tyler said something that made Erin laugh, and she was staring up at him like he'd just invented dancing. It was a special quality he possessed. Like earlier when he was asking me about my job. He had the ability to make whoever he was talking to feel special. Just by giving them his undivided attention.

How did a man like that, one who would sit in a car dealership most of the day entertaining a person he'd only recently met, date someone like Oksana? I mean, I knew why. I had seen most of her body, but . . . what would they talk about? World domination?

Maybe he makes her feel like she can tame lions, too, that perverse, annoying part of my brain said, and I ignored it.

The song came to an end and a twentysomething blonde I didn't recognize came up to Erin to hug her hello. Although I couldn't hear what they were saying, their body language made it pretty obvious what was going on. That the Erin greeting was cover for the blonde to meet Tyler.

And I was proven right seconds later when she and Tyler began dancing together. It set a pattern for the rest of the evening. He never got the chance to rejoin me. The way the women around my age were behaving, you'd think he was the only single man under the age of thirty-five at the party. His dance card was very full.

He shot me apologetic looks over his current partner's head, but I waved them away with a smile. This was what I had set out to accomplish and it had succeeded beyond even my expectations. Especially since I saw him pass out his business card to each and every dance partner.

And he had no reason to feel bad, as I was kept very busy by all the people who came up to me under the guise of "catching up" and then asked about Tyler.

Bitsie Fernley stepped up to the podium to announce the winners of the silent auction, and the music was turned off. Tyler said something to the petite brunette standing next to him and then he made his way over to me.

"I think we should call it a night," he said. "I'm beat."

"Amen." We walked out of the ballroom, collected our coats, and went through the lobby. This time I didn't let him help me because I wasn't sure I could handle another round of him touching me and standing close. When we were outside, he handed the valet his ticket.

"You know," I told him, "Bitsie missed out. If she'd just auctioned off a dance with you, she would have raised all the money she needed."

"Ha-ha."

"I'm serious. You were unquestionably the belle of the ball tonight. Did you leave behind one of your shoes just in case?"

This time he did actually laugh. "I'm not trying to land a prince."

"You'd be the only one."

His car arrived and we both got in after Tyler tipped the valet. As he put his seat belt on, his phone started buzzing. And buzzing. He pulled it out and stared at it. Then he handed it to me. "Do you recognize these names?"

He had like fifty new texts. I scrolled through them while he drove. I did recognize some of the texters. Every message was some variation of *I was hoping to meet with you to discuss my portfolio. Please contact me immediately.*

"I knew it. Did I ever mention that I get smug when I'm right? I told you this would work."

He looked worried. "So all these people, I danced with their daughters? And now they want to meet with me? In case I might marry one of them?"

"Sounds about right."

Rubbing the back of his neck, he said, "When you suggested it, I honestly didn't think this would happen. And now that it has . . . it doesn't seem right to have them come in and try to turn them into clients when I have no intention of going out with any of their offspring."

"I get it, but that's not really the point. You networked your butt off. They might come in with these hopes and ulterior motives and then you'll either turn them into clients or you won't. The dating thing will be irrelevant once you charm them with your business acumen."

"How do you know I have acumen?" I loved that teasing tone.

"A woman just knows these things."

He laughed, and the sound warmed me. It was one of the things I was coming to enjoy most about him. Brad never thought I was funny. We weren't that couple who sat around and laughed together.

Another text came in to Tyler's phone. It was from Mary-Kate Martinez. "Okay," I told him, "this one is weird because I happen to know her oldest daughter's in high school."

"I'm not into committing felonies," he told me.

I smiled. "Maybe they want to get a dating rain check for when she's legal. Or someday have her be your second wife after you get tired of your first one."

He made a sound of disgust and this time it was my turn to laugh.

"Or maybe," I continued, "what I told you was correct and rich people hate missing out and they're not all trying to get you to marry their daughters. Tonight you became the hot new finance guy that people want to use and the rest of them will line up to get your attention. You've become the new Birkin bag."

"What is that?"

"To get a Birkin bag you have to get on a waiting list. Which rich people hate doing. But it makes them want that thing even more. You're going to be swimming in appointments when you get back from Singapore."

We came to a red light and he grinned at me, his eyes bright. "Thank you. Seriously."

"You're welcome."

I looked at his phone again as three more texts rolled in. It seemed like I had done a good thing and helped him.

So why did it feel like I'd just made a big mistake?

~

Tyler spent the next morning with Pigeon until he had to leave for the airport. I was out at the grocery store when he left, and I came home to find a Post-it note on my door. It said:

Forgot to tell you—mi DVR es su DVR. Record to your heart's content. Also, don't buy any more cars unless I'm there to see it.

His note made me smile so hard that my face hurt a little. And he had no idea what he'd just agreed to. I spent Sunday afternoon and evening creating timers for my favorite shows. Pigeon came and sat next to me on the couch. At some point she rested her chin on my knee, and I held my breath when I slowly reached over to pet the top of her head. She closed her eyes when I did so, seeming to enjoy it. I almost texted Tyler to tell him about it because the moment seemed so monumental, but I was worried it might get lost in the avalanche of potential new clients. I opted for leaving him a Post-it note about it instead.

Part of me wanted to ask him how the text messages were going, but the bigger part of me was happy to leave all that in his hands and not think about it any longer. It was one thing to step into that world temporarily, for one night, in order to help a friend, but I wasn't interested in it as a lifestyle any longer. I hated having to worry about how I looked, what people were saying about me, if I was in with the right people and excluding the wrong ones. Where everything was about the facade and nobody cared about the things in life that really mattered.

I didn't envy Tyler having to still play those games. The one benefit of staying just friends was that I wouldn't have to go to those charity events all the time.

I tried not to think too hard about all the other benefits of being his girlfriend.

The next day I was back at work, and we had a teacher professional development day. Which meant time for us to work on our lesson plans, catch up on our grading, and then attend a meeting in the afternoon organized by the headmistress.

I grabbed lunch with Delia and Shay, and since the cafeteria was totally empty, we decided to eat in there. We were discussing our classes in part because one of our friends, Jennifer, had gone on maternity leave and Delia had filled in for her until a long-term substitute teacher could be found.

My teacher's pet, Brinley, had struck again with a question I didn't have an answer for. "One of my kids asked me if either the *S* or the *C* is silent in the word *scent*."

Delia twisted her mouth to one side. "I have no idea. Every time I fill in for a non-art class I realize how many things I don't know. Speaking of scents, we've been discussing insects this week and I learned a certain type of orb-weaver spider puts out a scent that smells just like a female moth in heat in order to attract and trap male moths. It made me wonder what my lure scent would be. You know, the thing that would make me fly blindly to my death. I think it would probably be warm apple cider and cinnamon sugar doughnuts."

Shay laughed. "I would have guessed patchouli and incense." Delia lightly shoved her shoulder, protesting, and then Shay added, "My lure scent would probably be expensive shoes and an Italian leather bag. What about you, Madison?"

"Chocolate and the promise of no more cleaning."

That made them laugh, but it wasn't my real answer. The thing that would draw me in right now was someone who smelled like . . . I tried to think of the right word, and the one that popped in my head was *freedom*. Like choices and options and dreams and possibilities. If that kind of man existed, he would be the opposite of Brad.

Like Tyler.

I brushed the thought away.

Shay asked me a question, interrupting my brain going down forbidden paths. "How's that thing with the little boy in your class going?"

"Denny? I still haven't heard from his parents. I'm going to try them again and then maybe bring the headmistress into the situation." Both women looked a bit scandalized, which I got. Nobody wanted to take things that far and I didn't want to be forced into a position where I had to resort to more drastic measures over Denny's behavior. Because here at the academy, at least as far as the parents were concerned, giving a kid detention was the first step into them becoming meth addicts.

Apparently looking to change the subject, Delia asked me what I'd done over the weekend. I filled them in on how much I was improving with my cleaning.

"I even dusted with one of those feather dusty thingies."

"Did you wear one of those cute little French maid outfits, too?" Shay asked, teasing me. "I bet Tyler would enjoy that."

"He wasn't even there," I shot back. "He's in Singapore at the moment. But he'll be back in a few days."

"Aw, look at you memorizing his schedule," Delia said, joining in on the make-fun-of-Madison party. "Do you make his appointments, too?"

"No, but we went out together the night before last." I'd said it to shut them up, to make them think that I was more than his maid or secretary, and it had worked. But I couldn't let my best friends believe something that wasn't true. "It was to help him network for his job because I'm good at talking to rich people. Friends only. Nothing more."

Shay studied me for a moment before announcing, "You like him. *Like* like him."

"I barely know him."

"That doesn't mean you can't have a major crush on him. And you do," she said.

I shook my head. "What? How could you . . ." I let my voice trail off when I realized that I couldn't deny it to my friends. "Yeah, okay. I have a crush on him."

"Why don't you go for it?"

"First off, he's been really clear that he only wants us to be friends."

"Easily surmountable," she replied with a wave of her fingers.

"Second, I've realized that I'm kind of over dating rich guys."

"Yes." Shay nodded. "The reason the Cinderella story has endured for thousands of years is because no one wants that. Is that it for your objections?"

"No. The third thing is he's sleeping with a Russian spy named Oksana."

"What?" Delia looked alarmed.

"Okay, she may not actually be a spy. But I'm pretty sure she's Russian. And possibly a model."

"How do you know for sure they're together?" Shay asked.

"Her lack of clothing and lying in wait for him in his bed was my first clue."

"We could probably take her," Shay offered.

Delia scoffed playfully. "She could have Bratva connections for all you know and then we'll all be dead. But seriously, what if she's like a stalker?"

"A stalker the doorman lets up?" I asked. "They have to know her or they wouldn't be letting her access Tyler's apartment." At least, I hoped that was true. What if she was that girl Tyler had taken a restraining order out on? Maybe I should say something about her visit to him.

But Delia was determined to figure out what role Oksana was playing. "Tyler hasn't mentioned whether he has a girlfriend? If he and this Oksana girl are serious? Or just hanging out?"

"No, Tyler and I haven't reached the point in our friendship where we braid each other's hair and talk about which boys or girls we like."

Shay collected up her garbage, shoving it all into her paper bag. "Well, methinks the lady doth protest too much. And so I am officially withdrawing my cap."

"Your cap?" I repeated.

"Haven't you heard that expression? Setting your cap at someone? It means you like them and you're planning to pursue them."

"No," I said. "Because I live in the twenty-first century. Nobody at this table needs to be setting any caps anywhere when it comes to Tyler."

"Delia." Shay turned to face her. "You think Madison should go for it, don't you?"

"I think both of them should do whatever makes them happiest." Delia reached over to pat my hand.

"Unhelpful as ever," Shay told her.

"Thank you."

"We're just friends," I said for what felt like the thousandth time. "Nothing more."

"Not yet," Shay said, mischief in her tone.

Before I could do my best to persuade Shay to give it a rest, the school's secretary, Miss Martha, stuck her head in the cafeteria door. "Oh, there you are, Ms. Huntington. Ms. Gladwell would like to have a word with you."

My heart rate sped up. Ms. Gladwell was our headmistress. It was never good news when she wanted to have a word with someone.

Both Delia's and Shay's eyes had gone wide, which didn't make me feel any better.

I'd been so caught up recently in my personal life dramas (the cleaning, the dog, Tyler, Brad, my family) that I hadn't stopped to consider any potential workplace problems. I was currently on probation at work, as was every new teacher who started there, for one year. If the school was pleased with my performance and my students' test scores, then I would be asked back.

Had I messed up somehow already?

Delia whispered, "It will be fine," but her words were undone by Shay looking like I'd just been issued a death sentence.

Pulling in a deep, shaky breath, I got up to follow Miss Martha while frantically trying to figure out what I could have possibly done to warrant getting called to the headmistress's office.

CHAPTER ELEVEN

I knocked on Ms. Gladwell's office door, which was slightly ajar. She looked up at me, over the rim of her glasses and said, "Ms. Huntington. Please come in and have a seat."

Doing as she asked, I pushed the door the rest of the way open and sat in one of the chairs in front of her desk. Her office was decorated very traditionally: dark wooden cabinets, a desk with thick legs, and leather armchairs. Ms. Gladwell was in her forties, and had the same look as so many of the older mothers here at the school—where her face was unnaturally smooth and tight. But in Ms. Gladwell's case I didn't suspect plastic surgery so much as wrinkles wouldn't dare to form on her face. She was a formidable woman. And very, very good at her job.

Which is why the next part surprised me.

She finished typing something on her computer and then swiveled her chair to face me. "Ms. Huntington, as you know, we expect the students here at Millstone to participate in extracurricular activities. Especially school-sponsored ones."

I nodded. I did know that.

"And we have the same expectations of our teachers. As you may or may not know, our annual winter festival is coming up. It is typically held in our gymnasium and is one of our primary sources for fundraising throughout the year."

Delia had mentioned the festival a couple of times, but I didn't know much about it.

Ms. Gladwell continued. "A problem has arisen and we find that we need one additional person to join the decorating committee."

"Oh." That was a bad idea. A really bad idea. I'd never decorated anything in my life. My mother had very-well-paid people for that. Even my classroom walls had started the year pretty much bare. I felt bad about it and had tried to do a Harry Potter theme, but it was all excruciatingly terrible. I couldn't spend the entire year staring at my hideous attempts at re-creating Hogwarts and the Whomping Willow. I'd been assigning my kids art projects so that we could hang them up and cover the walls that way.

Taking my "oh" for a yes, Ms. Gladwell called out, "Mrs. Adams, would you please join us?"

I'd been so intent on following Miss Martha to the office that I hadn't noticed the pretty and tiny woman sitting out front of Ms. Gladwell's office. She looked like every other mother of a Millstone Academy student, perfect hair, perfect teeth, name-brand yoga pants, and a hoodie. A look designed to be casual but screaming of expense—both monetarily and timewise.

"Hello, I'm Mrs. Adams." She had been carrying about ten grocery bags but set them down on the floor.

I shook her perfectly manicured hand wondering what Ms. Gladwell had decided that I'd agreed to. "I'm Madison Huntington. Nice to meet you."

"Well, I am just thrilled and delighted that you're going to be joining our little committee! We told Ms. Gladwell that we needed an extra set of hands and she was so accommodating. We have so much to do and we are in dire need of your help."

"What exactly did you have in mind?" If it was just stapling up Christmas lights or putting tablecloths down, I figured I could manage that.

Mrs. Adams pointed to her bags. "Just a couple of little things that we need you to make."

"Make?"

"Yes. We pride ourselves on our homemade decorations. We want our kids to be surrounded by things made with love. Not to mention that they're so much more impressive for the school's Instagram account over generic things that we could just buy."

Yes, why would anyone just buy the decorations that they could so easily afford and save themselves hours of work? I barely refrained from making my snarky comment out loud. I would instead try reason. "I am not a crafty person. At all. I'm the actual opposite of whatever crafty is. I really want to help out, but I don't think this is the best way to use me." It was hard to adequately convey just how bad I was at it.

"Don't even worry about it," Mrs. Adams said, but my relief was short lived. "These decorations are so easy even a child could do them."

Huh. I wondered if I could make my kids do it. Or if that would somehow be breaking child labor laws.

"First, we need you to make a bunch of poms."

What was a pom? I was afraid to ask.

"We need a hundred in these different shades of blue and white." She pointed at the bags and I saw bags and bags of tissue paper in various shades of blue.

"A hundred total?"

"No." She said it like I'd asked something silly. "A hundred in each shade. Our gym is huge! We also need you to create some snowfall out of fishing wire and cotton balls. We plan on hanging those up on the walls. I'm not sure how many we'll need of those, but they should be six feet long and I guess just make them until you run out of supplies."

I let out a noise that was a cross between a squawk and the sound of my blood pressure going up.

Mrs. Adams misunderstood my sound. "Don't worry. We've already bought everything you'll need. You have two weeks and we put completed examples in the bags for you. This will be fun!"

I told my kids the same thing when I made them do something they didn't want to do.

I guessed now I was the kid being assigned the art project.

She handed me the bags and I might have said, "Thank you," like some kind of demented person who didn't rightfully protest something she was going to screw up horribly.

Ms. Gladwell expected me to participate. That was the end of the discussion.

I dropped the bags off in my classroom, heading to the teachers' lounge to find Delia and Shay. The other teachers were starting to gather there, as we still had our staff meeting. My friends had staked out a prime location, nabbing one of the faux leather couches.

"Over here!" Delia waved. "We saved you a seat."

I dropped down in the empty spot and Shay asked, "What did Gladwell want?"

"She wants me to help out with the winter festival."

Shay smiled. "I love the winter festival!"

Nothing could have surprised me more. "You love the winter festival? Did three ghosts visit you last night?"

"I like the holidays," she said defensively.

"It just doesn't seem like you," I said.

"What does seem like me?"

Setting traps for Santa? Changing out candy for coal in little kids' stockings? Shoving Christmas trees up chimneys? But I didn't say any of those things out loud because I enjoyed living.

Delia intervened. "You know why Ms. Gladwell chose you, right?"

"My fantastic bone structure?" It couldn't have been because of talent. Of the three of us sitting there, Delia was easily best suited for the job I'd been assigned. Why hadn't they asked her?

"It's because they give the new teachers the crap work thanks to your probationary year. They know you won't say no. It's unfair, but that's the reality," she explained. "My first year I got assigned to clean out the cages of all the room pets before winter break."

Shay jumped in with, "Gladwell had me doing setup and takedown for all the PTA meetings."

"They're having me make decorations. Something called a pom. And something else that involves cotton balls and fishing wire. I don't even know what fishing wire is."

"Oh no!" Delia gasped.

"Do they not know how bad you are at that stuff?" Shay asked, equally horrified.

"I tried to tell them!" Well, I hadn't tried very hard because I really did want to please Ms. Gladwell and keep my job. This probably had something to do with my childhood, but I didn't have any time to unpack it just then. "You guys could help me!"

"Sorry, but I'm already in charge of organizing the donated toys for children's charities," Shay said. "And Delia's running the ice-fishing booth. We've all got to pay our dues."

I could tell the moment Owen walked in the room because of the look on Shay's face and the fact that the temperature dropped twenty degrees. I knew he was currently mad at her because she was threatening to fail the quarterback, which would mean he couldn't play Friday's game.

While I'd never gotten the full story of everything that had happened between those two, I knew it was bad. One night when Shay had been overly tipsy (her term, not mine), she had confessed that if she ever found herself in some life-threatening situation she was going to write Owen's name on her body with a Sharpie pen just so that he'd be the primary suspect. She later claimed to have been joking, but . . .

"Look at that, there's the new substi-cute teacher taking over Jennifer's class." Delia pointed across the room to a good-looking guy in his late twenties. "His name is Kyle. I think maybe he should be my new boyfriend."

My phone buzzed before I could properly assess Kyle. It was a text from Brad. I tried not to groan. He was supposed to be leaving me alone.

"From Brad? *We should talk.* I thought you guys were done. What is this?" Shay demanded.

Too late I realized that I hadn't thought to cover up my screen in case something like this happened. My hand flew up to cover the message even though the damage had already been done. "It's just—"

Her hand dropped to my wrist, where she noticed Brad's bracelet. I didn't know what had possessed me to put it on that morning. It didn't mean anything. I had just . . . wanted to wear something sparkly.

The hope that when Tyler got back he might notice it, might even ask where it had come from, maybe have a twang of jealousy about it?

Yeah, that had crossed my mind.

But considering that I couldn't be with him, I couldn't exactly confess my ulterior motives to my friends.

Shay said, "Where did this bracelet come from? And know there are only two acceptable answers here. One is from Tyler in his quest to convince you to become his girlfriend and the other is in your mother's couch cushions."

I couldn't have lied to Shay even if I wanted to. Not only because she was my friend, but because she'd always been able to see right through me.

It was annoying.

Covering up my wrist with my sleeve I said, "It was a gift."

"From bad Brad?" Shay had never liked Brad, and with good reason. The first time they'd met, he'd hit on her. I wasn't around and they didn't know who the other one was. He approached her saying, "Hey. My name is Brad. What's yours?"

"Not interested."

He didn't take the hint. "You look like a good girl. I make good girls go Brad."

She had rolled her eyes, trying to ignore him.

"Come on, I'll be the best you've ever Brad."

"No thanks. You've left a Brad taste in my mouth."

He'd somehow seen this as a sign of interest. "That's the idea."

She got rid of him by telling him to go away before she harmed the protruding parts of his body. When she told me later, after I had properly introduced them, I knew it was true. Partly because of the idiotic punning, but also because it wasn't the first time he'd done something like that. When I'd confronted him, he tried to play it off like he'd known exactly who she was and it was a joke/misunderstanding. He'd said by way of excuse, "Like I'd ever hook up with a girl who had purple hair."

The truth was, Brad cheated on me constantly. I would find out, he would beg for forgiveness and promise to never do it again. Then my parents would start in, telling me to take him back, that sometimes men couldn't help themselves, that everybody was human and made mistakes. And I did it. I kept taking him back. Over and over again.

I'd often wondered how many times he'd cheated when I hadn't caught him or heard about it from someone else.

Shay said, "It *is* from Brad. Why on earth would you accept?"

Reminding myself of all that had happened before should have convinced me that I was being dumb; instead it only made me slightly defensive. Like when you knew you were wrong but dug your heels in anyway because you were embarrassed. "What? How could I refuse?"

"Oh, I don't know, maybe with your dignity and self-respect still intact? You don't even like this guy. So much for you being over dating rich guys. Why are you accepting presents from him?"

"I . . . I don't know." Because it had been so long since I'd had something pretty? I knew how shallow and petty that would sound. "It's over. We both know it's over."

"Are you sure?" she asked, pointing at my wrist.

"Yes. And now I have this token to remember. It wasn't all bad."

"And what, you think the good outweighs the Brad? And you still haven't explained how you got the bracelet."

"He came to see me at my parents' house. You know, the night when I moved into Tyler's. Anyway, that's when he gave it to me. He apologized and promised to change and said he would be committed to me now."

Shay narrowed her eyes at me. "Does he know what the word *committed* means? Like, he understands that he has to stop having sex with other women, right?"

"He knows." At least, I hoped he did.

She shook her head. "I'll fall in love with Owen James before Brad is faithful to you."

Delia put her hand on mine. "But you guys broke up, right? I didn't hallucinate that part?"

"No. You didn't. It's definitely over. He said he'd give me space." Something he was failing miserably at.

I could see Shay winding up, could already imagine the words that she was going to say. But Delia's uncharacteristically snarky response shocked all of us. "Give you space? Well, he's good at that already."

"Nice." Shay nodded.

As if he somehow sensed that we were talking about him, another message buzzed in.

Thinking of you.

"Unless he's thinking of you moving on with someone else, he should just be quiet," Shay said.

Ms. Gladwell entered the room, raising both of her hands. "If I could have your attention please, I would like to start the meeting."

As the room began to quiet down, I wondered if I needed to make things clearer to Brad. That maybe I hadn't been as definitive as I could have been, since some teeny part of me hadn't wanted to write him off publicly and risk the wrath of my mother. Both of my parents would react so badly. But could things really get worse? I hadn't been invited home for Thanksgiving. While I'd had a great day with Shay and her mom, part of me had missed being at home. They had effectively written me off and had only called me when they wanted something from me. They'd dangled Brad and a possible relationship with them in front of me like a carrot.

I needed to cut that last tether between us. I needed both him and my parents to understand that this was over. It was going to be awful, but I was strong enough to do it.

It was time to let them know that things were definitely over with Brad.

No matter how scary that prospect was.

CHAPTER TWELVE

A few days later, I was hunting under the bathroom sink for a bottle of window cleaner. Which I had, in my naivete, assumed only cleaned windows. As per the label. While cleaning the mirror I'd been using the kitchen cleaner, which had falsely labeled itself as "all-purpose." It was not all-purpose and made bathroom mirrors streaky. "Deceitful advertising," I mumbled to myself.

Once I found the window cleaner, the internet recommended I not use paper towels but since this wasn't 1996, we didn't have any newspaper. I also highly doubted that Tyler had microfiber cloths.

The paper towels worked well enough. Which freed me up to indulge in one of my favorite pastimes: daydreaming about Tyler.

It was one of the few ways to make chores entertaining. I imagined him coming home, finding me in the bathroom, washing the mirror. He would sneak in behind me, wrapping his arms around my waist, nuzzling my neck. I'd lean against his brawny frame, loving the way he felt and how he touched me. Shivers of anticipation would rack my frame, making me rely on his strength to keep me upright.

Then he'd whisper words hotly against my ear. "There's something I want to ask you."

My rib cage would constrict my breathing, my heart speeding like a jackhammer. "Yes?"

"Madison . . . how did you get the mirror so clean?"

Ugh. It had been so long since I'd been with someone that even my fantasies were lame.

I scrubbed at the mirror harder and wondered how Tyler cleaned the one in his bathroom. Or if he had someone else do it for him.

Someone like Oksana.

"Oksana, Oksana, Oksana," I muttered as I continued cleaning the mirror. It was weird to be so deeply jealous of someone I knew nothing about.

I had just finished up when I heard a noise. I figured it was Pigeon, but then she came in to sit on the floor next to my feet. She was whimpering.

Which meant . . . I went down the hallway and found Oksana in the kitchen.

I tried not to gasp. I'd chanted her name and had accidentally summoned her.

She had spread groceries all over the counter. A large pot sat on the stove, and I heard bubbles popping, as if something was boiling.

For all that was holy, I hoped it wasn't a bunny. Whatever it was, it smelled a little like dirt and sulfur. Wasn't that how brimstone was supposed to smell?

Maybe she was cooking up something for her good buddy, Satan.

"Hello." I smiled and waved at her.

She had a cigarette hanging from her lower lip. She paused from cutting up a head of cabbage to glare at me and then resumed her cutting.

When it was obvious she wasn't going to respond, I opted to be more direct. "What are you doing here?" *Did somebody accidentally leave the gates of hell unlocked?* I hoped I didn't come across as too accusatory. I was genuinely bewildered to find her in my apartment again.

Her eyebrows went up, as if my question were stupid. "Cooking."

"Oh. So, what are you, uh, making there?"

"Borscht."

That was a kind of soup if I remembered correctly. "What do you use to make borscht?"

She glared at me again, obviously not in the mood to talk, and it kind of surprised me when she answered. She held the large knife she was using against her shoulder, making me feel the tiniest bit of fear. "Beets. Cabbage. Knucklebones. And other things."

Knucklebones? Like . . . from people? What other animals had knuckles? This concerned me.

"Well, that sounds . . . great. Have fun. I'm going to go clean." She so didn't care what I was going to do. I wanted to ask her not to smoke because I was a big fan of my own lungs and breathing in general, but I didn't know if I had the authority to say so.

I scampered away, trying not to think about how unfair it was that she not only looked that way but could cook, too. She'd probably never stick a cast-iron pan in the dishwasher.

When I got back to my room, I called Shay. Somebody needed to commiserate with me.

She answered and I said, "Oksana's back."

"Back where?"

"She's in the kitchen. Cooking." Something that had not seemed great initially but now smelled utterly divine.

"Is she clothed?"

"Yes," I said. "I'm afraid I may have accidentally used the dark arts and conjured her by saying her name three times while looking in a mirror."

Shay played along. "Obviously."

I knew that I was being weird about this Oksana thing. I figured some of it had to be, like, guilt. Or some manifestation of my subconscious and conflicting desires. I wanted to be just friends with Tyler but I also wanted to fight Oksana in a death match for his hand in marriage. So . . .

"Do you know her last name?" Shay asked. "I feel like we should do some deep diving into her social media."

"No. And there's no way for me to get it." Unless I asked Tyler, which was something I didn't really want to do. His girl situation was just that—*his* girl situation. I shouldn't be involving myself in it. Especially if I wanted to maintain some emotional distance from him. He was supposed to be home in a few hours. He could deal with it then.

"Okay, maybe if we just do a more general search. I'm looking up *hot girls named Oksana* . . . oh! No! Oh, whatever you do, don't do that. Ugh. I'm going to have to bleach my eyeballs now. But speaking of hot, you should tell Tyler."

I was confused. "That Oksana's hot? I think he knows."

"No, that you think he's hot. What's the worst thing that could happen?"

"Um, he could hear me when I say it? You seem to forget that he has a girlfriend who is currently making him soup. What can we do?"

She chose to misunderstand me. "That's the spirit! What *can* we do?"

"Nothing. I'm going to go. I need to vacuum."

"Spoilsport. I'm going to think of a good way to find out her last name. I'll call you back when I have an idea."

I hung up my phone and slid it back into my pocket. "Pigeon, vacuum." I always tried to warn her first, and she went running by me, into my room and presumably under my bed.

I'd gotten really good at vacuuming since I did it so frequently. I'd spent my last few evenings trying to create poms and failing miserably. I'd already had to replace two packages of tissue paper. At first they looked like giant garbage balls of tissue or a deranged loofah. Then they were squished, as if someone had sat on them, or flopping over too much on the top, like a dead fish.

After watching multiple tutorials I realized that I was making several mistakes, which included making the accordion folds too big and the wire in the center too tight. I learned how to round the corners and now they were sort of resembling the right shape. I had five that I thought weren't too bad.

This also meant that there were tissue paper slivers everywhere all the time, hence the vacuuming.

Of all my chores, so far vacuuming was my favorite. Barring the Sock Incident, the Penny Episode, and the other time that involved hoovering up the cord from the blinds, I had been doing well. I hadn't had to replace the vacuum yet, so I was putting that in the win category. It made me feel accomplished to witness the dirt container filling up. I could actually see my success. It wasn't the same with something like washing counters. I felt like they generally looked the same after I was done.

Although maybe that was an indication that I wasn't doing it right.

I went down the hallway and stopped where it met the kitchen and living room. Usually I'd go in and do the front room, too, but I sort of didn't want to go in there at the moment. So I decided, even though I didn't need to, to vacuum Tyler's room. Since he was coming home tonight I thought it would be a nice surprise while also being a way for me to avoid being in the same room as Oksana. Win-win.

Tyler's room was done in dark blues and grays that felt masculine and relaxing. I made sure to avoid the sheets and blankets on his bed so as to not add to my list of vacuum-related issues, and made my way over to his bathroom.

As I passed his walk-in closet I felt the urge to stop and investigate. I turned the vacuum off. When I opened the door, I was immediately hit with his distinct and amazing scent that probably could have lured me to my death like those moths Delia had told us about.

Glancing over my shoulder, I said a quick prayer that Oksana wouldn't catch me. The first thing I noticed was that Tyler was a secret slob. While he had an extensive collection of ties and suits hanging up, the floor of his closet was covered in clothes. Like the dryer had thrown up in here. Since I worked with second graders and tended to be messy myself, I ignored it as I stepped into the closet. Considering he was currently on a business trip, it was surprising how many things were still here. He had a wardrobe almost big enough to rival mine. Or, my old wardrobe back when I could buy whatever clothes I wanted without considering the cost. I was running my index finger down the length of an expensive blue silk tie that I'd seen on him before, one that made his eyes look even lighter and more piercing, when my phone rang.

The sound shocked me and I rushed out of his closet, like whoever was calling could see what I was doing.

It was Shay.

I swiped to answer. "Shay! You just scared the bejeebers out of me."

"What are you doing?" She sounded suspicious (rightfully so). Was her Spidey-sense tingling or something?

I was too flustered to come up with even a white lie. "I'm being creepy and going through Tyler's closet."

"Oh." She waited a beat before saying, "You should go through his drawers, too."

"What?"

"I mean, if you're going to violate his personal space, you might as well go all the way. And describe it to me, woman with no boundaries."

Laughing, I said, "The no-boundaries thing is not my fault. I didn't have personal space growing up." There was always a bunch of people coming in and out of my room to clean up or put something away or tell me my parents wanted to speak with me so that they could let me know all the ways I was disappointing them. "I blame my parents."

"I blame your parents for lots of things. Climate change, trouble in the Middle East, why men don't ask me on second dates."

"Mine is blaming them for me being emotionally stunted. But Tyler should have his privacy. I'm leaving his room now."

"Are you really choosing now of all times to be mature and respect-ful?" she asked.

I walked across the hall into my own room and set the vacuum down near my dresser. Pigeon intuited that I planned on cleaning up in here next, and she took off. I asked, "Did you ever consider that maybe this goes against my moral code?"

"And here I thought your morals weren't up to code."

My phone buzzed and it was a text.

From Tyler.

"I have to go! I'll explain later!" I don't know why I made Shay get off the phone; I could have just as easily read the text while she waited for a second. It said:

> Flight delayed. Will be back
> early tomorrow morning

I replied with a sad face and told him to fly safe. After I pressed send, I immediately felt stupid. It wasn't like he was the pilot. He had zero control over what happened with the plane and whether or not it flew safely.

He seemed to pick up on this when he replied:

> Will do my best. Can't make
> any promises as I'm still one
> semester short of getting my
> pilot's license.

I smiled.

> That's not how you get a
> pilot's license.

> Seriously? I'm going to
> demand a refund!

There was a loud clatter and what I guessed were swear words in Russian. I went out into the front of the apartment and found Oksana smoking outside on the balcony. I was glad she was doing it out there and not in here, although she'd left the sliding door wide open. She was taking a picture and leaning back over the balcony rail and I had a sudden flash of her tumbling backward like one of those Instagram influencers who fell off a cliff while trying to get a perfect selfie.

"Hey, Oksana?"

She paused what she was doing, blowing a ring of smoke in my direction.

"I just got a text from Tyler. His flight was delayed so he won't be back tonight."

She shook her cigarette, letting some ash fall to the ground. She held her phone back up, presumably to verify if I was telling the truth.

But from the look on her face, Tyler hadn't contacted her.

That should not have delighted me the way that it did.

"The borscht simmers until twenty minutes of the ninth hour."

I wasn't sure what time that actually was. 8:40? 9:20? I was about to ask, but she kept talking.

"Then you will pack it up and keep it for Tyler."

It took me a second to register her instructions. Soon-ish the soup would be done and she wanted me to put it away for her? And given everything still out on the counters, clean up her mess, too? I opened my mouth to protest, but she grabbed her coat and left before I could.

Yes, that's just what I'll do. I'll put away your homemade soup and clean up the kitchen and lie down like the pushover that I am and you can take him and love him and I'll just be pathetic, sitting on the sidelines.

I went into the kitchen and started putting the leftover vegetables into the drawer in the fridge. I turned the heat off on the soup. I didn't care when it was supposed to finish. I considered dumping it down the sink, but I couldn't bring myself to do it.

Why was it so hard for me to say no? I figured it was a combination of needing to please scary, cold women and having no money—I couldn't let this much food go to waste, especially since there was enough soup here to feed a platoon.

And it smelled delicious. I decided to have a bowl and it was amazing and I wanted to curse her name for being so good at everything, but I held back just in case I made her appear again.

I wanted to have another serving of the borscht but decided against it and finished cleaning the kitchen instead. When I started the dishwasher, I noticed that Pigeon had been hiding for a long time.

"Pigeon? Where are you, girl? The Wicked Witch is gone. Come out, come out, wherever you are!" I walked past Tyler's bedroom and that's where I saw her.

Lying on the floor, chewing up one of his shoes.

I'd forgotten to close his closet door!

"No, no, no, no," I muttered as I reached for what had once been a shoe. A very expensive one, from the looks of it. While I ran to the closet to find the matching one, Pigeon stared at me as if she couldn't figure out why I was upset. I had to throw a bunch of clothes around, ignoring the fact that everything smelled like him. I finally located the other shoe and I made sure to close the door nice and tight this time.

"Well, Pidge, I'll give you this. At least you have good taste." And considering what a mess his closet was, she also possessed a fierce determination in unearthing the shoe that I wouldn't have anticipated.

I had to get replacement shoes tonight. Before Tyler got back in the morning. I didn't want him to think that I was irresponsible. Especially after he'd specifically warned me not to leave closet doors open. First, I called Pigeon's vet. The number was listed on the fridge. Pigeon didn't normally ingest shoes; she just liked to gnaw on them. His vet told me to contact her if Pigeon started acting strangely but that, more likely than not, Pidge would be just fine.

Then I looked up his shoes online. Fortunately there was a store just a few blocks away that had the exact same name brand, color, and size of Tyler's shoes. I'd just go exchange them and he would never know that I had been creepily fingering his ties and smelling his dress shirts like some kind of deranged stalker.

If he knew, then he'd probably take a restraining order out against me, too.

I worried about leaving Pigeon alone, but she was curled up on my bed and seemed okay. Deciding to take the vet at her word, I was going to just run over, grab the shoes, and come right back.

I walked quickly, hoping the entire way that the shoes would be there. I didn't recognize the name of the upscale men's clothing store that had the shoes in stock. Admittedly, my expertise was limited to women's fashion. A salesman in a three-piece suit approached me.

"May I help you?"

"Yes, I need to replace these." I put the one good shoe on the counter. "Same size, same color."

He nodded. "I believe I have that in back. Let me go check."

It occurred to me only right then that the website might have been wrong and this particular store might not have them in stock. I leaned against the counter, not knowing what I would do. Even if I found them online someplace like Zappos or Amazon, they would arrive after Tyler got home. And what if he wanted to wear them to work tomorrow?

I had started to work myself up into a frenzied panic when the salesman returned, shoes in hand. "We do have them. Can I ring these up for you?"

Exhaling pure relief, I said, "Yes, thank you."

He scanned the shoes, opening it to show them to me and double-checking that they were both the same size. "That comes to one thousand and sixty-eight dollars and thirty-two cents."

Did he just say $1,000?

All my frenzied panic returned an actual thousandfold. One piece of sheer panic for every outrageous dollar.

I mean, it was so out of my reach financially that it might as well have been $10,000.

It was sad to think that six months ago I would have thought $1,000 for a pair of shoes to be totally reasonable and it would have seemed an insignificant amount of money. Now it seemed like all the money in the world.

I should have expected this. I knew that Tyler's clothes were expensive; it had been so long since I'd shopped somewhere upscale that it was like I forgot how much stuff like this could cost.

The problem was, I didn't have $1,000. I didn't even have an extra hundred. I also didn't have any credit cards that I could use because they'd all either been in my parents' names, or I'd defaulted in repaying them and the accounts had been closed.

This was too big of an ask for Shay or Delia. I wasn't sure they could even afford it.

If I called Brad, there would be so many expectations and strings attached to him helping me that I'd never get him out of my life. And I just couldn't be in debt to him. Not when things between us were over.

There was only one person I could call.

"That's a little more than I was expecting," I confessed to the salesman and his expression changed from someone eager to please to utter disdain. "Let me make a quick phone call."

I pulled up my contacts and clicked on the number.

"Madison? What do you need?" my oldest sister asked. It was probably as much my fault as it was hers that she would assume that I'd call her only because I needed something.

And in this case, it was a totally accurate assumption.

"I need your help. My roommate's shoes got chewed up and it's my fault."

"You chewed up your roommate's shoes?"

"No. There's a dog and she did it, but I'm the one who accidentally left the door open when he told me not to and the problem is that I have to replace them right away before he gets back and they're like a thousand dollars and I don't have any money."

There was a long pause and I fully expected her to say no. To say, *I told you so*, or, *What did you expect?* To my surprise she said, "I'll do this, but you're going to owe me."

"Yes, absolutely. Anything. Thank you, thank you, thank you." That was how things worked in our family. Tit for tat. I would say I hadn't expected anything less, but that would be untrue since I'd expected her to say no.

I turned to the salesman and said, "My sister is going to pay for it." I handed him the phone and he took down the credit card information and was able to run it through the system. Another store probably wouldn't have done so, but given that this was the sort of place that catered to the wealthy, they would do whatever their customers wanted.

Even the broke ones.

He gave my phone back to me and I said Violet's name, intending to thank her for what she'd done, but she'd already hung up. I took the receipt and the shoes and started back for my apartment.

I was wondering whether Tyler would notice that I'd swapped out his old shoes for new ones when two people stepped in front of me, exiting a restaurant. I looked up and saw the sign. Yuto's. It had been one of my favorite sushi places back when I could still afford it.

Boy, did I want sushi.

Feeling poor should have discouraged me from spending money, but I'd been finding the opposite to be true. When I had no money, I wanted to spend it more. It was an inclination I had to fight regularly.

Tonight I was tired of fighting. Tonight I just wanted overpriced sushi.

It meant I'd have to eat ramen for the rest of the week, but I was okay with that. I wasn't going to order very much; I wasn't all that hungry, given all the borscht I'd inhaled back at the apartment. This was definitely more of a symbolic gesture. I would just grab a small roll and eat it on my way back home.

I went inside and smiled with nostalgia. I'd forgotten how romantic the atmosphere was. Brad and I had had several dates here. There was low lighting and private booths. As I looked around, I spotted someone who looked familiar.

Blinking, I figured I had to be hallucinating. I checked again. Not my imagination. That woman over in the corner with a man who most definitely was not Tyler—it was Oksana.

Was she cheating on him? I had to call Shay right away. I got my phone out.

As if he knew I was thinking about him, a text came in from Tyler.

> Thought you'd like to see this.

It was a picture of the Singapore skyline at sunset, taken from the restaurant I'd recommended. My pulse sputtered as the air solidified in my chest.

He deserved so much better than Oksana. So. Much. Better.

The hostess returned and asked, "Is this for here or to go?"

It didn't take much to make up my mind.

"For here."

CHAPTER THIRTEEN

The hostess showed me to a table, but I couldn't see Oksana. "Do you have a booth available? Over there?" I pointed to where I could feasibly hide but still keep an eye on Tyler's cheating girlfriend. She would have to turn and look over her shoulder to see me, and given how wrapped up she was in her date, I didn't think that was much of a possibility.

And I was assuming a lot here. Like the fact that I had registered enough on her radar for her to remember who I was. Because the two times I'd talked to her, I got the distinct impression that she thought me beneath her notice.

I called Shay and before I could speak, she said, "Did you figure out a way to get her last name?"

"I'm at Yuto's and she's here and it looks like she may be on a date."

"Oooh." She sounded way too excited. "How does she look?"

Like she always did? The same way she had when she'd been in my apartment earlier? "Like a shark wearing a human costume? Gorgeous but deadly? And she makes me feel inadequate in every way that a woman can possibly feel inadequate?"

"Well, that's not true. You're not a mother yet and that's going to be a whole new level of inadequacies. I meant, is she dressed up?"

"I don't know. She's wearing a dress, but she was wearing the same thing at my house."

"What kind of woman makes a guy what we're calling *soup* and then meets up with another dude?"

Much as I didn't want to be fair, in this instance I had to be. "You can't mock the borscht. It was really good."

My waitress came by then to ask what I wanted to drink and I told her just water. This was not a situation that needed to be alcohol fueled. It was important that I stay low-key and not start shouting things across the room at her.

Which may or may not have happened in some previous situations.

Shay asked, "Why are you in a sushi restaurant?"

So I explained the situation to her, leaving out the parts about the cost and Violet. Shay wouldn't want me to have to owe anyone in my family and I wasn't really in the mood to hash it out.

"Can't you teach the dog not to chew on shoes?"

"Probably. But Tyler's not really into disciplining Pigeon. He likes to spoil her." Which I couldn't blame him for, because she was the cutest and was usually such a good girl.

"That's excellent," she informed me.

"Why?"

"Because a man who spoils his dog will definitely spoil the woman he's in love with."

"Which is not me and is a very scary Russian woman who may or may not be cheating on him right this very second." And if I was being honest, none of that was any of my business. I really had no right to be sitting here. "I shouldn't be doing this. I feel like I'm breaching Tyler's privacy."

"More than when you were playing with his clothes?"

"I never should have told you that," I muttered.

"Probably not," she agreed. "This is probably some psychological thing. Where you stood by while Brad treated you like garbage so you're not willing to stand by and see someone you care about get treated the same way."

"What?" I asked, shocked by her assertion.

"Or I could be totally wrong. What's she doing now?"

I glanced up, trying not to stare. "They're just talking and they're too far away for me to hear them. I should probably just go. Isn't this technically stalking?"

"I say desperate times call for desperate measures and he is desperately hot and you're just desperate, so stay put."

"I'm not desperate—" I tried to protest, but she interrupted me.

"Speaking of desperate, have you told Brad to leave you alone and stop texting you? He gives love a Brad name."

He had texted me two more times, but I didn't mention it. "He knows not to. Maybe I should block his number. I told him he's not the right guy for me."

"That's because Tyler is the right guy for you."

I wished she could see me shaking my head. She needed to let the Tyler thing go. Even if I couldn't do it myself. "I'm not ready to deal with my mother at the moment. One nuclear war at a time. Now shush. You're distracting me from my stalking."

"That's so I can tell the police I tried to stop you from committing your crime when they accuse me of being an accessory after the fact."

"Hate to tell you, Shay, but you're an accessory during the fact."

"Yeah, okay."

I went silent, covertly watching Oksana and her date. I wished I could hear them. I could see only the side of Oksana's face, so it was hard to tell if she was flirting or if she was just talking to him.

I tried to figure out why this bothered me so much. Why I was sitting here watching this woman when it literally had no bearing on my life. I figured it was probably because Brad had cheated on me so often and it infuriated me to think that someone might be doing this to a guy as nice as Tyler. He didn't deserve it.

And yes, there was probably some small part of me that thought if she was cheating on him, it would free him up. To, you know, pursue other possible romantic entanglements.

But it was mostly indignation that anybody would want to hurt Tyler.

There was a staticky noise on my phone, like Shay was settling onto her couch as she spoke. "If you're going to maybe commit a felony and invade someone's privacy, the very least you could do is have the decency to keep up a running narration."

"Nothing's happening."

"We will solve this mystery! All we need now is a Great Dane, a van, and a stoned hippie friend. Oh! Maybe Delia counts as our hippie friend!"

One of the servers dropped off my water, but I was too busy watching Oksana and her friend to take a drink.

Shay said, "Tell me about the other guy. What does he look like?"

"Older, silver-fox type. Handsome but definite gray in his hair." Tyler was vastly better looking, but I could admit this guy was a hottie. "Maybe he's her modeling agent."

"Or her handler," Shay offered. "Or her dad."

Then Oksana climbed into the man's lap. They started kissing and I said, "Oh! Oh! Not her dad unless she's a Lannister from *Game of Thrones*." I knocked my water glass over in my excitement at this turn of events. It clattered onto the ground, loudly. It didn't break but everyone around me turned to stare.

I ducked my head and tried to clean up the spilled water with my linen napkin. Oksana stopped kissing the man and started to turn in my direction. Ack! She was going to see me!

Without thinking I slid under the table. One minute I was sitting in my booth, the next I was under a table, praying she hadn't seen me.

My phone was still glued to my ear and I could hear Shay say, "You know I don't speak nerd television! What does Lannister mean?"

"It means he's definitely not her dad as they're kissing and I'm currently under a table to avoid being caught because I knocked over my glass and it fell on the ground and it was loud and now I don't know what Oksana's actually capable of and what she might do if she finds me."

"This evening in This Is Not Going To End Well . . ."

As if her words were prophetic, a pair of feet came walking toward me. *Please don't let it be Oksana, please don't let it be Oksana . . .*

The universe finally seemed to be on my side as it turned out to be my waitress. She stuck her head under the table. "Is there something I can help you with?"

"Um, yes. There's a couple across the room. Older gentleman, younger woman with black hair. They were kissing. Are they still kissing?"

She gave me a very concerned look but straightened up. A moment later she was back. "I don't see anyone kissing and I don't see the couple you're describing."

Had they left? Or was Oksana making her way over here right now to confront me? I debated the merits of staying put and getting out of this restaurant as quickly as possible. Would it be worse for them to see me walking by or worse to be discovered?

"Were you ready to order?" the waitress asked, her face back under the table. "I could tell you about the specials."

"No, I think I'll just take off. I wasn't that hungry anyways. Sorry for being your weirdest customer this week."

"Oh, you're not even my weirdest customer today," she told me with a grin. "Have a good night!"

I nodded and then slid back up into the booth, which was much harder going up than it had been going down. I didn't look to see where Oksana had been and instead stood quickly, grabbed Tyler's shoes, and headed for the exit.

"Now what's happening?" Shay demanded once I was outside.

"I escaped without detection. I'm heading home to check on Pigeon and I'm hoping that she's not throwing up leather." I glanced behind me to make sure I wasn't being followed. As if Oksana really were some kind of assassin. "And now I'm making sure that Her Royal Evilness isn't following me."

The light indicated that I couldn't cross and I came to a stop. "I shouldn't call her evil just because I don't like her and am jealous of her. Maybe she's not evil."

"Maybe she is. You ever think of that?"

"Why does that cheer me up?"

I heard Shay laugh. "Because I'm your best friend and that's my job."

"You're really good at it."

"I know. Hey, did you get a picture of Oksana kissing that guy?"

The thought hadn't even occurred to me. "No."

"Why not? Wasn't that the whole point?"

I wasn't exactly sure what the point was anymore. I tried telling myself again that it was to help protect Tyler because he was one of the few good guys left in the world. That practically made him an endangered species and I should get a humanitarian award.

But none of this was my business, even if I wanted it to be. "I don't know. I kind of feel like I crossed a line here."

"Sometimes you have to cross the line to see where it actually is."

"I don't think that's an actual saying."

She sighed. "Regardless, tell Tyler. And while you're at it, tell Brad to go away. Tell the men in your life what is going on so that everybody can make their own decisions and move on to something better."

I wondered if she was right.

$\sim$

When I got home, the first thing I did was put the new shoes in Tyler's closet and throw the old ones (along with the shoe box and the receipt) down the garbage chute in the hallway. I also made sure that both his closet door and bedroom door were shut. I checked twice.

Pigeon was right where I'd left her: curled up in the corner of my bed.

To decompress from my day, I decided to watch one of the movies I had recorded on the DVR. I was a sucker for the sweet, cheery, comforting Hallmark romances but I also loved the women-in-peril suspense movies on Lifetime. Tonight I chose one of the high-octane ones, and it was about a former soap opera actress who was being stalked by an obsessive fan who thought the actress was her villainous character from the show and needed to be taken out. The actress moved into a high-security smart home in an attempt to stay safe, but her stalker was a computer genius who disabled the whole thing. After a drawn-out fight scene, the actress was able to push the stalker down the stairs, and the stalker died.

In the past I'd always gotten a bit of a rush from movies like that, imagining what I would do if I were in the heroine's shoes, but this one felt like a bit too much. Like it had rattled my nerves in a way I didn't fully comprehend. It wasn't like I had anything similar happening in my life. I didn't have any stalkers.

Maybe it was more of my guilty conscience because I'd been basically spying on Oksana earlier. It could be the universe was warning me that karma could be unpleasant.

I resolved to be a better person.

I decided I'd had enough excitement for one evening. I got ready for bed, putting on a tank top and shorts, something that had become a bit of a necessity lately. Even though it was winter and Tyler kept the thermostat a bit cold for my liking, Pigeon exuded a lot of body heat and when I wore heavier pajamas I would wake up in a sweat. I climbed in next to the dog, scooting her over slightly to make some room for me. As was my custom every night, I scrolled through social media and my in-box just to see if there was anything that needed my attention.

Usually the answer was no, but today there was an email. From Denny's father.

It was short and straight to the point—he apologized for Denny's outbursts and said that Denny's mother had left the family and Denny was having a difficult time adjusting. He asked for my patience and said he'd be happy to meet with me after things had calmed down at their house.

I felt sick to my stomach for Denny. No wonder he'd been acting out. I put my phone down on the nightstand and began to think about what I could do to assist him now that I had this new knowledge. What did he need from me to help him be more successful behaviorally?

At some point I must have drifted off because a loud noise woke me up. It was one of those heart-pounding-unmercifully-in-your-chest moments, where you woke up suddenly and weren't exactly sure why.

I nudged Pigeon with my hand but she only grumbled and went back to sleep.

There was another noise, a shuffling. I grabbed my phone. It was three o'clock in the morning.

My first delirious thought was that Oksana had returned to finish me off. I got out of bed quietly, listening with each step that I took. My pulse was pounding so loudly in my ears that it was hard to hear. I slowly opened my door and looked down the hallway. I tiptoed to the kitchen, looking around and not seeing anything. I grabbed Tyler's cast-iron pan, because he always left it out on the stove top. Gripping it in both hands, I continued my search.

No one.

I glanced at the TV and silently cursed it. It was that movie that had me all worried and scared. I reminded myself, again, that I didn't have a stalker.

Although . . . there was every possibility that Tyler had one. It didn't even have to be Oksana. It could have been another woman that he'd bewitched who didn't know how to let go.

Wondering if I'd imagined the entire thing, I started back toward my room when I realized that Tyler's door was open.

A door I knew for a fact that I had shut.

My heart leaped up into my throat, making it hard for me to swallow. I pushed the door open slightly and saw a large, looming figure. Letting out a shriek of terror, I lifted the pan to swipe at the person when the lights suddenly turned on.

I blinked several times, feeling blinded.

"Madison! It's me!"

"Tyler!" I protested, letting the pan fall to my side. "I almost Tom and Jerry'ed you! Which wouldn't have been easy because this thing is really heavy!" *And expensive,* I almost added, but caught myself in time. "I thought you were a stalker or something!"

That movie had seriously rattled me.

He took the pan from my shaking hands, setting it down on top of his dresser. "It would be really hard for a stalker to get past one of the doormen."

I nodded. This made perfect logical sense. But my body was still feeling totally illogical. "I just . . . I feel really freaked out. I'm having a hard time catching my breath."

"Hey. Come here."

Next thing I knew, I was being enveloped in a warm, giant hug. It was like coming in from the cold to a roaring fire and a mug of hot cocoa. I leaned into him, wrapping my arms around his waist, letting him press me firm against him.

His hand ran up and down my back. "It's okay. Everything is okay."

I believed him. I couldn't remember the last time I'd felt so safe. Protected. I didn't trust many people but right here? Right now? I trusted Tyler.

As my breathing calmed, I realized that I'd been so scatterbrained that I hadn't even registered the fact that Tyler must have been getting ready for bed, as he wasn't wearing a shirt. It certainly registered now as my hands curled against his strong back, the side of my face pressed against his warm chest. I turned my head slightly and my lips were now touching his skin and it was almost like I was kissing him.

Almost.

Now that I was much more aware of my surroundings, I felt bad that I was enjoying this hug so much. That my blood pounded slowly through my limbs while my pulse frantically throbbed. It felt like he rested his cheek against the top of my head, and my lower abdomen tightened in response.

Nothing about this was very friend zone–ish.

I should have released him. Stepped back and put some distance between us. Not enjoyed his warmth and wanted to snuggle closer. Because this was, quite possibly, one of the best things that had ever happened to me and I didn't want it to end.

Where I'd been oblivious only a few seconds ago, now I was painfully aware of how smooth his skin was, of the sexy way his back muscles strained against my palms as he continued to move his right hand up and down my back to console me. Since he was just being nice, I probably shouldn't have been finding all this super hot. I was either extraordinarily lucky or desperately pathetic.

I pulled in a deep whiff of his naturally attractive and enticing scent. His particular brand of pheromone would a hundred percent make me fly to my death by getting caught in his web. I was definitely leaning toward pathetic. Which made me feel like I had to justify my behavior.

"I'm sorry," I finally said, my words going directly into his chest. "I watched a scary movie tonight and then you said you wouldn't be back until tomorrow morning and my mind just went weird places."

Which it was still doing.

"It is tomorrow morning," he reminded me, and I loved how his words rumbled their way out of his chest.

"Yeah, but I thought you meant morning as in a decent hour . . ." I lifted my head to look at him and suddenly realized just how close our lips were. Like if I leaned forward just a micro-fraction of an inch, we'd be kissing.

My breath caught and then sped up. My head started to swim, making me a little dizzy. Which was the only way to explain what I saw next—it looked like he was checking me out, his gaze hot as one side of his mouth lifted, as if he liked what he saw.

Which reminded me of how little clothing I was actually wearing.

Was he breathing a little harder, too? And whose heartbeat felt so fast—mine or his?

"Madison . . ."

The way he said my name sent shivers through me. Low and seductive, almost as if he were asking a question.

And the answer to that question was always *yes, yes, a thousand times yes*! Fortunately, I managed to keep that inside, although it took great effort.

Was he going to kiss me?

While I wanted to wait and see if it had just been my imagination or if something was about to happen, I remembered his rules. And that I was completely broke and still needed a place to live. I didn't want to jeopardize our friendship or our living arrangement.

"Thanks," I said as I extracted myself, willing my heartbeat to return to normal. I crossed my arms over my chest. "I'm glad you got home safe and I will see you in the morning."

Not waiting to hear his response, I practically sprinted back to my room and shut the door.

I got into bed and Pigeon lifted her head lazily. I realized that the reason she hadn't been worried earlier was because she'd known that Tyler was the one in the apartment.

"You're a terrible guard dog," I told her. She licked my face in response before laying her head back down.

And I was terrible at remembering that I was only supposed to be Tyler's friend.

I hoped I hadn't screwed anything up between us.

CHAPTER FOURTEEN

I didn't exactly fall asleep after that. Instead I kept reliving every moment of what was an innocent and kind gesture on his part and turning it into something it was not. I worried about having to face him over breakfast, but his door was shut and he didn't come into the kitchen.

Which left me the rest of the day to think about what I'd say to him the next time I saw him. I refrained from sharing the story with Delia and Shay since I already knew what they'd tell me. Shay would have lectured me about not taking advantage and pulling him onto his bed while Delia would have reminded me to just be true to myself.

Pigeon greeted me when I got home and I petted her head and the spot under her chin that she loved. Tyler's door was slightly open, and a quick glance told me he wasn't in there. Poor guy had to fly halfway around the world and then go to work the next day. That couldn't have been fun.

I decided to just behave normally and do the things I would usually do. I'd wait to see how he acted toward me, first.

Which meant that after a quick dinner of noodles, I was in the living room watching my recorded television shows and working on the poms. While the process had gotten easier, I didn't seem to be getting any faster.

My heart skipped when the elevator doors opened and Tyler walked in. It was only five thirty. I paused the show I'd been watching. "Home already?" I asked.

"Yeah. I just wanted . . . to be here instead of there." He paused when he saw what I was doing. "Why does it look like a present store threw up in here? I don't think I've ever seen so much tissue paper all in one place."

"Me neither," I agreed. "Except for maybe my mom's gift-wrapping room."

He totally stared at me. "Your mother has a gift-wrapping room?"

My first instinct was to lie and laugh it off because I knew how weird it sounded. While it was strange to everybody else in the world, it had just been my normal, how I'd grown up. But I didn't want to be dishonest with Tyler.

Well, more dishonest than I had been already in the name of self-preservation. "Of course she does. She's not going to wrap her presents on some random table like a heathen."

He laughed at that, but he sounded tired. "I guess that makes sense."

I couldn't have explained what possessed me to say to him, "I like your shoes." It was like I wanted to get caught. As if now that I'd decided to choose honesty, my brain decided to be honest about everything. I wanted to dig a hole in the floor that I could crawl into. What was wrong with me? Why had I said that? When you were hiding something from someone, it was generally a good idea not to act like an idiot and draw their attention to it.

"Thanks." He seemed distracted. "I've had them for a long time. But today for some reason they seemed really tight."

"Well, I think I remember hearing once that when you travel your feet can swell. All that sitting." I was so going to spend my eternity being the devil's permanent houseguest.

"Maybe. I'm going to go get changed."

Then he left and it turned out that I had no reason to worry about seeing him again because he acted just the same, as if we hadn't pressed our bodies tightly together while barely clothed in his bedroom in the middle of the night.

Not that I'd been thinking about it or anything. Not that I'd been harboring some secret hopes that maybe last night had meant something, that he might have changed his mind.

While I sat around feeling sorry for myself and my poor, misguided dreams, Tyler came back in the room. He headed straight for the kitchen and set a box down on the counter. "Are you hungry?" he asked.

"I already ate, thank you." I mean, I could have eaten again. But he seemed exhausted, most likely jet-lagged, and I was feeling guilty. Not to mention that the idea of sitting down with him at dinner and chatting about our days felt a little too cozy. Intimate.

"That's good, because, to be honest, I am feeling worn out and not really up to cooking. I think I'll grab a frozen dinner." He took one out of the freezer, tore off the outer packaging, and then slid it into the microwave.

"You never did tell me what the tissue paper is for," he reminded me as his dinner heated up.

"My school has a fundraiser coming up. A winter festival. And they put me in charge of these decorations and told me I had to make them by hand. It's something they do to new teachers. Because we're on probation they give us the grunt work. Joke's on them, though, I'm terrible at it."

The microwave beeped and he took his dinner out, tore off the plastic, and turned the contents onto a plate. It looked like some kind of chicken-and-rice recipe, and it smelled delicious. He grabbed the box he'd brought in with him and came into the living room.

Then, to my surprise, he sat next to me on the couch. He kicked his feet up on the coffee table, being sure not to disturb my stacks of paper. So much for not wanting to share a cozy moment with him.

"Here," he said, handing me the box. "I brought you something."

"You brought me something?" I repeated as my heart slammed into my chest, hard.

His eyes sparkled at me with delight. "Open it."

Gulping, I nodded. There were Asian letter characters on the outside, and I opened the box carefully, painfully aware of his gaze on me.

Inside, there was a small plush Hello Kitty holding an apple in one hand and a book in the other. She was a teacher.

He'd remembered the store in Singapore. I couldn't believe it. My pulse pounded so hard I was in actual danger of passing out.

"Thank you. This was so thoughtful." I didn't know what else to say. If I could say it. If I was allowed to tell him how much this meant to me. That I wanted to cry from the sweetness of it.

That I would keep this for the rest of my life, and that it was the best present I had ever received.

"You're welcome," he said, oblivious to my emotional turmoil. "Have you done anything fun over the past couple of days?"

I blinked a few times and cleared my throat. I needed to be normal. "Other than being terrorized in my own home last night and destroying tissue paper?" I teased, and was rewarded with his smile. "The most fun thing I've done lately is . . . my friend Delia lent me her label maker at school and it's kind of altered my entire life. Like, if she wanted to start a cult worshipping it, it's possible I would join." Since I had already filled out my paperwork to join the cult of Tyler, what was one more? "What about you?"

"Just work and more work for me." He gestured toward the TV. "What are you watching?"

"Oh, this is a show called *House Hunters*. I've seen so many episodes of this that I'm pretty sure I could pass a test to become a licensed real estate agent. It's about couples looking for a home and they walk through three different houses and then pick one. Usually you can tell in advance which one they're going to choose. It's always the empty one because they've already bought it but just haven't moved in yet."

"We should watch it."

"You want to watch TV with me?" I asked, a little alarmed. What if he hated my shows? Then I wouldn't be able to maintain my crush. Then again, this could be a good thing. Friends weren't really your friends until you'd forced them to watch your favorite TV programs.

And that was even more true for boyfriends.

"I like television. I used to watch it a lot when I was younger. But I went to college on scholarship and spent all my time working or studying. Then I got this job and most of my time is dedicated to working. I never really take the time to relax." He put his emptied plate onto the table, near his feet. Again I had that feeling that there was something more than what he was saying, a whole subtext I wasn't getting, but I didn't want to push or pry because I had the sense he didn't like it. That while he was very good with people and getting them to talk about themselves, Tyler wasn't the kind of guy who would tell you things about himself until he trusted you.

I hoped someday he would trust me that way.

"My parents forbid me from watching it and you know what happens when people say you can't have something and it makes you want it more?" All too late I realized that this also applied to him and me—I suspected that a tiny portion of my attraction was due to the fact that he was completely off limits. "Anyway, it kind of turned me into an addict. So allow me to be your guru to effective TV relaxation. And if we're going to start you off with reality television, we're going to do the granddaddy of them all. *The Bachelor.* Your life will never be the same again."

"I've heard of that one but I've never seen an episode."

I grabbed the remote and began clicking on the controls. "We're going to rectify that right now."

Tyler picked up one of the packages of tissue paper. "Hey, do you want some help?"

I nearly wept with gratitude. "Yes! I would love some! Bless you!" I had the show queued up, but I gave him a quick run-through of how to fold and then fluff out the pom. He seemed to grasp it pretty quickly and then I explained the premise of the show we were about to watch.

It was easier to focus on the show instead of on the way he was making me feel. Bringing me presents, being interested in my shows. It almost seemed like another one of my daydreams. Only better. "Okay, so there's a single guy—"

"That's the bachelor?"

"Yes. And there's, like, thirty women who are competing to end up with him. Each week he eliminates some of them until we get to the finale and then he proposes!"

"How long does this show film for?"

I shrugged. "A few weeks, I think."

"And they get engaged in the end? That's what they win?" He looked dubious.

"What did you think they'd win?"

"I don't know. All of America's sympathies when this goes south?" He laughed as I pushed him on the shoulder. "It sounds to me like the real winners will be the divorce attorneys in two years."

"Okay, Mr. Cynic. Don't you believe in love?" I'd meant to say it in a teasing manner, but suddenly his answer seemed very, very important to me.

Instead of joking around, like I'd half expected him to, he seemed to be taking my question seriously. "I'd like to think that true love is real. I've never been in love, so I can't personally testify to its existence. What about you?"

"I thought I was in love once." But I'd discovered that it was hard to be in a loving relationship when only one of the people felt that way. "I'm not sure that I really have been, either."

When he asked, "Having problems with your boyfriend?" I realized my mistake. My living here was predicated on the belief that Brad and I were together and everything was fine between us.

"It's not really worth discussing." Not only because I didn't like thinking about Brad when the vastly superior Tyler was sitting next to me, but because I didn't want to give Tyler any reason to throw me out. I hated lying to him, especially when he was such an honest person. "Let's watch the show instead."

"Done," he said, holding up the perfectly constructed pom he'd just finished.

"What . . . how . . . why did you . . ." I couldn't form a sentence. On his first try he'd made a better pom than the example Mrs. Adams had given me, and in a fraction of the time it took me to put one together. Of course he'd do this just as well as he did everything else. "How are you so good at that? You should have seen my first one. Here! I took pictures to send to my friends."

I handed him my phone and he laughed as he handed it back to me. "If this investing-money career doesn't work out for me it's a relief to know that I have pom making to fall back on. Plus, you're forgetting that I had a really good teacher." His praise sent my heart fluttering faster than a hummingbird's wings as he grabbed some more tissue and floral wire and started on another one.

I started up the show and despite his initial teasing, I could tell he was getting caught up in it. We were making comments back and forth about the contestants and the ridiculous things they were doing to catch the bachelor's attention.

"Is that a pool of Jell-O being wheeled out?" he asked.

It was. And the next woman out of the limo introduced herself as a women's empowerment / life coach and then scored a point for women's empowerment by wrestling in the Jell-O pool with another contestant.

Tyler shook his head. "All this for the chance that they might get to go on a date with this bland, mediocre guy who won't remember either one of their names? Why are we watching this again?"

I shushed him and said, "Because it's about true love winning out and . . . I have to watch it."

"Why?"

"To find out what happens next!"

At that he laughed again, thoroughly amused by my response. When the show ended, he got up to get himself a drink from the kitchen. "Do you want anything?" he asked.

"I'm fine—" I stopped speaking when he went for the fridge. Oh no, I'd totally forgotten about the . . .

"What's this?" he asked, holding up a large plastic bowl.

Oksana again. I didn't really want to hear from him how fantastic and gorgeous she was and what a good cook and a good everything else. I was having fun with him watching TV. I didn't want the specter of her to ruin that.

"That's . . ." My brain ran through a million different answers but I sighed as I settled for honesty. Maybe it would be a good thing to hear about how much he liked her. It would remind me where I stood with him. "That's your borscht."

He looked alarmed. "My what?"

"It's the soup that Oksana came by and made for you."

I got myself all ready to view the heart-wrenching list of emotions that I was sure were going to show up on his face at the thought that his beloved girlfriend had made him food, but he just looked bewildered. "Oksana was here?"

Why did he seem so confused? "I thought you knew. Isn't she your girlfriend?"

"No!" He put the container away in the fridge. He grabbed a bottle of water and came back to sit by me on the couch. Was it my imagination or was he sitting marginally closer than before? "We went on, like, two dates months ago and then she basically dumped me."

"Who would do that?" I hadn't meant to say it out loud, but realized that I did when he laughed. It wasn't a joke, though. I couldn't imagine someone telling Tyler, *Thanks, but no thanks.*

"Oksana did. Pretty convincingly."

"And what, she changed her mind?" That I couldn't blame her for. Maybe she woke up one morning and realized how stupid she had been.

"My guess is things didn't work out with the Saudi Arabian billionaire she left me for."

"Wow. That's . . . shocking." If only because I'd been rich and didn't have a Tyler in my life, and I much preferred now, being broke and having Tyler. As a friend and roommate, but still.

"I thought so at the time. I don't intend to be anybody's backup plan."

"I know the feeling," I confessed. And without thinking, without weighing the ramifications when something similar had happened just a few minutes ago, I said, "My . . . friend, Brad? He's broken up with me more than once to date somebody else." Someone prettier, thinner, or from a socially superior family. It made me ill to think of all the times I'd been told to take him back and had done it.

"I'm sorry." Tyler reached over briefly to rest his hand on top of mine and it was like time stood absolutely still and nothing existed beyond the feel of his skin on mine. It was electric.

And I keenly felt the loss of him when he moved his hand away.

"Thanks. I was actually worried about bringing her up because I didn't know what her status with you was. Or whether we had that kind of . . . relationship."

He grinned. "I definitely think we've reached the a-stranger's-in-our-apartment-and-I'm-letting-you-know stage of our friendship. Right?"

I nodded. Yep. That was me. His friend. His nonappealing buddy who did hilarious things like letting his former hookup hang out and make him borscht.

As one does.

Now that I knew the truth, I wanted him to know everything, too. "Does that also mean that we have the kind of friendship where I tell you I saw her in a restaurant yesterday making out with some older man?"

"It doesn't surprise me."

That made one of us. "I assumed she was your girlfriend. It surprised the crap out of me."

After he finished laughing, he said, "To be honest, we never should have dated in the first place. I went out with her because she seemed like the kind of girl I should be dating. The sort of woman the other guys at the office are dating. We never had anything in common, and I definitely didn't see it going anywhere. Like, I couldn't imagine her and me sitting here on the couch, watching television and talking, like you and I are doing. If she hadn't ended things, I would have."

While that was truly excellent news, one thing didn't make sense to me still, and instead of guessing I decided to just ask. "Then how did she know about me? And when you'd be back from your trips?"

"She's been texting me lately."

That wasn't an explanation. "So?"

"So, wouldn't it be mean for me not to answer? I told her about you because she texted me the day you moved in and asked what I was up to. And when she asked about my future plans, I told her about my trips."

"You know you don't have to reply to a text if you don't want to, don't you?"

"It just seems a little rude."

"It's not rude!" I protested. "I do it all the time with . . . people that I don't want to talk to. You can be rude to people who aren't respecting your boundaries." Was he seriously the one hot guy in America who didn't understand the concept of ghosting someone? "You can even block her number if she's annoying you, Grandpa. It's called technology."

"To be fair, I hadn't really set up any boundaries with her. But I'll call her and thank her for the soup and tell her that I'm not interested in rekindling anything. And I'll call downstairs and tell them not to let her up anymore without letting us know first."

"Good plan. Especially since I was going to resort to leaving a wooden stake in one of your nightstand drawers. Just in case."

That got him laughing again. "Now that we have that straightened out and no one's going to be in danger of getting puncture holes in their neck, you should start the next episode."

"You still want to watch it?"

He settled back onto the couch. "Yeah. Like you said, now I have to know what happens next."

I couldn't stop the grin that spread across my face. I got the remote and hit play. There was nothing going on with Oksana and I wasn't going to randomly find her in my apartment, smoking and saying mean things. No more James Bond villain for me to contend with.

And Tyler was watching *The Bachelor* with me.

This shouldn't have felt like a win.

So, then, why did it?

CHAPTER FIFTEEN

Tyler left another Post-it note on my door the following morning. He'd gone to bed early due to his exhaustion and had already left the apartment when I got up to get ready for work. Pigeon had spent the night in his room and I'd found myself missing her.

It was funny how quickly your life could change, how something that seemed so foreign at first quickly became your new normal.

Anyway, his note read:

Remember, it's okay not to let people you don't know into the apartment.

I will admit that I tucked that note into my pocket and carried it around with me the rest of the day, smiling at it each time I saw it. Every time that Denny acted out in class, I would take out Tyler's note for the little pick-me-up it provided.

When I got home that afternoon, I decided to do two things before I started on my pom making; I wanted to research ways to help Denny, and I needed to sit down and figure out what was happening to all my money because I never seemed to have any. I set up at the dining room table with my laptop, a notebook, and a pen.

When it came to my expenses, there was the obvious: food, gas, insurance, replacing the things of Tyler's that I'd ruined. But given that I wasn't paying rent, I should have had lots of extra money.

Pigeon ran past me and headed for the foyer, where she sat, her tail wagging. I wondered what she was doing and then there was Tyler. Home early again.

When the calendar said he had a flight for New York in about an hour. "Aren't you going out of town?" I asked.

"Hello to you, too," he said. "I was supposed to go, but my boss canceled my next two trips and is sending someone else in my stead."

"That doesn't sound good."

He ruffled Pigeon's fur and she stared at him adoringly. I hoped I wasn't looking at him the same way. His tie was loosened, the top button undone. I was chewing on my pen and thinking how I'd like to undo the rest of the buttons, especially now that I knew what he was hiding under that shirt when I realized that he'd said something and I hadn't heard him.

"What?"

"I said, it actually is good and you're the reason why."

"Me?" What had I done?

He shrugged off his suit coat, laying it and his briefcase on the kitchen island. "It's because of all the people who want to meet with me from the charity event. The appointments were set up to start a couple of weeks from now but today my assistant made phone calls to reschedule and I'm going to start talking to people tomorrow. Apparently not being able to get in with me made me seem even more valuable."

That was definitely how rich people worked. He'd accidentally turned himself into an unobtainable, precious commodity and it had made everyone want him more.

It had certainly worked on me. "That's fantastic! Your boss must be thrilled."

"He is." Tyler sat down in the chair across from me. "And I don't have any other trips scheduled until the new year, so I'm going to be around."

This was also fantastic. I could only smile.

"Although I will confess to being a little worried about what I'm going to say to these people when it comes to my love life."

He was really putting too much thought into this. Even if these potential clients were meeting with him in hopes of setting him up, that wasn't why they would sign with him. "Tell them you're living with someone. Because technically, you are."

"I don't want to lie."

Just like my mother's gift-wrapping room was weird to other people, it was weird to me that regular humans hadn't been raised in a world where white lies and half truths were necessary for your survival. "I don't think it is. I live here, you live here. I am someone. Hence, you are living with someone."

"Right. But the implication is that you are my girlfriend."

And would that be so bad? I swallowed the words back, trying to calm down my racing heart. Because all it had heard was *you* and *my girlfriend.* "Your personal life is nobody's business and if they're intrusive enough to demand answers about it, then they deserve to be shut down. But I'm not too worried about the whole thing because I know you'll win them over."

"How do you know that?" I loved that smile, the one that said he was amused and enjoyed what I was saying.

How did I know? Besides the fact that he was charming enough to convince a rattler not to bite? "I saw you schmoozing people at Bitsie Fernley's event. You're good at it. And you'll be good at it at work, too."

He thumped his hand against the table and then leaned forward, as if declaring the matter over. He gestured toward my laptop. "What are you up to?"

"Before I begin my nightly indentured servitude of molding tissue paper into a somewhat recognizable decoration, I've been working on a couple of things. The first is trying to figure out some good ways of working with that little boy in my class, the one who's been misbehaving. His dad emailed me and said that his wife left and that's why his son's been acting out. Second, I'm trying to figure out how to budget because no matter what I do, I never seem to have any money."

"I can help you with both of those things."

"Oh yeah, Superman? And how are you going to do that?"

"Your first problem, I called my stepsister. She's an elementary school teacher, too. I asked her for some advice about your situation."

"You . . . you talked to your stepsister? About me?" Why did that make my breath catch?

"Yes, and she said to try really utilizing positive reinforcement. Because right now he's learned that if he misbehaves, you'll respond, even if it is negatively. Catch this little boy being good and verbally reward him for it. Do the same for other kids so that he sees positive behavior getting praised. She was guessing that it's all about the attention. Which I understand. I kind of went through something similar when my dad . . . when he left us. My mom basically checked out and I wanted the attention of my teacher at school. Just to know that there was some adult in my life who still cared about me."

It was the most personal thing he'd ever told me, and my chest felt tight. I wanted to cry for him, for the little boy who had felt unloved by his parents.

Because I had grown up feeling exactly the same way.

I wanted to ask him about his family but was afraid of being shot down. "It sounds like you had a really good teacher."

"Ms. Sparr. I put her through a lot, but she stuck with me. She used to give me these little assignments in class like cleaning the chalkboard or sharpening her pencil. She used to let me be the line leader a lot, too. Small things but they made me feel special. I really needed that attention." He cleared his throat. "Anyway, maybe you could give it a shot. Because if she had looked like you, I can only imagine it would have been a lot worse."

"Um, thanks?" I asked it as a question because I didn't know what in the crap he was talking about.

Was his implication that my face would scare small children into being bad? Or that he thought I was pretty and that would have made him want my attention more? I was so confused.

"I'm going to go change and then I'll come back and help you with your second problem. Because that just happens to be my area of expertise."

Then, heaven help me, the man winked at me. Actually winked at me and it was one of the sexiest things I'd ever been a part of. My blood pressure spiked and I grabbed my phone.

I texted Shay and Delia. We needed to parse out every possible meaning of what he'd said.

> Tyler just told me he'd acted out as a kid in class and wanted his teacher's attention. Then he said that if his teacher looked like me it would have been a lot worse.

Shay instantly responded:

> He wants you. Lock. This. Down.

Shaking my head, I texted:

> He wants us to be just friends. I can't go there with him.

> You're already there with him. It will be a short commute. Somebody should be hooking up with this man.

I really couldn't fault her logic there.

Delia didn't answer, and I was disappointed. Also, a little concerned because she usually responded to texts quickly, and recently, the past few times I'd texted, she'd stayed silent. Had she bewitched the new substi-cute teacher into going on a date with her? I made a mental note to check in with her and see how she was doing.

I also wanted her more objective opinion on this. Shay was a bit unreliable when it came to this situation because she wanted Tyler and me to get together, given that he was incredible looking.

Which, again, no faulting that logic.

Tyler came back in the room and I hid my phone under my leg, as if he could read it from six feet away. Pigeon followed him but came over to lie down on the floor next to my feet. I reached down to scratch behind her ears.

"I am going to order some takeout. Do you want some?" he asked "My treat."

"While I know my answer is supposed to be 'no thank you,' because of dignity or pride or whatever, I'm going to say absolutely yes."

He grinned. "I do like how you speak your mind. What should we get?"

Inspiration struck. "Oh, remember how we were talking about getting you some culture? One of the ways of doing that is to eat foods from different countries. And we've got so many different international restaurants nearby to choose from. Maybe Korean? Vietnamese? Thai? Turkish? Indian? Egyptian?"

He thought about it and then said, "Let's do Thai. What do you recommend?"

"I'll look it up and see what's close." I did an online search and found a restaurant half a mile away. I showed the menu to Tyler, who read it over my shoulder. I could feel the heat from his chest next to my neck, making my skin tingle. He braced his arm on the table as he read it and the screen in front of me started to swirl and swim, so that I couldn't focus. I noticed that he had such strong, nicely formed forearms.

I sighed. I was truly pathetic.

We decided on a few different dishes, like pad thai, noodle soup, and green-curry chicken. More accurately, he decided and I nodded, as I was so distracted by him that I couldn't have said words even if I wanted to. It was both a relief and a disappointment when he moved away to call in the order.

When he hung up, he sat back down at the table with me. "We should go over your budget while we wait. Why don't you show me your last month's expenses?"

I quickly and mentally ran through what I had bought and whether it would show up on my account. Most of the replacement stuff I'd done through Amazon and Violet had paid for the shoes. I didn't think there was anything too embarrassing.

After I logged in to my bank account, I pushed my laptop toward him. "Do you mind if I download some software for budgeting?"

"Sure."

He mentioned one by name that was free and would sync up with my bank account. After a few minutes, he angled my laptop so that we could both see it. "So it seems like your biggest expenses fall in this miscellaneous category. Part of setting a budget is figuring out how much you should be spending and then discipline yourself to stay under that amount. You should also be looking at monthly expenditures that maybe are unnecessary. Like . . ." He scrolled down a bit and said, "Do you really need Netflix?"

That was like asking me if I needed my firstborn child. "Uh, yes. I need it. That's nonnegotiable. If for no other reason than it allows me to consume television the same way I do ice cream and alcohol."

He laughed and said, "Okay, okay. You win. Netflix stays. What about this expense for Sephora? A hundred and thirty-two dollars?"

While I'd had to downgrade my hair dye, makeup, cleanser, and toner, I was not willing to give this up. "That's for my moisturizer."

He blinked at me a couple of times, as if he hadn't heard me correctly. "You paid a hundred and thirty-two dollars for lotion for your face?"

"It's not lotion. It's *moisturizer.*"

"For one bottle? What's in it? Dragon's blood and the scraping of a unicorn's horn?"

I wasn't about to tell him it wasn't for a whole bottle, but for like two ounces. "Ha-ha. I need it. My face needs it."

"You don't need it. You're beautiful."

"It's why I'm beautiful!" I was caught between sheer delight and disbelief at his words, and partial terror that he was going to make me stop using it. But then I started thinking about the way he'd complimented me—he'd said it so matter-of-factly, like it wasn't his personal opinion, just a truth he happened to agree with.

I wasn't sure how to feel about that.

While I was trying to figure out his deeper meaning, he chuckled and shook his head. "Come on, you're easily the hottest girl in this apartment."

If I thought I'd been thrilled before, it was nothing compared to what I was feeling now. A flush started at the top of my scalp and went down to my toes—unpainted because I couldn't afford to get a pedicure. Then I realized that Tyler was quoting back to me what I'd said about him at the charity event. Did that mean . . . it was a joke? A callback and he didn't really mean anything by it? Or was he trying to butter me up so that he could pry my moisturizer out of my cold, soon-to-be dehydrated hands?

Not willing to be taken in, I said, "You're not going to flatter me to get me to change my mind. I'll remind you that I'm the only girl in this apartment."

"That's not true. Pidge is here and she's gorgeous. Aren't you?" he asked his dog, bending over to pet her. She licked his cheek and I had never felt more of a kinship to her, ever. He turned his attention back to me. "Do you really need it?"

"The only time I get a facial now is when I open the dishwasher midcycle and the steam hits me in my face. I don't buy the moisturizer every month. I'm really careful with how much I use on a daily basis. But I've had to give up so many other things. Let me have this one."

"All right, all right." He threw his hands up, as if I'd defeated him. "But there's something I've been meaning to ask you. If your parents are super wealthy, don't you have a trust fund?"

"My trust fund is gone." He raised an eyebrow at me. "Not because I spent it all on moisturizer. My parents took it back."

"Revocable or irrevocable?"

"My understanding was irrevocable for the tax benefits." I'd over-heard Violet and Vanessa discussing their trusts in the past.

"That means they can't take it away just because they're mad at you."

I shrugged. "They employ attorneys by weight and volume, and as you can clearly see, I'm in no financial position to fight them."

"That sucks."

I nodded. It did, indeed, suck.

He turned back to the screen. "What about your gym membership? Do you go enough to make that worthwhile?"

"I don't have a gym membership. I used to, but when I left my parents' house I called them and canceled."

"That's not what your bank account says."

I'd never really been a going-to-the-gym kind of girl. I'd always preferred my exercising to be things like yoga at a feminine and relax-ing studio. Not lifting weights or running on treadmills. I'd joined only because Brad had insisted so we could work out together.

We never had.

And as I thought about when I'd initially signed up, solely to make him happy, I remembered something. "They told me they preferred a debit card."

"Yeah. So they could keep pulling the money directly from your banking account. It's harder to prevent than a credit card charge."

"Those . . . fiends. I am going to cancel it right now." I couldn't believe I'd been paying a monthly fee for something I wasn't even using. It was like they were stealing my hard-earned money from me.

There was a buzz from our intercom and Tyler got up to answer. It was our food. "I'll go grab it," he said.

I was intent on calling the gym, but couldn't help but text Shay first.

> Update: he called me
> beautiful. Like in a completely
> non-romantic way, but still.

It felt like her answer arrived only a second after I'd pressed send.

> I TOLD YOU!!!! For all
> womankind, please make this
> happen.

I sent her some laughing emojis and put myself back on track. I was going to get rid of this useless membership and then go over my checking account again to see where else I might be hemorrhaging money pointlessly.

Somebody at the gym picked up on the third ring. It was a young woman with a bubbly and high-pitched voice. "Standford Fitness and Training, this is Kiki. How may I help you?"

What kind of made-up Barbie-sounding name was Kiki? "This is Madison Huntington, and I want to cancel my membership with you. I called several months ago and canceled my membership, but you guys are still taking money out of my checking account and I would like that to stop."

"Do you know who you spoke with?"

"No." It wasn't Kiki. Because I was pretty sure I would have remembered. "But I know I did because I lost all my money and I couldn't afford it anymore."

"Oh, I'm so sorry to hear that. But we don't cancel memberships over the phone. Whoever you talked to must not have known that."

Wasn't it the phone answerer's job to know things like that? How to cancel a membership seemed like first-day training material. "Okay, well, I need to cancel it now. How do I do that?"

"You can do it one of two ways."

Two ways? Like I was being sent on a quest in *Lord of the Rings*? "Okay, Gandalf the Grey, what are my options?"

"Um, no, it's Kiki?" She sounded like it was a question and I could hear her chewing gum while she paused. "The first way is to send in a certified letter."

"A letter?" I repeated. Why? I hadn't signed up for my membership during the American Revolution. And I didn't know if I was even sure what a certified letter actually was, having never sent nor received one. "Then what? I carry it to Mount Doom and throw it into the fires?"

"No, you mail it to us. You need to include all your personal information, name, address, phone number, Social Security number, birth date, along with your membership identification number and your agreement number listed on your contract. Once we have all that information, then it takes us about eight weeks to get everything processed."

Did they want my measurements and shoe size, too? Sheesh. And two more months of them robbing me blind? No thanks. "What's the other way?"

"You would need to come to the gym in person and do it manually."

Manually? What did that even mean? "I will be there tomorrow during my lunch break to cancel." Then I hung up the phone before I could counsel Kiki to make better life choices and stop working for places that took money away from completely broke teachers.

Tyler returned with the food, putting it on the table. I moved my laptop to the side to make room and then got up to grab some plates and forks.

When I sat back down, he had already opened all the containers, and he asked me, "What are your plans for later tonight?"

I looked down at my outfit. "I have my Netflix pants on. That means I'm planning on being in for the night."

"I was thinking we could go to that art exhibit after we eat. The one you were talking about with Walter Loveless. You want to come with?"

My heart raced and I had to swallow a couple of times before I did my best nonchalant response. "Sure."

"Cool. Then it's a date."

Was he serious? Teasing? Was it a date? I felt like I didn't have enough information to suss out whether he was serious or just saying "it's a date" because in all other ways it would seem like a date only we both understood that it wasn't really because we were only friends so ha-ha, it was just a joke?

Boys were the worst.

My phone buzzed with a text from Shay.

> You kiss him yet?

What was wrong with the two of us? Why did my and Shay's brains keep trying to turn this into something it wasn't? It sometimes felt like I was so caught up in my imagination that I had practically started hallucinating things that weren't there. Looks, lingering touches, feelings.

I'd always been a dreamer. I liked hoping for a better world and doing what I could to make it happen. But in this situation? The reality was pretty clear, even if I kept resisting it.

My reply was short and to the point.

> No. Not going to happen.

Something both of us needed to remember.

CHAPTER SIXTEEN

"So what's the verdict?" I asked. Tyler had gone through most of the exhibit with me. He carefully followed my instructions to read the titles of the artwork, along with any wall text that would further explain the piece, and to just let himself absorb each painting, see if he had any kind of emotional response to one.

"I'm a . . . what's the word? *Troglodyte? Philistine?* Because I don't get any of this. I feel like I'm missing something."

"You don't have to get them," I explained. "In fact, I think the mystery of not knowing what the artist was thinking makes it more of a challenge. Where you get to decide the outcome and how you feel about it. I think the great thing about abstract art is that there are no rules. It's all about freedom of expression."

"If you say so."

I giggled at his frown. "It's not that bad. Like this one. I love that the splotches of colors are so vibrant and happy. What do you think?"

"I don't want to be that guy in the art museum, but I think this is . . . not all that impressive. If I'm being honest, it looks like the colors got drunk at a party, threw up, and then started procreating with the other colors in the room, creating color-spot babies and then they also threw up and this is the end result. It's too bad we can't talk about reality television at society functions. That I think I could do, and with conviction."

"Unfortunately, nobody here considers reality TV to be art, and you're right, it's not exactly something you can bring up with socialites at parties. Well, except for the ones that starred on *Real Housewives.*"

"I don't consider any of this art, either. I'm sorry. Am I being too blunt?" he asked as we started walking away from the color-vomit love-in painting.

I found it refreshing, considering the other men in my life. "Your honesty is one of the things I like most about you."

"Oh yeah? What else do you like about me?" He sounded flirtatious, but I wasn't sure if I was again projecting my own feelings onto him.

And there were so many things I liked about him. His devotion to his dog, his kindness, his charm, his sense of humor, his intelligence, his thoughtfulness, the way he made everyday things seem like adventures. And then there was that thing where he was in possession of a face that would make an angel hurl herself from heaven just for the chance to be with him.

None of which I could say. "I like that your name can't be turned into a pun."

"That's kind of a weird thing to like."

"You didn't say it had to be normal." We passed into another room and I said, "They do have a couple of Rothkos here."

We walked over to stand in front of one and Tyler said, "I hate to tell you, but they're just rectangles of color. Again, I'm not getting it."

"Don't worry about it. My guess is ninety-nine percent of people don't, either, and just pretend they do. But in Rothko's defense, one of his most famous paintings sold a few years ago at auction for over eighty million dollars."

His eyebrows shot up. "On purpose?"

"On purpose."

"Miss Huntington?"

I turned to see Mrs. Adams, the destroyer of souls and giver of pom materials, standing just behind me. "Mrs. Adams! How nice to see you. This is Tyler Roth."

They shook hands, exchanging pleasantries, and then Mrs. Adams asked, "How are the decorations coming along?"

Ignoring the amused glint in Tyler's eye, I said, "It's . . . a process." After my initial meeting with her and the headmistress, Delia and Shay mentioned that the Adamses were heavy-hitting donors for the academy and that it was in my best interests to smile and play nice.

"Well, I'm so glad I ran into you because I've been meaning to call you. I don't know if Ms. Gladwell mentioned it, but in addition to making the decorations we will also need you to hang them up."

Was she serious? Had I not already done my penance?

When I didn't respond, she just kept talking. "Feel free to bring your boyfriend here to help out. I'll see you at the festival!"

I tried to protest that he wasn't my boyfriend, but she just wiggled her fingers at us and was gone.

I had really thought that I was going to make the decorations and then pass them along to some other poor schmuck to take care of. I'd never considered the possibility that I'd be the poor schmuck.

Tyler's voice interrupted my woe-is-me train of thought. "I guess that makes it official. I'm going to help you hang up decorations at the winter festival."

The last thing I wanted was for him to feel obligated toward me. "You absolutely don't have to."

"I was there when they were born. I feel like I should keep going on this journey with them, all the way to the end."

It made me feel better that I wasn't in this mess alone. "Only if you really want to."

"Hanging up decorations in a school gym? Does it get more exciting than that?"

I laughed softly and we walked over to another art piece that was bright red with various slivers of other colors showing through.

He pointed at the canvas. "That kind of looks like the borscht Oksana made me, doesn't it?"

"A little." Bringing her up made me wonder if he had someone else in his life that he hadn't mentioned. I knew it wasn't really my place to ask, but I had to find out the truth. It felt really important. "So I know Oksana's not your girlfriend, but do you have a girlfriend? Or people that you're dating?"

"Not at the moment. Not for a long time, actually. I've been too busy. The only special lady I have time for in my life is Pigeon."

He flashed that megawatt grin of his at me and I pressed my arms against my sides so that I wouldn't visibly react to his news. Because I wanted to jump up and down and that would get us thrown out of the art museum. Not to mention that he'd specifically said he was too busy to spend time with anyone yet that's all we'd been doing recently. Spending time together. Was I becoming a little bit special to him, too?

He walked over to a painting that was mostly yellow crescents and circles, making me think of bananas and lemons.

Tyler doesn't have a girlfriend, Tyler doesn't have a girlfriend was on a singsong loop in my head, so I was startled when he said, "You're stroking your purse."

"Am I?" I glanced down and my hand was on my bag. "Sorry, I just really love it."

"It's a purse," he repeated, as if I couldn't possibly love an inanimate object.

"It's not a purse, it's a Birkin bag." I took it out only for special occasions like this one. I'd had more than one nightmare about what my second graders might "accidentally" do to it if I was ever foolish enough to bring it to school. "It's a very special type of bag by a designer who made a limited edition a long time ago and my grandmother gave it to me when I graduated from college. It's easily my most prized possession. You should have seen my mother's face when—"

I was cut off by the sight of my actual mother's face. She was with my father talking to the mayor.

This was the problem with society events. Society tended to show up.

And I did not want to see or be snubbed by my parents. I didn't want them to notice Tyler or have my two very separate worlds colliding. Because I knew they would automatically jump to the worst conclusion—that I was here with Tyler on a real date and at some point they would give me an earful over my "cheating on Brad and disgracing the family name."

Not only that, much as she hated making a scene, there was a very real possibility that my short, pink-clad mother would try to physically fight me to get this bag. I never took it anywhere that I thought she might be.

I let out a little cough. "Hey, I'm suddenly not feeling all that great, could we go?"

Tyler said yes so quickly that I felt guilty for not suggesting it sooner.

When we got to the front of the building, he told me to stay put, that he'd get the car and bring it around. The museum had not provided valet service, something I'd overheard being repeatedly criticized. I believe the phrase "having to park like peasants" had been used.

It was a little nerve-racking waiting for Tyler to come back. I was afraid with every moment that passed that my parents would spot me and this evening would turn into a whole thing that I didn't want to deal with.

Fortunately, he drove up a minute later, opening my door from the inside.

When I got in I said, "Thanks. You didn't have to go get the car alone. I could have walked with you."

He pulled forward, making his way through the parking lot and back out to the main road. "You said you weren't feeling well. I was happy to do it. Besides, what are friends for?"

There it was. My daily reminder as to how he felt about me.

But if he was trying to make sure we were only friends, he was failing pretty miserably. Because the more time I spent with him, the more I liked him.

~

Before I went to bed for the evening, I'd put up a note on Tyler's door (after our night that most definitely *was not a date*, especially considering that I'd ended up with a dog as my only sleeping companion) reminding him that we needed trash bags. I couldn't help but add:

Also, Pigeon says to tell you she loves me more.

There was a reply from him on my door when I woke up the next morning. He said:

Lies. Don't try and brainwash my dog.

My response?

Too late. She has a deep and abiding love for Snausages and I'm the one who provides them.

I went to work and started trying out the positive reinforcement plan. At first it felt unnatural for me to be constantly verbally praising the children for doing what I asked, but I could tell the kids weren't sure what to think about it, either. But they quickly adapted and I saw that even Denny began to respond to it. I'd have to thank Tyler and his stepsister for the advice.

Lunchtime I'd had to bail on my friends to go to the gym to get my cancellation straightened out. Shay was particularly displeased since she had wanted to go over my conversation / museum outing with Tyler minute by minute so that we could analyze everything he and I had said under a microscope.

I wasn't really in the mood. Or maybe it was the fact that I was spending so much time in my own head trying to uncover any possible subtext that I was tired of doing it and didn't want to rehash the lies I kept telling myself and the truths Tyler kept forcing me to acknowledge.

When I arrived at Standford Fitness and Training, I asked the woman at the front desk to please get the manager.

"Is there anything I can help you with?" she asked.

"Yes. You can get me the manager. That would be the most help." I was being rude, which she let me know from her expression, but I wanted this to be over.

She came back with a guy so buff I could barely see his neck. He shook my hand with a grip so hard he might have actually bruised some bones. He introduced himself as Billy. I explained the situation, including my financial hardships, and told him that I really needed my membership to be canceled.

"Tell you what," Billy said. "How about we sign you up for six more months at only half price. If you're not happy then, we can reconsider."

Anger bubbled up inside me and I clenched my teeth together before saying, "Considering I've already paid you two years' worth of membership fees for a gym I haven't stepped foot in since I initially signed up, under duress, I might add, by a boyfriend whose idea of a good time is spending four hours looking at himself in mirrors while he works out, I think you probably owe me quite a bit more than six months at half price. I'm not interested in any specials or deals. I'm not going to change my mind. Can we please cancel this?" I was past being polite; I wanted it done.

Billy must have recognized my determination, because he didn't offer me any other deals and simply said, "I'll get the paperwork."

And I decided no matter the outcome here, I was going to stop by my bank either today or tomorrow and get a new debit card that the gym wouldn't have access to.

It would be worth the hassle to know that this wouldn't happen again.

Speaking of things that wouldn't happen again, I heard my name being called.

It was Brad.

This was the problem with Houston. It was supposed to be a big city, but it so often felt like a small town where I was constantly running (or almost running) into people I did not want to see.

It looked like Brad had just finished his workout and showered, and was probably headed to his father's offices. For his "job."

Since I was already on a canceling kick, I decided to add Brad to my list.

"What are you doing here?" he asked. "Did you come to see me?"

It was the delight in his voice that threw me. Like he was truly happy that I'd finally made the effort to come to his gym. But this place was another reminder as to why I needed to end things; we were not made to be together.

Like, for example, Brad loathed television and spent all his time watching videos on social media.

"I'm here to cancel my gym membership." I hoped he caught my double meaning there, that by ending one thing having to do with him I was also planning on ending the relationship, but I figured it was probably too subtle. "Because I never wanted to be a member here."

"Sure." He sounded disbelieving. "The same way our relationship is 'over.'" He made air quotes and I had never wanted to punch somebody more.

"It is over. I don't know how else to explain it to you so that you'll understand." I wanted to tell him that I liked someone else so much more, but that would be humiliating if I was somehow forced to admit that Tyler didn't like me back.

He looked angry. "I told you I was waiting for you. That I could commit myself to you. What more do you want?"

"Love? Respect? Fidelity? I'll never have those things with you."

"Let's go somewhere and talk about this," he said. "Someplace private."

I really didn't want to be alone and/or private with him. "I can't. I have to get this membership thing straightened out and then I need to get back to work."

Anger flashed across his face before he said, "So skip work. Shouldn't an eight-year relationship, shouldn't I, be more important than your job?"

He wasn't. "I can't just skip the rest of my day. People rely on me to show up and actually do my job. I don't work for my daddy."

"Whose fault is that?" he asked. Before I could respond he said, "I suppose none of this really matters because you'll quit once we get engaged."

I was so dumbfounded that it was several seconds before I regained my ability to speak. He was ridiculous and I knew, then and there, with a hundred percent certainty, that I was never ever going to marry Brad. And I couldn't believe what he'd just said. He really thought he could make me stop working? If I'd been angry before, it was nothing compared to the total rage that threatened to consume me. My whole life my parents had tried to control me: what subjects I could study, who I was allowed to date and marry, where I could go to school, what kind of job I could have. I was so tired of other people assuming that they got to tell me how to run my life. Brad and I were never getting engaged or married. Was he delusional? "This is over. Please get that through your skull."

Before he could respond, we were interrupted by one of Brad's best frat buddies, Chip. He was carrying a gym bag, which made me think they'd been working out together. Or trying to hit on women together, since Chip seemed to enjoy encouraging Brad to cheat. I'd never liked the guy and I suspected the feeling was totally mutual. "We need to go. Sorry, Madison. But we have plans. You know how it is."

Ha. Plans. I knew none of them would include Brad pretending to go to his job that his father provided, where he was paid an exorbitant salary and spent his days working out at the gym and playing Xbox and going clubbing with his idiot friends.

When I looked at Brad, there was nothing left. No lingering feelings, no teenage part of me that still held out hope. It was really over. I realized that I didn't respect Brad. I couldn't respect a man who treated life as if he were still in college, content to let his parents pay for everything so that he could prolong his adolescence. Who wasn't passionate about anything besides himself.

Unlike Tyler. Who came from nothing and through hard work and ambition had created a great life for himself.

And who had helped me, someone who had been a virtual stranger to him. I couldn't imagine Brad doing anything similar. He'd never done anything for anyone unless he benefited from it in some way.

Then Billy was back with a manila file folder in his hands. "I have the paperwork ready for you to sign."

I turned my back on Brad and reached for the paperwork, ignoring him and Chip as they left.

The only way to get him to stop and to leave me alone would be to tell my parents the truth.

I had to stop putting it off.

CHAPTER SEVENTEEN

The next few days passed by in a blur. Every evening, Tyler came home only a couple of hours after I did, making me think that his claims of always working long hours and being devoted only to his job seemed to not really be a thing. Because that wasn't the reality that I was currently experiencing.

He would make us dinner, I would clean it up. We would talk about our days. I told him how well his stepsister's advice was working, and Denny was like his old self again (although we still had some issues). Tyler entertained me with the stories of the colorful potential clients who came through his door, wanting to work with him.

Then we would retreat to the living room, where I would work on the winter festival decorations while watching television. He would either help me or do work on his laptop. I worried that the TV would distract him, but he said he didn't mind.

We were settling into a routine that was so comfortable and . . . homey.

Tonight he was on his laptop while I watched an episode of *Survivor* and one of the particularly weaselly contestants reminded me of Brad. Which made me flash back to our last infuriating encounter. I paused my show.

"Would you want your wife to work?" I asked.

It was a weird question, but that didn't seem to faze him. He paused whatever he was doing and said, "I don't have a wife. I'm pretty sure you would have noticed by now if I had one."

Ha. Noticed her? I would have already tried to choke her out from sheer jealousy by now. "I know that. I mean, you make good money. When you get married do you expect your wife to stop working? Even if she loves her job?"

He looked at me like I was a crazy person. "I would want her to do what she wants and what makes her happy. And if she loved her job, of course she should keep working."

That made me smile with satisfaction. I knew Brad was not normal, but it was nice to have it confirmed. As was verifying that Tyler was awesome and guessing that he would probably be an awesome husband.

While I was daydreaming about our wedding, he asked, "Speaking of strange and out-of-the-blue questions, have you ever done a marathon?"

I was confused. "You mean like on Netflix? All the time."

He smiled. "No, I mean like an actual marathon. Running. If I get this promotion and I stop traveling, I was thinking I would have some extra time on my hands and maybe I could train for a marathon."

That just . . . did not sound fun to me. "You know the first guy who ran one of those died right after? That's not exactly a ringing endorsement in my book."

"I like exercising."

"I can tell." Whoops. I clamped my lips shut, hoping that it didn't come across the way that I'd intended.

Apparently not picking up on my innuendo, he said, "I've always found running to be relaxing."

"If you think running a marathon is a way to relax, I'm not sure we can still be friends."

He laughed while clicking something on his computer. Which made me curious.

"Is that what you're looking up?" I asked. "Information on local marathons?"

"This?" He actually looked a little embarrassed, which made me more intrigued. "No, I'm not looking anything up. It's actually, that is, I'm . . . well, I'm doing something fun for me."

Did I want to know what that was? "Like what?"

"I'm creating a game."

Was this a Dungeons & Dragons thing? "What kind of game?"

"Growing up, I was fascinated by computers and especially programming. I loved the idea that I could create something out of nothing. I really wanted to be a software engineer. Lately I've been designing a game for mobile devices. It's simplistic. You pop bubbles on it. I'm doing it to teach myself how to make programs that interact with smart screens so that later I can create something more sophisticated."

"So all the programming you know, is it self-taught?"

"I had a couple of classes in high school, but that was it. As much as I wanted to take them in college, there didn't seem to be a point because it wouldn't make enough money."

"If it's something you love so much that you do it for fun, shouldn't that be your career? I'll admit that I don't know a whole lot about salaries, but I thought computer programmers made decent money."

"That's the problem. It's only decent money and I had to make a lot more than that," he said with a wry smile.

"Why?" As someone who'd chosen a job because she loved it, it was hard for me to understand when other people didn't do the same.

He closed his laptop and set it on the coffee table and I got the feeling that something very important was about to happen. Then he turned toward me, his arm along the back of the couch, almost touching me.

"You asked me once if I grew up with money. I didn't grow up with it, but I was born into it. When I was five years old, my father was convicted of insider trading and running a Ponzi scheme. He stole a lot of money from a lot of people and got fifty years."

Wow. I did not even know what to say.

"My mother had come from money herself, but my father had stolen most of her parents' money in the scam, so there was practically nothing left when he was incarcerated. My mom had never been to college, had never held a job, and didn't know what to do. From the time I was little she told me that I had to take care of her and our family, that it was my responsibility. I got a job as soon as I was old enough and later I went into the same line of work as my father so that I could support her."

"Support her?" I echoed. I wondered if she was sick. Or elderly. "Like, is she in a nursing home?"

"No. She's forty-eight. Not quite old enough for a nursing home yet. She just doesn't work and I'm the one who pays for everything in her life. I mean, occasionally she'll get married again but her husbands tend not to last when they see how she spends and there's always a prenup."

That explained the stepsister. Which prompted me to ask, "Do you have any siblings that could help?"

"I have a younger brother, but he's one of those get-rich-quick schemers. There's always another big, overblown plan for how he's going to make a fortune that inevitably fails and he's constantly broke. Do you have one of those in your family?"

"Not really. Mostly they're just rich. Not a lot of failing. A ton of scheming, though." I paused, wondering whether it was okay for me to say anything about his situation, but deciding that if I was really his friend, I would. "Why don't you just tell her she needs to get a job?"

"I'm not sure she would even know how. She just relies on me to keep sending her more and more money."

That first day when we met—this was why he loved Pigeon. Because her love was unconditional and she didn't ask for anything in return. So many other things were starting to make sense now—why he didn't

181

drive a flashier car. How he was good at budgeting. He was so sweetly generous, even though his mother was totally taking advantage of him. I wished there was a way to kindly let him know that he deserved to live his own life without this hanging over him. "I hate to ask this, but what if something happened to you? What would she do then?" After she presumably burned through whatever life insurance he had?

"I don't know."

"My guess is she would find a way to survive, without your help." People like that usually did. I was formerly rich and I'd done it. The irony that Tyler was the one helping me do it, though, was not lost on me.

"She would probably get married again," he said. "Sometimes I feel like I'm doing a public service for all the men of Texas by financing her lifestyle. And I know it sounds ridiculous. Me working at a job just to make my mom happy and comfortable."

"Trust me, it doesn't sound ridiculous at all. I understand." I'd been raised similarly, only with a different set of expectations. It was never in the plans that I would take care of my parents; only that I would be a credit to them and their business and social standing. When you were raised a specific way, it was really hard to just let it go.

"Most people don't. Most women don't."

Now I understood the disconnect of him being the way that he was and looking the way that he did but not having a girlfriend. A woman like Oksana would not take too kindly to his money being spent on somebody besides her. "That must be tough. But I really do get it."

"Only you stood up to your parents and went against what they raised you to do."

"I think you were the one who told me that we always have a choice. I try to keep choosing the things that are right for me. I'm not even completely free of the burdens of their expectations yet. I'm still a work in progress. And I know how hard it is."

He nodded, giving me a wry smile. "Wow. Thanks for letting me unload. I've never told anyone any of this before."

A spark of joy pierced my heart that he would trust me. "Really?"

"It's sort of humiliating to admit that your father is a felon and your mother is selfish and a leech. It's not really something you want to advertise."

My heart melted, again. "I think it makes the man you've become even more admirable, given how you were raised."

"Thank you." His gratitude was deep and serious sounding and it took all my strength not to reach out and hug him. "And it's not like I don't ever get to use my programming skills. Part of being good with computers is being good at logic and math, which helps me out in my day-to-day. I also designed a program that helps me more effectively monitor investments."

"See? I told you that you had acumen."

His bright-blue eyes danced. "You were right. Now, I think we should find out if Lauren confronts Mandy P. for lying about her on their two on-one date."

"Definitely," I agreed.

"Lauren never should have trusted her," he said as he reached for his laptop and flipped it open.

His words were like a massive thud against my heart and made it settle heavily in the pit of my stomach. I should tell him the truth. About everything. I should be worthy of what he'd told me, but how could I be when I was keeping so many things from him?

Tyler's trust felt like a precious thing and I wasn't sure I deserved it.

~

When I was younger, I always used to sleep in on Saturdays and Sundays. But as I grew up, I realized it was better for me to generally try to get up at the same time every day. I hated it, but it made me feel more rested overall.

My morning was instantly made a little bit better when I found a Post-it on my door.

Have purchased Snausages. Let the games begin.

His door was still shut and I could hear Pigeon moving around on his bed. Sometimes she was a restless sleeper, which I assumed was due to her anxiety.

I started up the coffee machine, a skill I'd recently had to acquire. Since it was basically my medical treatment for being morning impaired and it was much cheaper to make it at home, I'd learned how.

Not to mention that the barista at Starbucks had said, "Here's your receipt," and I'd blissfully called back, "Hey, you too!" So now I was too humiliated to show my face there ever again.

Looking at the calendar, I realized how quickly the holidays were approaching and that I hadn't done anything to get into the spirit of the season yet. When I was younger, my grandmother used to have us come over and had her servants make Christmas cookies with us. Strange as it sounded, it was a good memory.

So I decided to make sugar cookies all by myself. I found a recipe online, preheated the oven, and started combining the ingredients. The recipe said to refrigerate the cookie dough, but I didn't want to wait, and we'd never done that when I was small.

When the ingredients were all in and mixed, I rolled up some balls and put them on a cookie sheet. I wished that I'd had some cookie cutters to make shapes, but round was good enough. All that mattered was how they tasted. I put the cookies in the oven, set the timer, and waited impatiently for them to finish cooking.

Just before the timer rang, Tyler walked into the kitchen. His hair was adorably mussed and he smiled wide. My heart leaped at the sight of him. "Are those cookies I smell?"

"It is."

Pigeon came in next, yawned, and then went for her food bowl. Tyler went to grab her some kibble when she sat in front of it and looked at him mournfully.

"Cookies aren't exactly the breakfast of champions," he called out from the pantry.

"It's a breakfast for people in the mood for Christmas."

"That's hard to argue with." He came out with Pigeon's food, pouring it into the bowl for her. He then returned the bag to the pantry and closed the door.

"Does your family have any Christmas traditions?" I asked.

"Only if getting blackout drunk and blaming your children for being a burden counts as a tradition. It's my mother's favorite."

The thought that anyone could treat Tyler that way made me sick. And unfortunately, I could relate. "My mom's favorite is making a You Suck list that she checks twice so that she can spend Christmas dinner telling me all the ways I've failed as a daughter."

The timer rang and I took out my cookies. They looked perfect. A nice, golden shade. It was hard to believe that I'd done it. I'd made cookies without burning them or setting an oven mitt on fire or some other terrible disaster.

"Hello, my name is Tyler Roth and I'm here from the IT department. I've been instructed to delete your cookies," he said with an exaggerated drawl, using a spatula to pick up a cookie. He blew on it and then popped it in his mouth.

I giggled at his impersonation but fell silent at the expression on his face. "Is something wrong?"

He ran over to the sink and spit the cookie out. Was he trying to tease me? He grabbed a cup and poured himself a glass of water.

This had to be a joke. I got a cookie myself and had already put it into my mouth when he said, "No, wait!"

My eyes watered. This was the saltiest, grossest cookie known to mankind. I followed his actions and spit it out, too. Only I didn't make it to the sink and it landed on the floor. Pigeon was there to investigate, but one sniff proved she was smarter than both of us as she ignored it and went back to her own food.

Tyler handed me his glass and I gulped down the rest of the water. I put the empty glass in the sink and grabbed my fallen cookie from the floor and threw it away. Then I washed my hands, like I could wash the stink of this mistake off me.

"How much salt did you put in those?"

"What the recipe said. Half a cup." I pulled the recipe back up on my phone and realized that I had somehow confused the salt with the measurement for the powdered sugar just above it. "Oh. It was supposed to be half a teaspoon of salt. I'm sorry. I already knew I was a terrible cook. I didn't know I was bad at baking, too." Had I not learned my lesson with the chocolate macaroni and cheese?

"Didn't you taste the dough?"

"I may not know a lot of kitchen stuff, but I do know you don't eat batter with raw eggs. That's how you get salmonella." Or at least that was the excuse one of Grandma's cooks had given us as kids to keep us out of the cookie dough.

"So basically, if I didn't feed you, you'd starve."

"Something like that," I agreed.

He went over to the refrigerator and pulled out a carton of eggs. "How do you like your eggs prepared?"

"By somebody other than me."

"Excellent choice, as that's what we're serving here today." He got out a frying pan and put some olive oil in it. I loved watching him do physical things, the way the muscles tightened and relaxed across his shoulders and back, his arms flexing as he reached for the eggs and the spatula.

"You know, I feel bad that you are always feeding me," I told him. That he was spending his money on groceries that he would then use to cook for me. Since he'd told me about his mom I'd become uncomfortably aware that I was relying on him too heavily. It made me even more determined to get my finances straightened out so that I could start paying him rent.

"We have a bartering system in place here. You get what you want and I get what I want."

That was dangerous territory because what I wanted when it came to him did not involve scrubbing toilets or sweeping floors. "You should let me chip in on, like, apartment groceries. I don't want to be someone else you have to take care of."

"Maybe I don't mind taking care of you."

My pulse quickened, but his back was to me, and I couldn't see his face. His voice had a weird tone to it and I didn't know what to make of it.

It felt important, though. But I was too afraid to make a fool of myself by asking him what he meant.

He made the eggs scrambled and we chatted while we sat at the kitchen island and ate. I was in the middle of explaining why my only experiences with baking Christmas cookies didn't involve me doing any of the creating or baking when he interrupted me, his eyes bright and his voice giddy.

"You know what we should do today? We should go get a Christmas tree. There's a lot a few blocks over selling them for charity. What do you think?"

I thought it sounded fun and I told him so.

"Then let's go get ready!" He sounded so excited, like a little kid. It made me laugh.

We put our plates in the sink and retreated to our separate bedrooms. My phone buzzed as I pulled off my yoga pants.

I rolled my eyes when I saw who it was from. Did Brad somehow just know that I was having fun with a man who was not him?

> This can work. I am all in. Please call me. I'll wait for however long you tell me to.

I wanted to text him back and ask if never ever worked for him.

Wanting to get the Big Brad Wolf out of my head, I put on some music and stuck my earbuds in. I danced around the room for a couple of minutes to one of my favorite songs before I took off the rest of my clothes, put on a robe, and headed for the bathroom.

I was singing along when I opened the bathroom door and spotted Tyler . . . getting out of my shower.

For a moment all I could do was gawk, taking in his naked, glistening self.

Then I realized what I was doing. I yanked out my earbuds. "Sorry! I'm so sorry!" I quickly closed the door and started back for my bedroom when the bathroom door swung open.

"Madison! Wait!"

I turned around slowly and tried to keep my gaze at eye level.

"I'm the one who's sorry. I forgot to tell you the drain in my shower's not working so I have to use yours for a couple of days. The super is sending a plumber on Monday to fix it."

"Yuh-huh." My eyes did not stay put and while he had a towel around his waist, he was still dripping wet and my imagination was getting quite the vigorous workout. "Maybe"—my tongue felt dry and too big for my mouth—"you should go, uh, put some clothes on."

"Yes! Sorry!"

He brushed past me smelling like soap and Tyler and I actually stopped my arms from reaching out for him.

I went into the bathroom, where I let out a deep, shaky breath and locked the door. But whether that was to prevent him from walking in on me or to stop myself from going into his room "by accident," I wasn't sure.

The water heated up quickly and I realized that was at least one benefit to sharing the shower. I got in and let the hot water rush over me.

I probably should have felt embarrassed or sorry. But I didn't.

Well, that wasn't precisely true. I did feel sorry.

For me.

Because now I knew exactly what I was missing out on.

CHAPTER EIGHTEEN

I offered to take my car, as I figured I would care less about any potential damage from tying the tree to the top. He was so enthusiastic about our trip and next thing I knew we were at the tree lot thanks to his very precise directions, which mostly consisted of things like, "Turn right now! Right now! TURN!"

But unlike my last boyfriend, it didn't seem to faze Tyler that I was bad with directions. He just took it in stride.

I liked that about him.

I liked a lot of things about him.

Naked, wet things.

I shook my head, trying to get that image out. I was so glad reading minds wasn't a thing. Especially since Tyler seemed the same as usual while I felt totally awkward about what had happened earlier. He chatted about the research he'd done online about how to pick out the right tree and all the while, like a bad person, I was still mentally undressing him. I knew I shouldn't be objectifying him so much.

I mean, more so than usual.

He said, "Do you know that I've never had a live Christmas tree before?"

"You haven't?"

"My mom had a fake Christmas tree that she would sometimes trot out. Usually only when she had a new husband or boyfriend she was trying to impress."

I felt that kinship with him again, a line that connected us because, while our experiences hadn't been identical, we both knew what it was like to have terrible parents. "Our trees were always just delivered to the house, so this will be my first time picking one out."

"Trees? As in plural?"

"Christmas at my house was like living in a tinsel-covered forest. What kind should we get?"

"I haven't narrowed it down," he said. "Let's go look and decide."

We passed by a couple of booths that were selling basic Christmas tree decorations. Lights, multicolored glass balls, that sort of thing.

It caught Tyler's attention, too. "I don't have any decorations."

"Should we get some?"

"Oh." He looked disappointed. "I thought you could just make some."

When I shoved his shoulders he started to laugh. "Just kidding! Come on, let's buy some. On me."

"Yeah, it's going to be on you. Because now you owe me." And because they would be his decorations, not our decorations. Someday when I moved out, he'd put them on a tree with someone else.

The thought made me sad.

"Hey, are you okay?" he asked.

I smiled, hoping he wouldn't see past it. "Yes. It's just a little strange not to be shopping for pink ornaments."

He picked up some silver beads. "Why would you buy pink? That's not a Christmas color."

"It's my mother's signature color."

"I didn't realize that was a thing."

I picked up a cylinder container that had red, green, and silver balls in it. "I don't think it is for most people. Hey, grab some hooks. And a Christmas tree stand," I told him.

He did as I instructed. "Do you have a signature color?"

No, because I wasn't a crazy person. "I don't. I like wearing dark green and purple because my eyes are hazel and when I wear those shades, they look more green than brown."

"You could get colored contact lenses, but I don't think you should because you already have beautiful eyes. I like how they change." He walked away to pay for our purchases, pointing to the cylinder I still held in my hands when he spoke to the cashier.

My heart had stopped and I worried I might need CPR. What had just happened? Had he just called me *beautiful*? Again? Or at least just my eyes, which were a part of me, so that counted for the rest? I was feeling giddy and bewildered and, quite frankly, overwhelmed. He'd just dropped a second *beautiful* bomb on me and it happened to be the same day I'd experienced the gloriousness of his entirety.

It was too much.

"Come on," he said. "What are you waiting for? Let's go find our tree."

Oh, I was waiting for a lot of things. At the moment, clarity topped my list.

I tried to put everything out of my mind, every confusing thing he was saying, and focus on our hunt. We discussed the merits of each tree, deciding which kind of needles we preferred. I pulled in a deep breath. I absolutely loved the smell of pine trees.

We ended up deciding on a Douglas fir that had one bare patch down toward the bottom, but we both agreed that we could just turn that side to face the wall.

Which seemed silly since we were the ones who were going to see it every day and we already knew the patch existed. Tyler handed me our bags, grabbed our tree, and we brought it over to one of the employees.

The employee rang up the tree and then put it on a machine to shake off the extra needles. It felt a bit pointless because no matter how hard we tried there were going to be pine needles all over the floor at our apartment.

And this year I was the one who would have to clean them up.

We brought all our stuff back to the car, loading our bags in the trunk, and then I helped Tyler center the tree on the top of my car.

"Now what?" I asked him.

"Now I go find somebody who knows how to tie the right kind of knots so we can lash this thing down."

Why did this make me smile? "You don't know how to tie knots? Weren't you a Boy Scout?" I could so picture it.

"Nope."

Interesting. "And you're not going to go the guy route where you pretend like you know exactly what you're doing and hoping it doesn't fall off on our way home?"

"Again, nope."

"I like that you don't try to impress me."

"I aim not to please."

I very much doubt that. My eyes went wide. Was that my inside or outside voice? Inside or outside voice? I started to panic.

When he didn't react and just headed off to find someone to help with the tying and didn't run away screaming in abject terror, I breathed out a sigh of relief that it had been my inside voice that only I could hear.

My phone rang. Shay.

"Hey—"

She cut me off. "I feel like we haven't talked lately. We need to catch up. I want to spend some time with you and celebrate. My Mathletes placed first in regionals yesterday, which means we're going on to state!"

"That is so great!" I told her. "We should definitely celebrate!"

"So tonight, you, me, and Delia are going to Gilded." That was a new club that had recently opened downtown.

"I'm in!"

"I'll text you the time," she said. "Don't flake out!"

"I won't," I promised, just before hanging up. I turned back around and saw Tyler and one of the lot employees getting the tree snug and tight.

"Looks good and secure. Too bad you didn't have any part in it," I teased Tyler.

"Hey, I helped. Sort of. When he said, *Cut here*, I did. Which means I get to keep my man card."

It didn't take us very long to get back home, but when we parked we realized we had no way to get the tree off the car. Tyler took all the bags out of the back of my car and then ran inside to get a knife while I waited with the tree. I knew the likelihood of someone stealing a Christmas tree off the top of a car was pretty minimal, but this was *our* tree and I didn't want anything to happen to it.

He returned a couple of minutes later and quickly cut all the thin rope. "I'll grab the bottom of the trunk, you hold on to the top."

It was easier than I'd thought it would be maneuvering the tree through the lobby, into the elevator, and up to our apartment. Pigeon came over immediately to investigate, her tail wagging as she sniffed the tree.

"This is not a bathroom tree," Tyler told her.

"Where do you want it to go?" I asked. He pointed to a spot near the gas fireplace, and I agreed that it was perfect. I put the Christmas tree stand down and Tyler brought the tree over.

"Ready?" he asked. "You make sure it stays in place and I'll get it in."

Nodding, I knelt on the floor next to the stand. He lifted the tree up and the trunk wasn't fitting. I told him, "It's too big. Do tree stands have sizes?"

"I don't think so." With a grunt he picked up the tree and laid it down on the floor. "Oh. Those three bolts? Loosen those and then once the trunk is in, tighten them to lock the trunk in place."

Boy, did I feel stupid. Just another one of those basic life skills I'd missed out on growing up the way that I had.

The next try was successful and the tree slid into place and I tightened the bolts. "I think that's it," I said.

He carefully let go of the tree and I felt like celebrating when it stayed in place.

"We did it!" I exclaimed, standing up to see our tree. "We make a great team."

"Yeah, we should get T-shirts," he joked, then he held up a hand to high-five me.

I was being high-fived. I slapped his hand, hoping my disappointment didn't show. If that action wasn't putting me solidly in the friend zone, I didn't know what else would. Other than him making a sign that said, MADISON, I'M NOT ATTRACTED TO YOU. Maybe that would be clear enough for me.

"It looks taller than it did on the lot," he commented. "I hope we got enough ornaments."

"When did you want to decorate it?" It might be good practice for me before I had to do it at the winter festival.

"I was thinking maybe we could leave it bare until tomorrow to let Pigeon get used to it. And then we could have our own official decorating party where you don't make Christmas cookies."

"Ha-ha." I had the feeling I was going to be hearing about my salt cookies for a long time.

"It'll be great," he said, as if he had to sell me on the idea of spending time with him. He did not, but I appreciated the effort. "We'll put on some Christmas music and then maybe afterward we can watch a movie."

I didn't know what kind of movies he liked, but given that we always watched what I wanted, I figured it was his turn to choose. With one exception. "You pick. Only no horror movies. If I wanted to spend an hour and a half feeling anxious and slightly terrified, I'd just have dinner with my mother."

He laughed and said, "I was thinking a Christmas movie."

"That sounds . . . really nice. Perfect, actually." I'd been sad thinking about all the family traditions I was missing out on, and this somehow helped make up for that.

Like Tyler was moving past just being a friend and roommate and settling into a spot that felt more like family.

~

We spent the rest of the day doing our own things; Tyler went to work out and run some errands while I went over my lesson plans and made more winter festival decorations.

Shay texted me and said to be ready in an hour and a half. Then she added:

> P.S. – I'm getting us an Uber because I am going to drink my body weight in alcohol.

I replied with a laughing emoji and found myself excited to be going out with my girls. It had been a long time since the three of us had done something fun, like going dancing. It was also nice to be making actual plans with people. My social life with Brad often had consisted of me waiting around to see if he would call and want to get together.

I had a night out with my friends and a private decorating party with Tyler tomorrow. I was hoping that one of these events would help me understand the other. I wanted Shay and Delia's input, biased as it might be. But I needed an outside perspective to tell me if I was making stuff up where Tyler was concerned or if things had somehow shifted between us and I was too dense to realize it.

Because I'd recently come to the conclusion that Brad had messed me up not only with trust issues, but also made it impossible for me to read and/or understand men. The only boy I'd ever dated had lied to me constantly, so I didn't know what real communication looked like. Or signals. Or flirting. I was all screwed up and that's why Tyler's words and actions confused me so much. I didn't know whether I was supposed to be seeing only friendship, or if there might be something more.

I needed my friends to help me figure things out.

It was also fun to get dressed up again. Not because I was trying to please my family or impress Brad or make sure I would fit in wherever I was going. No, I put on a short sparkly black dress, glittery silver eye-shadow, and red lipstick just for me. So that I would feel pretty.

When I finished getting ready, Tyler was back and moving around in the front of the apartment. Shay texted that she was on her way and I decided to go down to the lobby and wait for her so that the Uber wouldn't have to park.

I was feeling pretty and sparkly and even though I hadn't dressed up in order to get validation, I was finding myself in want of some. Especially from Tyler.

"You'll have to tell me if this dress looks okay," I called out, baiting my hook as I fished for my compliment. Hopefully he'd let me land one.

"The perfect situation for any man to find himself in," he called back, his voice brimming with humor.

With one final nod I came out into the front room. Tyler was sitting on the couch with one of his spy novels. Pigeon was curled up next to him and he was stroking her fur and I again thought that she was the luckiest dog in the world.

He looked up and saw me and just . . . stared.

Like, awkwardly.

Or maybe I was the only one feeling awkward. But it seemed to last a long time and there was a strange tension in the air that I didn't know how to explain. Or I was imagining it.

He cleared his throat. "Going out?"

"Yes." My voice sounded shaky. "With some friends from school." That made me sound twelve. "They're teachers, too. From my school."

I was dangerously close to babbling. I grabbed my purse from the table in the foyer, trying to collect myself. What was happening? "You didn't tell me what you think of my outfit."

"You, uh, you look . . . yeah."

My heart sank. Was that bad?

And should I ask?

I decided against it. My fishing expedition had been fruitless. With a sigh I reached into my purse with the intent of transferring over my wallet to my handbag and felt a lump. I'd forgotten that I'd stopped by the pet store yesterday and picked up a Christmas present for Pigeon. It was a girl stuffed pigeon with pink wings and I thought she might like it. I took the wrapped box out of my purse and put it under the tree. "Before I forget again, I got a present for Pigeon. And now the tree doesn't look so bare."

Placing the present brought me closer to him and he was studying me again in a way I didn't understand.

"You bought a Christmas gift for my dog?" There was a strange catch in his voice.

"Of course. I love her. She's a good girl, aren't you, Pigeon?" She barked at me happily in reply, her tail wagging.

Still, Tyler didn't speak. Wanting to break whatever this bizarre tension was, I said, "I'm going to go. Don't watch *The Bachelor* without me."

Then he was back, his blue eyes bright, a smile hovering on his lips. "There is zero chance of that happening."

My joke made things feel somewhat normal and I decided to leave before I said or did something to mess it up again.

It actually felt a little weird to be going somewhere without Tyler. We'd been spending, well, almost all our free time together lately.

But it would be good. I thought a little distance couldn't hurt. And I hoped my friends would be able to help me untangle the mess that my life had become.

Because I no longer felt equipped to figure it out on my own.

CHAPTER NINETEEN

Both Delia and Shay had come to pick me up. They scooted over and all three of us were crushed in the back seat. Our driver was a middle-aged man with a deep Texan drawl who introduced himself as Jimbo.

I'd just said hello to him when Shay demanded, "We've waited long enough. Spill!"

So I did. I told them everything that had happened since we'd last chatted. I told them about the weird run-in with Brad, and how he told me I couldn't have a job once we got "married" and that he'd failed to grasp the concept that we were done. Then I quickly shifted gears to fill them in on every amazing and glittery thing that had been happening with Tyler. Shay was so excited she practically had hearts in her eyes.

Well, I told them *almost* everything. But I didn't tell them about his mom. That was between Tyler and me.

"What else?" Shay asked.

So I filled them in on the present from Singapore, the beautiful comment, and the thing with the shower, which made Shay laugh.

"Oh, yeah, right, he 'forgot' to tell you," she said, using air quotes around the word *forgot*. "He probably wanted that to happen. On a subconscious level."

"I don't think so. He seemed pretty mortified. Although I can tell you, he had nothing to be embarrassed about."

That made both of my friends dissolve into giggles. The car wasn't moving and I noticed that we were sitting in bumper-to-bumper traffic. Jimbo muttered something about construction, and it probably would have been quicker for us to walk to the club than it was to drive.

But it worked out in my favor because I still had stuff to tell them before a thumping club mix made it too loud for us to hear each other.

I told them about this morning, about the cookies and Tyler making me breakfast, buying the Christmas tree. I was warming up to what had happened right before I left when Delia announced, "You've basically kissed him."

"What?" I asked, not sure I had heard her right.

"He gave you his glass. Your mouth was where his mouth was. Same thing as kissing."

I laughed, wondering if she'd been pregaming and had already had something to drink before she left the house. It was extremely silly, especially given that I assumed kissing Tyler would be nothing like pressing my lips against a cold glass. Because I had imagined that very act many times and knew that there wouldn't be anything cold about Tyler.

Which gave me a little heated shiver.

Shay had to add in her two cents. "Buying a Christmas tree together feels like a very couple-y thing to do. And then making plans to decorate it? With hot chocolate and mini marshmallows and Christmas music and a movie? You've basically been married for six years because everything you're doing screams *couple*."

"The problem is, I can't tell the difference between what I want to have happen and what is actually happening. I want to respect his boundaries and stay just friends." Especially since Brad had been so unable to respect mine. I knew what that felt like, and it sucked. "But the truth is I do have a crush on him and am maybe even falling for him. But I can't tell if he feels the same and it doesn't help that my attraction barometer is all off because the only guy I've ever dated lied to me all the time."

They both nodded, looking at me seriously for the first time that night. I kept talking. "Like tonight. I came out to get my purse and he just . . . stared at me. But did he stare at me? Or am I making it up in my head? And if he was, why?"

"Did he say anything?" Delia asked.

"He started to say something about how I looked but he was kind of hemming and hawing and didn't finish his sentence so I don't know if that was a good thing or a bad thing."

Shay said, "Oh, please." She dragged the word *please* out to, like, six syllables. "Look at you in this black dress. You basically rendered the man speechless."

My chest felt light and sparkly. I wanted so badly to believe her. "Do you really think so?"

She rolled her eyes at me and said, "This guy could write *I think you're hot* in Sharpie on your forehead and you'd still be asking us if he liked you."

I was a little offended. That wasn't true. If he wrote it in Sharpie on my forehead, I thought I'd believe it then.

"Here you are, ladies," Jimbo said, pulling up in front of the club. "And even though it's none of my business, I'm glad you dumped that Brad guy and you should give this Tyler a chance."

"And that's why you're going to get a big tip," Shay said as we climbed out of the car.

As Jimbo drove off I said, "If Tyler is attracted to me, then why isn't he doing anything about it?"

"Other than spending his every waking moment with you?" Shay asked sarcastically.

Delia linked her arm through mine. "Doesn't he think you're still with Brad? Maybe he's trying to be a good guy and not hit on his room-mate who has a boyfriend."

I'd never considered that. Part of me immediately wanted to blame my aunt. She'd made him think that Brad was this serious thing in my life when he hadn't been a real part of it in a long time. Of course, I'd played a part in that, too, by staying quiet. "That makes sense. But Tyler keeps reiterating that we're friends. He high-fived me today. It's like our only house rule."

"I think your options here," Delia said, "are you either need to bring it up to see if he still feels the same way about the rule, which could be potentially embarrassing, or you're going to have to wait and see if he makes a move. After you break up with Brad, of course."

If I brought the rule up with Tyler, the problem wasn't just the potential embarrassment. It was also that I could lose my place to live if he rejected me.

Not only that, but what if we dated? Wouldn't it be weird with us already living together? What would happen if we broke up?

Maybe I was getting ahead of myself.

Shay shook her head. "I think you should just get him drunk. See what happens when his guard's not up."

"That's not really a plan," I told her.

"Speaking of getting people drunk"—Delia began tugging on my arm—"I feel like I've been neglecting my liver by letting it get too healthy. Let's go do some damage."

We followed her into the club. It was packed to the brim even though it was still a little early in the evening. The inside was decorated like a modern speakeasy. There were stuffed armchairs and benches that lined the walls, all covered in a dark-purple velvet. Glittering chandeliers hung overhead and a grand piano was set up next to the DJ. The walls were covered in a shimmery peacock feather wallpaper that somehow sparkled under the dim lighting.

The music wasn't nearly as loud as I'd anticipated it to be, which was nice.

We stopped off at the coat check and followed Delia to the bar. She flagged down a very cute bartender. "Bring us three Grey Gooses with soda. Wait. That can't be right. Three Grey Geese with soda? Which one is it?"

Shay shrugged. "We're teachers. We should probably be able to figure this out."

"Never mind, just bring us a flock of vodka and sodas!" Delia said. Vodka was Delia's favorite poison and she always insisted we drink with her.

The bartender returned quickly with our cocktails and we cheered each other, clinking our glasses.

"Maybe Shay is right," Delia told me. "If nothing's going to happen with Tyler, we should find you a new guy. What is your type?"

"So far it seems to be guys who suck up to my father." Which meant Tyler was out. I sipped my drink. It was strong. Meanwhile Delia practically chugged hers. I could never figure out how someone as tiny as she was could drink like a sailor on leave.

She set her empty glass down. "That guy's cute. The blond at the end of the bar. His dark-haired friend's not so bad, either."

I looked in the direction Delia pointed and she was right—the guys were cute. I just wasn't interested. "Eh."

As if this was a challenge, she said, "Okay, what about that guy sitting near the post? He reminds me of that actor who plays Iron Man, only younger."

"If you're feeling desperate," Shay added, "that guy over there kind of looks like Brad. You should hook up with him and then dump him. It'll help your ego."

It took me a moment to realize that the man didn't just look like Brad.

He was Brad.

And he was kissing another woman. Not just kissing her. It was like she had been deprived of all oxygen and he was single-handedly keeping her alive by providing her with a steady stream of it.

Shay seemed to have come to the same realization just after I did and I heard her swear as I stalked off toward him. I had to make sure.

I tapped him on the shoulder and it took him a bit to break off his kiss. It almost sounded like suction being broken.

When he turned around, his eyes went wide. "Madison! What are you—"

Before he could accuse me of stalking him or being in any way irrational, I said, "So your text this morning, about waiting for me, you forgot to mention that you only planned on being faithful for less than twelve hours. You said you were committed. Which I guess could still be true if your definition of *committed* means sticking your tongue down other people's throats."

His date tried to intervene but Brad told her to be quiet. Then he turned back to face me. "This isn't what it looks like."

I was incredulous. Was he seriously going to try and gaslight me here and now, when I had literally caught him cheating on me? Well, not technically cheating since we weren't together anymore. But he had been making promises to me. Promises that he'd had no intention of keeping.

How had I ever believed him? How had I ever given him the benefit of the doubt? Why had I taken him back so many times? But I knew why and it just made me sick that my own parents had been complicit in this mess. That I had been complicit.

That I had been so stupid somebody really should have taken my picture and hung it up in the hallowed Halls of Stupid as the stupidest person who had ever lived.

"I know I'm repeating myself here, but that's because you seem to not be getting it. We are totally done," I told him. "This is over. We are never getting back together. I don't want to see you. I don't want to talk to you. I can't believe I wasted so many years of my life on such a pathetic excuse of a man who is nothing but a liar and a cheat."

His eyes flashed angrily. "What did you expect, Madison? A man has needs. I'm sorry you saw me kissing Amber. I just wanted to remember what it felt like to kiss someone who knew what they were doing. I wouldn't need to cheat on you if you'd ever bothered to learn how to be better in bed . . ."

Oh, that was a low blow. It was like he'd just punched me in the gut. When we were fifteen, we'd been making out in the stands at a football game. The head cheerleader, a girl named Fallon, had irrationally hated me for years and it only got worse when Brad and I got together. I overheard her making fun of how I kissed him and how stupid I looked. She and all her friends were laughing at me. I was already so insecure at that age and when I went to Brad and told him, when I had expected him to comfort me and say that he loved kissing me, he had cocked his head at me and said, "Well, she's not wrong. You've got a lot to learn. You're not great at it."

Which made me feel like I was always running a race I couldn't win. With every physical thing that happened between us, I was always unsure and questioning myself. It wasn't until this moment, when he weaponized those fears against me, that I realized all of it had been a way for him to manipulate me. By making me feel like I was never good enough for him, he had ensured that I spent all my time trying to change his mind.

A favorite tactic of my parents, and one I should have recognized sooner.

Any remorse I might have felt, any fear I had of my family's expectations, it was all gone. He had just wiped it out with one fell swoop. I didn't even have the strength to care enough to hate him. He was toxic and terrible and I just wanted him out of my life permanently.

He'd spent years showing me what a snake he was and it was about time I started believing him.

"And to think some part of me actually felt bad about possibly hurting you." I just shook my head. "The only good thing now is that

I never have to see you again. Don't call me, don't text me, don't even think about me. We're finished."

I needed to get out of this club. Away from him. Because right now I was furious with both of us. Furious with him for being such an awful human being and furious with myself that I'd put up with it for so very long.

I felt rather than saw Delia and Shay just behind me, one at each shoulder like they were my royal bodyguards ready to protect me. I went to the coat check and I heard Delia saying that she'd ordered another Uber and it was on its way.

Brad ran over and said, "You're still wearing my bracelet. That has to mean something."

I'd forgotten that I'd put it on. The only thing it meant was that I didn't have any other bracelets to accessorize my outfit. I yanked the bracelet off my arm and threw it on the floor at his feet.

"All it means is that I'm an idiot and I deserve so much better than you."

Shay got our coats and Delia put her arm around me, taking me out the door. As I walked outside I heard him yell, "What are my parents going to say?"

That was so not my problem.

Fortunately, he stayed in the club and our Uber arrived a minute later. Shay and Delia took me to a quieter bar but I only sipped at the martini they put into my hands. What I wanted was to go home and crawl into bed. I felt embarrassed that tonight had happened and how my friends didn't seem to know how to act around me. I wanted to tell them I was fine. That I'd been over him for a long time and that I was ashamed I'd put up with him and his lying, cheating ways for so long.

Tonight I was mostly mad at myself and there was no way they'd be able to talk me down from it. "Guys, I really just want to go home. Thank you for all the support. All of it. You are the best friends anyone could ask for and I adore you. You mean the world to me but I sort of just want this day to be over."

Thankfully they understood and got an Uber to take me back home. They made me promise to call, said they would be there when I was ready to talk.

When I got inside my apartment, what I saw was such a sharp contrast to how I was feeling that it startled me.

Loud music was playing and Tyler was gleefully dancing around the room with Pigeon yipping at his heels and bouncing along with him. He was so adorable. I drank in the sight of him and his happiness. It was like a soothing balm for my soul.

He came to a stop when he saw me. His expression was excited, giddy. "Madison! You're home! I was hoping I'd get the chance to celebrate with you!"

I saw an open bottle of champagne on the coffee table. "It looks like you're a little drunk."

"Little bit," he agreed. "Care to join me?"

He grabbed my hand and spun me around, then unexpectedly circled me back into his arms so that I crashed against his chest. My body hummed with awareness, my skin heated in response to being pressed flush against him.

"Hi," he said, and that tension was back. This didn't feel like some friendly hug. It felt like more.

But I distrusted myself too much to see things clearly. I coughed and moved away from him, not entirely believing that my shaky limbs could accomplish the task. "What are you celebrating?" My voice sounded a little too bright and fake.

He grabbed his phone and turned off the music. "I got the promotion!"

"That's amazing! Congratulations!" I was genuinely delighted for him.

"Thank you. I've had to sacrifice a lot to get here and do things that I'm not . . ." He trailed off. The light in his eyes dimmed and his voice sounded distant, like his body was here but his mind was somewhere else. The entire mood had changed and I wanted to bring him back to being happy Tyler.

"How did you find out today?" His office wasn't open.

My question seemed to do the trick, and that gleam was back. "My boss is in London and he'd put in the request but upper management had to sign off on it and with the time difference . . . they sent the email late afternoon and didn't get it until the following morning and then he had meetings but he wanted me to know as soon as possible. He emailed me this morning but I hadn't checked my email until an hour ago. Hey, have a drink. Let me get you a glass."

He came back with an empty champagne flute and filled it two-thirds of the way. "To you," I said, clinking my glass against his. "In celebration, I won't cook for you."

"Aw, that's the sweetest thing you've ever done for me."

Shaking my head, I proceeded to down the entire contents in a single gulp.

Letting out a low whistle he said, "Wow. That was kind of impressive."

"Pour me another," I said, holding my glass out to him.

He did so but asked, "Is everything okay?"

Was I so transparent? Here I thought I'd been hiding it well. "I don't want to bring you down. You seem really happy. And you should be. I know you worked hard."

"You helped me with this. I think bringing in those new clients is what pushed me over the edge. I kind of owe you. And I hope you know that you can talk to me." He put his hand lightly on my wrist and led me over to the couch so that we were sitting down. I stared at his hand, wondering how such a simple touch could make me feel like the champagne bubbles were fizzing in my blood. He asked, "What's going on?"

"I broke up with my boyfriend tonight." I took another big gulp of champagne. I was starting to feel the effects. My head felt a little light, my body warmer than usual. "It's the man my parents picked out. The one I'm supposed to marry. And so I've put up with him and his crap for a long time. He would lie to me and cheat on me and my parents demanded I take him back. Then when they cast me off, he was nowhere to be found. I needed his support and he disappeared. Recently he came back, saying he was committed to me and wanted another chance. Tonight I saw him in a club making out with another woman."

"Huh." He paused a beat. "That guy sounds like a real winner."

I wanted to both laugh and cry. "Believe it or not, he's the best boyfriend I ever had."

"Jeez. Who did you date before? Satan?"

Now I did laugh. "Brad has been my only boyfriend."

Tyler took another sip of champagne. "Wait. But when you and Frederica came by—"

I cut him off. "I don't know how much she knew about what was going on with me and Brad. But she might have played it up a bit for your benefit because of your rule. Because you were so worried I'd be psycho and fall in love with you and then stalk you."

He smiled wryly. "That seems a little silly now, doesn't it?"

Other than the Everest-size crush I had on him? "Yep. Silly."

"Well, it sounds to me like you're better off without him. Good riddance."

"Definitely. Especially when his parting shot was about what a bad kisser I am. Among other things."

"Wasn't he the only guy you were kissing?" When I nodded, he added, "So wouldn't that kind of make it his fault if you were?"

"Good point. He was just trying to make me feel bad about myself. And it might have even worked a little. He knows I'm self-conscious about it." Liquid warmth was spreading through my limbs and I kicked off my shoes to make myself more comfortable, tucking my legs up underneath me.

He seemed to be considering what to say to that and what he came up with nearly knocked me off the sofa.

"I could kiss you."

CHAPTER TWENTY

"What?" I asked. Was I drunker than I thought? Recently I hadn't been drinking very much, mostly because I couldn't afford it. I'd also been so busy with my decorations and setting up my new life and getting accustomed to it that I hadn't really found the time for alcohol. I must have become more of a lightweight because I was obviously feeling the effects from my drinks at the clubs and the two glasses of champagne.

And If It wasn't affecting me, then the alcohol had clearly affected Tyler. In some ways it was kind of fun—he was like Tyler on steroids. More charming, more playful, more fun.

Somehow more attractive.

"I could kiss you," he repeated. "As an impartial third party, I could judge for myself whether or not you are a bad kisser. Then you would have empirical proof that he was wrong."

Why did this sound logical? I knew that it wasn't. "But we're friends. Just friends."

"And don't you think this is something a friend should do? If they could?"

Again, totally reasonable.

My conclusions meant that I was not myself because I knew somewhere deep inside me that this was not a good idea. And what if I was truly bad at it? Did I really want him, of all people, to know it? "Maybe we shouldn't. Since we're both a little drunk."

What are you doing? Shut up! He wants to kiss us! But he didn't really want to kiss me. He was just offering to judge me and I was pathetic enough to agree to it because I had wanted to kiss him and more than kiss him for what felt like a very long time.

"I'm not drunk," he said, his eyes glittering with a look I didn't recognize. "I consent to it if you consent to it."

That almost sounded like a dare and something inside me rose to respond. "Okay." After I'd said it, I felt unbelievably awkward. What was I supposed to do now? For a judgment kiss? Was I supposed to kiss him first to prove my talents or was he supposed to kiss me?

Suddenly some part of my brain buzzed, like an annoying fly, that this was a Bad Idea. "You know, we don't have to . . ."

My voice trailed off as he moved closer to me. Oh. I guessed he was going to kiss me. He moved in close, reaching up with his right hand to hold the side of my face. I drew in a trembling breath, unprepared for the onslaught of feeling that came just from him barely touching me. Every nerve ending crackled and sparked with excitement.

"You bought my dog a present," he whispered.

I looked into his beautiful eyes, noticing that there was a ring of gold around the pupil, something I'd never noticed before. Mostly because our faces had never been this close before. Well, not when there was light and I could see him.

"Yes," I whispered back. "We already established this earlier." It felt like a weird thing to bring up, given the moment.

Then he smiled and moved toward me, like he was underwater or going in slow motion. It took me a second to realize that he was doing it so that I could say no.

He confirmed this when his lips hovered above mine. "Are you sure?"

Every cell in my body hummed with anticipation and desire. "Yes."

Then his lips were against mine, softly, sweetly, a featherlight touch. The kind of kiss you imagine when you're a tween dreaming about your first kiss. He'd obviously intended for it to be sweet and gentle. Which meant that it should have made me feel dreamy and nostalgic and swoony.

It did none of those things. From the moment his lips touched mine, it was like someone had plugged my mouth into an electrical socket. A surge zipped through me, giving me goose bumps and heating my blood.

It lasted for only a few seconds but it almost zapped my ability to hold myself upright.

He pulled back slightly, still within kissing range. I felt his warm breath against my face and it took all my restraint not to press my mouth against his and keep this going. Which he may not have wanted. I swallowed, trying to figure out what to do next. I settled on finding out what he'd thought of our experiment.

"How," I started to speak, surprised at the breathy quality to my voice. "How was that?"

His lips pulled up into a smile. "I think I need more data before I can draw any conclusions."

Again, perfectly sound logic. I nodded, feeling as if I couldn't quite catch my breath. I noticed that he was looking at my lips. As if he'd only had a fleeting impression and now needed to do a more thorough investigation. The look in his intense blue eyes made the air around me feel charged with energy, like lightning could strike us both then and there.

That feeling didn't lessen when he pressed his lips against mine again, this time kissing me. Not just a peck, but moving his mouth against mine with a gentle firmness that left me weak and shivering. He made the nerve endings in my lips explode from sheer pleasure.

Now both of his hands were on the side of my face, guiding my head this way and that as he kissed me over and over again.

Some detached part of my brain was warning me to pay attention to the technical aspect of the kiss, so that he wouldn't think I was terrible at it, but I was so caught up in what was happening that I couldn't focus on anything except the feel of his strong mouth on mine.

He tasted like champagne, and it was delicious. He was delicious.

Time passed—seconds, hours, I didn't know—and somehow, something changed. A sense of urgency crept in and I didn't know whether he was the cause of it, or if I was.

I suspected myself. Because while kissing him was almost transcendent, better than anything I could have imagined, I wanted more. More kissing. More of him.

At this point I didn't even care if I was truly bad at it. It didn't matter because obviously Tyler had been created solely to kiss women into oblivion. Yet another thing he was fantastic at.

The pressure of his mouth increased, his movements faster, and I immediately responded. A buzzing sensation whipped through me, and I wanted to get closer. My hands moved of their own volition, wanting to touch him. Hold him close. Feel the strands of his soft hair against my fingertips.

His arms went around my waist, tugging me up. I got to my knees so that I could be closer to him. He shifted his body up into a kneeling position, too. The sensation of him wrapping his arms around me, holding me tight, made me sigh with pleasure, every part of my body tingling in response.

The sound I made did something to him, as if the electricity passed through me and traveled into him, and he groaned against my mouth, deepening the kiss. A lightning storm burst to life under my skin, making my lungs constrict and my heart feel as if it were about to explode.

We kissed and kissed, building and building the storm until it threatened to rage out of control. I couldn't have guessed how long we stayed locked in our embrace, only that I wanted to spend the rest of time kissing, and being kissed by, this man.

I'd never known anything to be quite as glorious or as intoxicating.

Then he suddenly stopped, resting his forehead against mine. His hands moved to my shoulders, and I didn't know if he meant to push me away or pull me back in. I was confused, but felt a primal surge of satisfaction that he was breathing as hard as I was.

I heard his husky intake of air, and it made my shivering intensify.

"You," he said, his voice raspy and harsh, as if he could barely control it, "are *not* a bad kisser."

The tingly sound of his voice made me want so badly to lean forward and capture his clever lips again. I was about to do just that when, without another word or touch, he got up and left the room. I heard his bedroom door close.

What?

My nerves still buzzed, and I had the residual feel of his mouth on mine, as if it had been permanently imprinted there. I collapsed back against the couch, not trusting my legs to work.

Pigeon cocked her head at me, seeming confused. She wasn't the only one.

"Is there anything written in Sharpie on my forehead?" I asked her. Because I worried that would be the only way I would understand for sure what had just happened.

～

I slept in a little later than normal because all night I couldn't stop thinking about that kiss. I understood that it had been some kind of weird tipsy/friend/pity kiss, but if somebody compiled a list of Top Ten Kisses of All Time, that one would have to be put on there. Which then made me wonder what it would be like if he really kissed me. If he did it because he wanted to and not because he was drunkenly trying to make me feel better about myself.

When I finally dragged myself out of bed the next morning, I smelled bacon. One of my favorites. It was also one of Pigeon's favorites, so this didn't necessarily mean anything.

I wasn't sure how this morning would go when I saw him again. Would he just pretend it had never happened? Could it possibly move toward being something more? Although I'd already decided before the kiss that maybe trying to have a relationship with him was a mistake. I didn't want to jeopardize our living situation or our friendship.

But truth be told . . . if I saw him and he said that the kiss had been incredible and that he wanted to try an actual relationship? I just couldn't picture myself saying no.

I came out into the kitchen and he turned when he saw me. "Madison, good morning." He finished up the last couple of pieces of bacon, putting them onto a paper towel–covered plate, and turned off the stove. "I made you breakfast."

"Thank you." He made me breakfast pretty frequently. There was no need to announce it, which made me think there was more he wanted to say.

He ran his fingers through his hair and said, "Last night, that was a mistake. I was buzzed and I shouldn't have . . . it was wrong for me to . . . can we just forget it ever happened?"

Ha. As if that were possible. That kiss was seared into my memory banks for all time. But that didn't mean I wanted things to be more awkward between us. And it sounded like I had my answer as to how he wanted things to move forward. As if none of this had happened. "Of course."

I just didn't think that I'd be able to forget.

Giving him the response he wanted made him grin. "I'm glad. We got a little carried away."

Yep. I was there. But I didn't want to make a fool of myself again and admit that I'd hoped he might have a different reaction to what we'd done. I could play along with this game, tell him what he wanted to hear. "I was upset and you were just being a friend. Which I need, because I think I'm done with men for a little while."

Especially since I was so emotionally involved with Tyler, even though he had no idea. I didn't really have it in me to try and find someone new.

"Oh," he said, nodding. "Do you want some bacon?"

"The answer to that question is always yes." I hoped I wasn't radiating my disappointment. Disappointment that I had no right to feel since he kept being clear with me. I was the one who wanted more so I was the one who was going to have to keep my feelings to myself.

Our intercom buzzed just as he finished serving me three pieces of bacon. I had taken a bite; he somehow always cooked them perfectly. I hated chewy bacon where the fat felt greasy in my mouth, and I didn't like it too crisp. I loved them just the way Tyler made it.

"Hello?" he asked.

"Good morning. I have a Julio here for Madison."

I stopped midchew. Julio? That meant only one thing.

He had been sent to retrieve me and this time my mother hadn't even given me the courtesy of a heads-up. Which shouldn't have surprised me. It was like the universe was trying to balance itself back out. I'd been part of something amazing last night so, obviously, I had to suffer for it today.

"Tell him I'll be right down."

Tyler relayed my message and then asked, "Who is Julio?"

"One of my family's drivers. Which means one or both of my parents wants to talk to me and I need to go get changed and head out to their house."

"You don't have to go."

Was he going to tell me I had a choice? He wasn't really in a position to be giving me parental advice. He lived his life just to take care of his mom. He didn't tell her no because he knew the fallout wouldn't be worth it. Just like me and my mother. "I think you, of all people, know that I do."

I looked at the bacon he'd made me and suddenly I didn't feel very hungry. My mother had a natural talent for appetite suppression. I pushed my plate away. Pigeon could finish it for me.

Normally I would get dressed up to go back to the house, but if they were willing to be rude, then so was I. I put on a pair of comfortable leggings and a dark-green tunic. I put my hair up into a ponytail and brushed my teeth. Then I went to get my coat and purse and I called out, "See you later!"

He stuck his head out of his bedroom door. He looked concerned, but all he said was, "Good luck!"

I was going to need more than luck. I was going to need all the strength and willpower I could muster to stand up to them, because I knew what was coming next. I didn't have to wonder why they'd sent for me. I knew.

I greeted Julio as he opened the back door of the black SUV for me. We'd been on the road for only a few minutes when my phone buzzed.

Brad had texted me.

> Can we please talk about this like adults?

I wondered why his grasp of the English language was so very poor. Since he couldn't follow basic directions, I blocked his phone number. I blocked his email. Then I went into every bit of social media I had and blocked him there. I felt satisfied that I had done my best to cut him out of my life completely.

I knew that the only reason he'd bothered to reach out was that he was probably getting yelled at, too.

About a half hour later Coughlin let me into the mansion and told me that I could wait in the library. As I got closer to the door I heard someone crying and talking. Did my parents have a list of people they planned on torturing today?

"No. I know. I love you, too. But you don't understand. I have to marry him . . . You know I don't want to. I only want to be with you. No, Santiago, please, they will disown me and—"

Violet was walking back and forth, talking into her phone, her free arm wrapped around her waist as if she were trying to hold herself together. Never once in my entire life had I seen my sister cry. My father loved to tell the story of the time Violet was thrown from her horse and fractured her arm in two places. She didn't cry once, not on the way to the hospital, not when they put a cast on her, not when they had to rebreak the bone because it was healing improperly.

I said her name and she stopped short. "I have to go," she murmured.

"What was that about?" Who was Violet in love with? "Are you okay?"

"Mom and Daddy are making me marry Howard Hurley." At my blank expression she added, "The man I had with me at dinner the last time you were here?"

Oh yeah, the guy I'd wanted to tell to run. But Howard was not the name she'd just said on her phone call. "Then who is Santiago?"

She looked sad and conflicted, and I thought she wasn't going to tell me, as we'd never been especially close. But then the words came rushing out of her, as if she couldn't help herself. "Santiago is my personal trainer. And I'm in love with him. But Howard works at Weston Wilshire. He's set to become president of our overseas division and our parents think he's the perfect match for me. I have to marry him."

This was insanity. My sister should be able to marry whomever she wanted. "No, you don't. I broke up with Brad. In fact, I'm pretty sure that's why I'm here. So that I can get yelled at. But they're not going to change my mind. Mom and Daddy don't get to dictate who you marry. You're the CEO of one of the biggest companies in the entire country.

Nobody should be telling you what to do. Tell them you're in love with someone else and you're not marrying Howard."

There was a brief spark of hope in her eyes, but I saw the way she immediately squashed it. "They'll cut me off. They'll fire me. I'll lose everything I've worked for."

I shook my head. "Not everything. You'll have Santiago. You have your degrees and your experience. I bet there are forty companies out there who would hire you as CEO in a heartbeat. You can get another job." I took a step toward her, not sure what she would do. "And you'll have me. I know what it feels like not to have any support. But that's not your situation. I'm on your side and I'll stand by you. No matter what decision you make. But it is your decision, hard as it may be. Someone told me recently that we always have a choice. Make the one that will make you happy. Not our parents."

She nodded, clearly miserable, and I wondered what she would do if I tried to hug her. This was probably the most personal conversation she and I had ever had. Part of that was due to the ten-year age difference, but it was also due to our parents pitting us against one another, trying to make us compete for their affections.

Another game I was no longer going to play.

"I have to go," she said, and I stepped aside, wishing I could offer her comfort but knowing she wouldn't accept it. I let out a deep sigh as she left the room. My poor sister. Her personal trainer? My mother was going to break her favorite pearl necklace from all the clutching she was about to do. That image made me smile a little.

Sitting down in one of the overstuffed armchairs, I considered my sister's fate. I knew how hard it would be for her, probably even harder than it had been for me as she'd been under their thumb for longer and was more reliant on them than I was. Her entire career, which had always been the main focus of her life, was due to their benevolence.

But that also meant they could withdraw it any time they chose. It was like having a sword hanging over your head that hung by the weakest thread. It could drop at any moment and you had all the constant stress and anxiety of not knowing when or how that would happen.

Except for today. I knew that sword was headed straight for my head.

I was a little proud of Violet that she'd found the time to fall in love. That she'd taken a risk and chosen something for herself.

Just as I'd started to wonder how long my mother was going to make me wait, another one of her favorite tactics, I smelled her Chanel perfume. She came into the library a moment later.

"Madison."

"Mother."

She sat down across from me, perched on the edge of her chair, her legs crossed at her ankles. Her pink business suit was perfectly pressed, her french knot elegantly done. She looked over my slouching, comfortable form and her dismissive gaze let me know I'd been found wanting.

I didn't feel less than. She was mistaking my appearance to mean I wasn't prepared and that I would crumble under the weight of her disapproval.

She was wrong.

My mother could bring on her own personal Spanish Inquisition. I was ready.

CHAPTER TWENTY-ONE

"You are going to call Bradford and you are going to patch things up with him."

I wanted to sigh. How predictable. Same song, different verse. Actually, I couldn't even say that. Same song, same verse. She made her demand imperiously, like she was the queen of her kingdom and expected all the peasants to do her bidding.

What she'd forgotten was that made me a battle-ready princess. "I will not be doing that."

The look on her face was so priceless it made me wish that I could have taken a picture of it. "I beg your pardon?"

I knew that I had shocked her, because that wasn't how I normally behaved with her. When she and my father were busy casting me out and disowning me, I stayed silent. I didn't cave, I went ahead with the choices I'd made, but I didn't talk back. I hadn't verbally stood up for myself, just nodded and went along with their punishments.

Something else that was about to stop.

"I know you're not hard of hearing, Mom. I'm not going to call him. This may be a surprise to you, but this isn't the twelfth century. Your daughters are not your chattel and you don't get to arrange our marriages."

Somehow her back straightened even further. "I demand to know why you won't call him."

"Um, because he sucks and is a crappy human being?"

"I fail to see your point."

This was it. Time to throw away my get-out-of-jail-free card. She was never going to forgive me for this, and I was okay with it. It wasn't like I had anything left to lose. "I'm done with Brad. I'm not marrying him."

"You say that now—"

"No. Not now, not ever. He and I are through and should have been done a long time ago. If I hadn't been so caught up in trying to always please you and Daddy—"

Now it was her turn to cut me off. "When have you ever tried to please me? You've always done exactly whatever you wanted with no thought to how it affected me. Have you stopped, even once, to think about what you breaking up with Bradford would do to me?"

She was never going to get it, because she couldn't think of care about anyone besides herself. "This isn't about you, Mom. If you want to be connected to the Branson family so badly, you marry him. I'm not going to do it."

That made her gasp. "After all I've done for you, all I've given you, I'm overwhelmed by the sheer ingratitude! Give me one reason why you won't marry him."

"Just one? Wow. That'll be hard. I have so many." I leaned back in my chair, considering. "There's the fact that I don't love him, that he makes me really unhappy. But I think if I can only pick one, I'm going to go with he can't stop sleeping with other women."

"Do you think you're the only one who has to deal with that?" she snapped. "Sacrifices have to be made to have the life you want."

"I don't believe that."

"You should. I raised you to be smarter than this."

She was right. I was smarter than this. Smarter than all this. "I'm not going to put on a brave face in public while my husband humiliates me time and time again."

She snarled, her entire face twisting. "And you think you're too good for that? That you're better than me?"

Something had changed inside my mom. She was usually so much more controlled, so smooth in her condescension and disdain. I found myself feeling unexpectedly sorry for her. I didn't pretend to understand my parents' relationship, and after that outburst I certainly didn't want to know more. Part of me wanted to tell her that it wasn't my fault her life was terrible. To tell her all the ways she'd failed me as a mother and how I was trying to live a decent life in spite of the way I'd been raised.

I wanted to tell her that none of this was normal. That this was not how parents treated their children. I'd seen my kids at school with their parents. Watched my friends with their families. Blind obedience didn't equate to love.

But I knew it wouldn't do me any good. She wouldn't hear anything I had to say unless it was what she wanted to hear.

"It's not about being better than you. It's about making the choices that are right for my life. And one of those will include marrying a man I love, that I respect and I trust. If you want to be a part of my life, if you can support my decisions, then we can talk. Otherwise, I think we're done here." This conversation was definitely over.

I stood up.

"Where do you think you're going?" she demanded. "I haven't dismissed you."

"Despite what you seem to think, I'm not your servant."

She stood up, too, anger racking her entire frame. "Do you think you can just walk out on me? On me?"

I nodded and the level of quiet, self-assured calm I was feeling seemed to only infuriate her more. "The next time you call or send someone to fetch me, I'm not going to come."

"Oh, yes you will!"

"What are you going to do?" I asked her, genuinely curious. "Disown me again? That's the problem when you go nuclear. You can only play that card once. You have nothing else to hold over my head."

I went out into the hallway and she followed me to the door, huffing and puffing with frustration. "You are going to regret this! I promise you, you will regret it!"

That did make me stop and look over my shoulder at her. "No, Mom. I don't think I will."

As I walked toward the kitchen for what I assumed was the very last time, I thought that I probably should have felt sad.

Instead I felt like a great weight had been lifted from my shoulders.

~

When I got home, Tyler was in the living room with Pigeon. "How did it go?" he asked, the concern in his voice making my heart feel wonky.

"Fine. I mean, I guess not really," I said as I hung up my coat. "I told my mother I was done with Brad and wasn't going to marry him and she went volcanic."

"That bad?"

"There will be enough magma to bury a city." I went into the kitchen and got myself a glass of water. "I can't be who they want and so they don't want anything to do with me." The words stung a little, but not as much as I'd once thought they would.

"Is there a chance you just accept them for who they are and move on from there?" I couldn't tell if Tyler was just trying to be helpful, or if subconsciously he was trying to defend his own choices when it came to his mother.

"I do accept them. I know them and understand them. Probably better than they realize. But this is not up to me. I don't think they'll change, no matter how much I want them to. They've made it clear that

I'm not in charge of this relationship. They are. They make the decisions. And the only way I'll be their daughter is if I do what they want when they want it. I'm not going to live my life that way anymore."

"I respect that," he said. "I know how hard that must be to realize."

"In some ways it is, but in other ways it's not. It makes me feel . . . free. Like the whole world has opened up to me in a way that it never was before."

I put my glass in the sink and walked into the living room. I considered sitting down next to him, but I still felt a little edgy around him. "What have you been up to?"

"I was actually just going over my finances because I was hoping that I might be able to go down to Guatemala this year. I've done it in the past for this charity I work with. They build houses down there."

Nodding, I said, "I know. I mean, I saw it on your Insta." Then I realized how that would sound. Like I was cyberstalking him. I rushed to try and explain. "Frederica showed me your picture on Instagram when she was telling me about your apartment and then . . ." Then my best friends had gone through all his posts and shown them to me and that was creepy and I needed to shut up. "That sounds like it would be a nice trip. Maybe you could take Pigeon."

My eyes went wide. Oh crap, I had just done it again. Referenced his Photoshopped pictures of him and Pigeon on Instagram, which I had also ogled.

He didn't seem to notice. "I'd love to take her all over the world." His eyes flicked up to mine and the intensity that I saw there made me feel like my heart was trying to beat its way out of my chest. "Traveling is always better when it's with someone you care about. Maybe someday."

I wrapped my arms around my chest. He wasn't talking about me and I needed to stop hoping that he was. "When are you going?" I asked, fighting to get the words out.

His face fell at my question, the blue flame in his eyes dying out. "I can't. My mom sent me an email today saying she wants to replace her car and have this elective procedure done and . . ."

His voice trailed off but I knew what he was saying. He was going to have to put aside his wants again so that his spoiled mother could have everything she wanted. How he couldn't even have the job he really wanted because he had to earn enough money for her wish list. Having the career I wanted had been so important to me that it really upset me to think that Tyler was being trapped in the same way.

I knew I should stay quiet. This was none of my business. Even if I was telling him everything about my crazy life, it didn't mean that he wanted to do the same. Or that he was interested in my advice. His situation wasn't exactly like mine, and I should probably remember that.

But I couldn't help myself. I saw a long, lonely road in front of him, one that I'd been headed down but had veered off. "We're friends, right?"

"Yeah. Of course." He said it like I'd surprised him. As if it were a ridiculous thing to ask.

"I don't want to be rude to you, and you've been a good friend to me, but I think because I'm on this truth-telling bender at the moment I want you to know that it would be okay for you to tell your mom you're not going to bankroll her life any longer. It's not a bad thing for an able-bodied adult woman to support herself." I thought maybe I should stop there, but I'd already let the horses out of the barn, so I kept going. "You don't have to cut her off completely. You could put her on a budget. You're good at making those. And if she doesn't like it . . . .well, I guess she could find a job. Or get married again. You should have the job you want and not care about whether it's enough to support her. Or anyone else."

That made him smile a little, and he asked, "Anyone else? What about if someday I end up with someone who expects me to be wealthy? Who came from money herself?"

Someone like me? It felt like he meant me. Which was obviously crazy. I wanted to ask, but didn't. "Any woman who loves you, any woman who is worthy of your love, will not care what you do for a living. Only that you're happy and doing what you want to be doing. And it would be one thing if you had this job because you were ambitious or because you wanted to make a lot of money. At least then it would have been your choice. But if you want to be a software engineer, you should be a software engineer. Go back to school. Do what you love. But don't let somebody else take that decision away from you."

"I'm a little too old to go back to school," he said.

"There are plenty of people your age still in college."

"Yeah. They're called graduate students or doctors."

Now that he was joking with me, I knew we were okay and that I hadn't stepped too far over the line. "Your mother won't like it. Mine certainly didn't. But we're supposed to grow up and be independent, right? I mean, if there's one thing I learned from this Brad mess, and the blowout with my mother, it's that drawing boundaries is okay."

He nodded and held his laptop up. "I should probably get back to this."

Yes. He should. Maybe spending time looking at his bank account, at how hard he was working and how much of it was going to his mom, would allow him to take some steps forward and live the life he wanted. Not the one that had been forced upon him.

I went into my room and shut the door and lay down on my bed. I felt emotionally drained. I reached over and grabbed my Hello Kitty doll, holding it tight against my chest. I probably shouldn't have said anything to Tyler. He seemed happy with his life and his mother's selfish demands. But if I could help him, if I could maybe get him to see that things didn't have to be this way, then it would have been worth it.

We both deserved better.

~

That night we decorated the tree as we'd planned. It ended up being a little more difficult than we'd initially thought since neither of us knew how to string lights properly. Then Pigeon kept trying to knock the balls off and tugged at the garland. She was more fascinated by the ornaments than she had been by the tree itself.

As the days passed by, Tyler and I fell into an easy routine. Eating dinner became almost like a dance as we anticipated what the other one needed before either of us had to ask, moving like a well-oiled machine to set the table and eat. He still watched reality television with me and we either made the festival decorations or he worked on his laptop. Sometimes on his actual job, other times on his mobile game. I took that as an encouraging sign.

He even asked me to beta test it on my phone, which made me feel special because I was the only one who got to play it. The game was simple. Just popping bubbles that slowly moved around the screen.

"It has options," he told me, bringing up a Christmas theme. Now instead of bubbles it had floating Christmas trees.

I popped them with great delight. "You did a really good job on your game."

"It's basic. But I've learned so much doing it. Look at the menu, click on the other themes, and tell me what you think."

I did as he instructed and nearly gasped when I found a Hello Kitty level.

"You're kidding me with this," I said. The smile on his face let me know that he'd done it for me. I felt tears welling up, and I forced them back down. I so wanted this to mean something even though I knew it didn't. "Don't you need a license for this sort of thing?" I asked, popping a Hello Kitty head.

"You do. I'll take that theme out before I publish it."

It really had been just for me. I couldn't bring myself to look him in the eyes for fear that he'd see how it made me feel.

I found myself doing that on a pretty frequent basis, hiding my feelings, because we were always together. Especially since Tyler never seemed to stay late at the office. I figured that although he'd cut out most of his traveling, his new position would still mean a lot more work and responsibility. During my childhood my father typically hadn't come home until after nine o'clock every evening. A tiny part of me hoped that I was the reason Tyler was home so often. That he enjoyed spending time with me just as much as I enjoyed spending time with him.

Although at the back of my mind there was this nagging sensation that things weren't quite the way they had been before the kiss. And initially I couldn't tell if it was him or if it was me, but eventually I came to understand that the thing that had changed was me.

I didn't want to be just his friend. I definitely didn't want to be just his roommaid. I wanted more than a crush. More than this unrequited limbo I was currently living in. I wanted to be with him, to be his partner and his girlfriend, for him to love me the way that I loved him.

Knowing that I loved him wasn't like being in a dark room and then having a bright light suddenly turn on; I didn't look at him one day and realize that I'd fallen for him completely. It was gradual, more like a sunrise, where it got brighter and brighter until it became something that I just knew—I'd fallen in love with him. Slowly, day by day, he had become the most important person in my life.

It also made me realize that I'd never been in love before. What I felt for Tyler compared to what I'd thought I'd felt for Brad? It was like comparing a grain of sand to a giant mountain. So much of my relationship with Brad had been motivated by my fear of losing him, of trying to change myself to be what he wanted, feeling like I never measured up.

But with Tyler? I could be me, even the lounging-in-sweatpants version of me, and he liked who I was. I didn't have to change for him. And he made me feel amazing about myself. His compliments, his laughter, his banter, how he listened to me, the way he took care of me by feeding me and giving me a place to live; it all added up to a security and comfort and adoration like I'd never known.

I loved that we laughed together, that we shared so many personal and intimate parts of our lives. That I could tell him his mom was overstepping and he didn't get angry at me or shut me out. How my heart would flutter every time he smiled at me. The way my stomach got that light, flappy sensation whenever he walked into a room. I'd thought eventually I'd get accustomed to him, but so far it hadn't happened.

There was a nagging thought at the back of my mind at how quickly this could all end. That while I had scoffed at my mother, telling her she had no power over me, if there was anybody who could figure out a way to hurt me, she was the one.

Of course this could have been some bad residual energy from having grown up in my household and always expecting the worst.

Maybe it was time to try expecting the best. Or, at least, hoping for it.

And that was my new plan, right up until the moment I nearly wrecked everything.

CHAPTER TWENTY-TWO

The poms were finished. I stored them in my room and it looked like a cotton candy machine had exploded in there. Making the fishing wire with cotton balls was difficult until I figured out that if I hot glued the cotton balls, they stayed put. Delia had lent me her hot glue gun, because, of course, she had one.

"Who says you can't teach a still somewhat youngish dog new tricks?" I asked Pigeon. Feeling full of myself, I wasn't paying attention when I went to cut the fishing wire with the razor I'd been using and sliced across the fleshy part of my palm.

Blood spilled out—all over my hand and all over the couch. I wrapped the bottom of my T-shirt around the wound and ran into the kitchen. Thanks to the one time I had tried helping Tyler by cutting vegetables for dinner, I knew he kept a first aid kit in the cabinet above the stove.

I reached up for it and then put my hand in the sink so that blood wouldn't keep spilling everywhere. At least I knew something about caring for cuts, as second graders seemed especially adept at getting them.

Washing the wound out, I opened the kit with my free hand and grabbed a bottle of rubbing alcohol. I poured it over my palm, gritting my jaw as it stung. Once I'd cleared out the blood, it seemed the cut wasn't as deep as I'd thought it was. I used my teeth to help open the packaging for a large gauze bandage and put it on my palm.

I'd be fine.

But the couch . . . I ran back into the living room. Splotches of blood were standing out brightly against the light-gray fabric. How did I clean up blood?

I knew you could soak it in cold water to get rid of a bloodstain. But I couldn't soak the couch in cold water. What was I going to do? What could I do? My heart jackhammered in my chest and I felt like I couldn't think straight, until my brain finally came up with an idea. What about bleach? I'd used that before for blood.

Running to the laundry closet, I grabbed the bleach off the top shelf. I went back into the kitchen and snagged a white rag, rinsing it in cold water.

I went back to the couch and started scrubbing at the blood with the rag. Only that made it worse; there were now streaks of blood instead of just splotches. "No, no, no," I muttered. I then opened the bleach, setting it down on the cushion, and poured a little bit of it onto the rag. This time I tried dabbing at the stain.

It seemed to be working until I realized the reason why. It was turning the fabric white. I had ruined the cushion.

What was I going to do? Maybe I could just flip the cushion over and no one would ever be the wiser. Although I knew I would feel guilty every time we sat here to watch TV. Maybe there was, like, a cushion-covering store and I could bring it in and have them put on new fabric. That couldn't be that expensive, right?

I reached for the bleach, intending to put it away. Not knowing what I was going to tell Tyler. Because some part of me knew I had to tell him. I couldn't keep being dishonest with him about little things like this. I wanted him to know everything about me.

But just as I got my hand on the bottle, Pigeon chose that moment to nudge my arm and everything seemed to happen in slow motion. The bleach bottle tipped forward; I gasped and tried to grab it, but it slipped through my fingers. The bleach splashed all over the back cushion, as well as the one I'd been trying to clean.

I righted the bottle and then I put my body between the spill and Pigeon. I didn't know what bleach might do to dogs but I figured it couldn't be good. I took both the cushion and the bleach to the patio and left them outside.

Pigeon seemed fine when I went to check her, but I was not a vet and didn't know if she was okay. I brought her into my room in case there were fumes or something.

We sat on the bed and I thought about what had just happened. Although I couldn't guess at how much that couch had cost, especially one chosen by an interior decorator, I knew it had to be on the expensive side. I didn't have the money to buy a new one. I couldn't call Violet again; she had enough of her own problems to deal with.

How could I replace it? I didn't have anything saved up. I'd been paring down my expenses one by one, trying my best to stick to the budget Tyler had helped me create, but there was no way I had what I would need to pay for that couch. Maybe I could pay him off in installments?

Or maybe I could sell something of mine. But even if I combined everything I owned, it still wouldn't be enough.

Except . . .

Even though it made me heartsick, I knew there was only one way. I went into my closet. First I changed my shirt, putting the bloody/bleached one into my trash. Then I grabbed my Birkin bag. I closed the closet door and sank onto the floor, holding it. I would have to sell the bag. I'd been so desperate to move beyond my past, to give up everything that had to do with my parents. Maybe this was some kind of cosmic reminder that I had to let it all go.

I wrapped my arms around my bag and I started to cry. Pigeon came over and licked my face, trying to cheer me up, but I couldn't stop sobbing. If I'd believed in karma, I might have taken this as a punishment for not telling Tyler the truth about all the things in his house that I'd wrecked already.

He was going to kick me out. I was going to lose my apartment, Pigeon, and, most importantly, I was going to lose him.

Curling up into a ball, I kept crying. This was so stupid. It was so stupid to be this upset. Pigeon lay next to me, warming my body with hers. Which, for some reason, made me cry even harder. My chest started to ache, my lungs to burn, and my eyes became swollen and sore.

That was how Tyler found me.

"Hey, Madison? Why does it smell like bleach in here? And what happened to the couch?" His voice came closer and I felt him get down on the floor next to me. "Are you all right? What happened?"

"I'm a terrible person!" I lamented. I kept my eyes squeezed shut, too humiliated to even look at him.

His strong hand rubbed my back, trying to comfort me. "Why do you think you're a terrible person?"

"Because I ruined your couch!"

"It's okay."

"It's not okay!" I wailed. "You don't understand. I don't know how to clean."

"What?" He sounded so confused.

"You said you needed someone to move in and clean up. And I had never cleaned anything in my entire life. I messed up so many times! I made the dishwasher shoot out bubbles because I put dishwashing liquid soap in it and then I put your cast-iron pan in there and had to buy you a new one—"

"You did?"

"Yes! And I almost wrecked the vacuum I don't know how many times and I cleaned the windows with Dawn and the bathroom mirror with all-purpose cleaner and I sucked a sock into the dryer and had to have a repairman fix it and then . . . then I forgot to close your closet door and Pigeon chewed up one of your shoes! I had to replace them and they were over a thousand dollars. The ones you thought were too tight."

"I bought those shoes used at a consignment store right out of college and they've held up really well. But I don't think they were worth a thousand dollars."

I howled, "Now you tell me!"

"How did you pay for all that?"

"It's why I'm broke. And my sister had to lend me the money for your shoes."

He went silent and I knew he had to be regretting asking me to move in here. I was a liar and a destroyer of his nice things and he should have a roommate who wasn't either of those.

I announced, "And now . . . I'm going to sell my Birkin bag so that I can replace your couch."

"The bag your grandma gave you for graduation?"

"Yes. And then I'll move out and you can bring in someone who won't mess up your stuff and hide it from you and who will clean everything perfectly."

"I didn't ask you to move in here because I wanted some expert cleaner. I invited you to stay because I liked you and you seemed like you needed the help."

Why did he have to be so wonderful? "That is so much worse!" I sniffed. "Do you hate me?"

His hand moved to my shoulder. "Madison."

I didn't move.

"Look at me," he said gently. I shook my head. I wanted to screw my eyelids shut even tighter. I couldn't bear how often I had deceived him. "Madison."

Sighing, I relented. I opened my eyes and there was so much goodness in his gaze I wanted to start crying again.

"I could never hate you."

"But I lied to you. About Brad, about cleaning, about your things I ruined."

He shrugged one shoulder. "I understand why you did it. I know you felt desperate that day and desperation can drive people to do crazy things. Come here."

Then he pulled my arm up until he was hugging me. This felt so good, so right. I knew he was only being friendly, but this was where I wanted to be. In his arms. He felt like home. Not the horrible one I'd grown up in, but the one I'd always imagined for myself, where I would be safe, loved, and happy.

Resting my head against his shoulder, I let him soothe me. He stroked my hair and it was wonderful.

"I've felt so awful. I wanted to tell you everything but I was afraid."

"I'm glad you told me now." There was a beat and then he asked, "So what did happen with the couch?"

I explained how I'd cut my hand and that I thought I was supposed to use bleach to clean up blood, which I was kicking myself for. I should have looked it up online instead of blindly panicking. How Pigeon had bumped into my arm and the bottle had spilled and that I'd tried my best to keep her away from the bleach. "I didn't know if it could hurt her. And I don't know how much the couch costs, but I'll pay you back."

"Don't worry about it. It sounds like it was partly Pidge's fault anyway and she's my responsibility."

"No, I should contribute."

"You do contribute," he said, his voice sounding low and serious. "In more ways than you know."

This was no time for me to try and search for hidden subtext. "I mean, I need to pay you back for replacing it."

"You're not going to sell your purse," he told me. "So forget about that." He even took the bag out of my hands, as if I were going to run to my computer and post it on some auction website. "If it's that important to you, we can work out a payment plan. Later. When your budget involves less dragon's blood purchases."

That made me laugh through my tears. "How do you do that?" I asked. "Make me feel like everything's going to be okay?"

His mouth was against the top of my head and I both felt and heard his words. "Because everything is going to be okay."

"You're not going to kick me out?"

"No! Why would you even think that?" His arms tightened around me. "This is your home, too. And I'm so glad you moved in. It's hard to remember a time when you weren't part of my life, and even though we came together under some unusual circumstances, I'm really grateful for you."

That made my heavy-laden and exhausted heart practically sing with glee. "Me too. I mean, not that I'm grateful for me, but I'm so glad that we're . . . roommates."

"Friends," he corrected me.

I wanted him to be right. I wanted everything to be okay.

I should have known better.

~

A new couch arrived quickly and they took away the old, bleach- and blood-stained one. The new couch was exactly the same as the old one. I figured Tyler must have called his decorator, but when I asked him how much it had cost, he just waved his hand and wouldn't tell me.

He did help me finish the snowfall decorations and he jokingly refused to let me handle the razor and cut all the fishing wire himself.

Then the day of the winter festival arrived and my next pressing issue became how to transport all these stupid fluffy poms. He suggested sticking them in giant trash bags.

The method concerned me. "But that might kill the fluff."

"Then we'll have to re-fluff them."

Once we got them into the trash bags it was obvious that there was no way they would all fit in my car. Even if we did squish them.

He said, "We'll stuff your car full and then we'll put the rest into mine. I'm going to grab some things to help set them up and I'll meet you there."

We got my car loaded up and I waved goodbye to him. Delia and Shay, despite their other responsibilities, had agreed to show up early to help me decorate. For the past week I'd had recess duty while they'd been scheduled to cover lunchtime. We hadn't had a chance to really sit down and talk since the Brad blowout. They had no idea Tyler and I had kissed.

I pulled into the school parking lot, wondering how exactly I should break the news. Wondering if they might be mad that I hadn't told them yet. Although I should have learned my lesson by now about being distracted, I somehow managed to get out of my car and lock it shut, leaving my keys in the ignition.

With all the poms inside.

"No!" Why did this stuff always seem to happen to me?

Leaning my forehead against the cold car frame, I called Shay. "I'm in the parking lot and I locked my keys in the car."

"I'll be there in a minute."

True to her word, she arrived quickly. I'd hoped she'd know some magical trick, but she only looked worried. "Do you have an extra set of keys?"

I did, but they were back at the apartment somewhere. In my dresser? My nightstand? I couldn't remember where I'd put them.

Delia came up behind us. "What's going on?"

"Madison's keys locked her out of the car."

This caused Delia to reach inside her big bag and pull out a long rectangular piece of metal. "I've got this."

She had the door unlocked in less than half a minute.

Shay and I just gaped at her.

"What?" she asked.

"How do you know how to do that?"

At the same time Shay said, "It's always the quiet ones."

I made sure to get my keys and they helped me grab all the trash bags. We brought everything inside the gym. The other decorations were on par with any formal event my mother had ever thrown. Christmas trees lined the walls, white lights twinkling softly. Dark-blue tablecloths with pine cone and pine branch centerpieces were set up throughout the room with silver plates and pale-blue linen napkins. A string quartet was warming up in the far corner.

I suddenly felt very bad about the things that I had created. Somehow I'd imagined this would be geared more toward children. With, like, homemade snowflakes or candy canes made out of pool noodles. I felt underdressed in my red sweater and jeans. Shay and Delia both had on casual dresses, but they were still more dressed up than me.

A little heads-up would have been nice.

I started unpacking the poms, trying to fluff them back up. They most definitely had been squished and it killed me to think about all the time I'd spent making them look nice only to have them end up being lopsided and flat.

My despair must have been showing on my face, because Delia said, "Don't worry. We'll fix this."

The three of us sat on the floor doing just that, getting little shreds of tissue paper all over the place. I felt bad for making a mess, especially considering how nice everything else looked. "Someone's going to need to sweep this up."

"Isn't that what you're into now?" Delia asked.

"I thought this cleaning thing would get easier. Or that I'd like it more," I confessed. "But neither one of those things has happened. I feel like fairy tale princesses have been lying to me for years now. Especially Snow White. She tried to make it seem like going from being a princess to a glorified maid was fun. It's not."

"You're forgetting that those princesses had all those woodland creatures to help them out. Cleaning definitely might be more fun if tiny animals did most of it," Delia reminded me.

"You know the moral of the Snow White story," Shay said.

I raised my eyebrows at her. "Don't eat poison apples?"

"No. Do housework and maybe wind up with a prince. Speaking of handsome people you live with . . . how have things been going with you lately? I feel like we haven't talked in forever."

While she had specifically referenced Tyler, I kind of wanted to work my way up to it. "My mom summoned me. And I told her not to do it anymore and I wasn't ever getting back together with Brad. She threatened me." And I'd been expecting her wrath to fall down on me in some way ever since. I wasn't sure whether the silence meant that she'd backed off, or if she just hadn't come up with a good enough way to punish me yet.

"Good for you! Look at you with your adamantium-covered ovaries, standing up to your mother. I am impressed. And glad that she didn't turn you into stone," Shay said.

"Thanks. Also, I kissed Tyler."

Shay shrieked while Delia just frowned at me and asked, "Why do you do that? Hold on to these things and not tell us? You should call us right after it's happened! If not during."

There was no way I would have called them during. Nothing could have gotten me to stop kissing him. Other than, you know, him stopping kissing me. "It was the night we ran into Brad at that club."

Shay grinned. "And you told him about your terrible ex-boyfriend and then Tyler kissed you because he felt obligated to show you what it's like when a real man does it."

"No. He was a little drunk and trying to make me feel better about myself."

"He can make me feel better about myself anytime he wants," Shay responded, then threw up her hands. "See? This is why you need to carpe date this guy already. He should not be running around single. It's dangerous for womankind."

I shook my head. "I can't date him as he hasn't asked me out."

"No, he's only kissed you."

"While he was drunk."

"Which could happen again," she retorted.

"The kissing or the drunkenness?"

She waggled her eyebrows at me. "Both."

I laughed and then Delia said, "I think Madison should ask Santa to put Tyler under the tree as her present this year."

Shay disagreed. "Mrs. Claus is the one she needs to hit up for that wish. She gets it."

"You guys, he doesn't want to date me. He asked me to forget about the kiss and move on from it. It was a mistake and we got carried away."

"Hm," Shay grunted. "Some men don't know what's good for them."

"So now I'm the kale of the dating world?" I asked. I was on the verge of telling them all about how I'd wrecked his couch and then told him all the bad things I'd done to his possessions and that I didn't know anything about cleaning, when I noticed rustling whispers and murmurs. I turned to see what the commotion was about.

It was about Tyler.

Who walked into the gym wearing a tool belt, holding a ladder with one hand and a drill in the other.

Shay gasped. "I don't know what he's here to fix, but mine just broke."

CHAPTER TWENTY-THREE

"Again, I find myself siding with Shay here," Delia said. "Maybe just make out with him a little more. Let him take the edge off."

I glared at her.

"What?" she said defensively. "He looks like he's a great kisser."

"I bet he's taken off more edges than a carpenter." Shay nodded fervently.

They were going to humiliate me in front of him. Absolutely mortify me. I could feel it.

It was then that I noticed Mrs. Adams trailing after him, like a duckling falling in line after its mother. I was sure nobody in the room blamed her for following him.

Before he could speak, she said, "Hello, again. I'm so glad you made it."

I wanted to say, *I made it, too,* but I needed to behave.

Then she launched into a boring explanation of the false ceiling hanging above us (filled with balloons that would drop at the end of the party) and said that we could attach the poms to it.

"We'll take care of it," he said.

"I have every confidence that you will!" she said, flirtatiously waving her fingers at us before she left.

He turned to face me and I was about to introduce my friends, when he said, "Hi, Shay. Nice to see you again." I shouldn't have been impressed that he'd remembered her name, but I was. It had taken Brad three months to remember Shay's name without me prompting him.

She greeted him in return and then introduced him to Delia, who looked a little starstruck.

Then Shay announced, "Okay! So we're going to go hang up these cotton-ball strings. Over there. And leave you guys. Here."

While she didn't say, *Alone,* she might as well have. I didn't know what they thought might happen. We already spent tons of time alone together. It wasn't like this one incident at a dance was going to suddenly make him figure out that he couldn't live without me.

I looked over his shoulder as they walked away and they were both making faces at me. Shay mouthed, *Go for it!* And while I couldn't figure out what Delia was saying, it was a long sentence that probably involved respecting our feelings and each other, and she looked very enthusiastic about it.

Tyler started to turn around, presumably to see the craziness I was staring at, and it made my two friends scatter in opposite directions.

I gestured at him. "So, what's with the accessories?"

He looked down at his tool belt. "I did some construction work in college to help pay for school and I still had this stuff in storage down in the basement. I thought it might help. Don't you think it makes me look like I know what I'm doing?"

"It does kind of make you look like you should be hosting your own HGTV show." What he really looked like was the hottest man alive, but I couldn't tell him that. "Shall we?"

Tyler had just set up the ladder when Miss Martha found us. Again her gaze was anxiety provoking. "Ms. Gladwell needs you to come to her office." She didn't wait to see if I would follow and just immediately left.

"Okay." I handed the poms in my hands to Tyler and said, "I'll be right back. Ms. Gladwell is my boss."

"I'll be here," he told me.

Shay was talking with one of her math students. "It's due tomorrow. You can't do this whole assignment the night before."

"Challenge accepted, Ms. Simmons."

"That wasn't a challenge!" she called after him just as Delia asked, "Out of idle curiosity, how much nonedible glitter can a student eat before I am technically a terrible teacher?"

Shay saw me and said, "Where do you think you're off to?"

"Gladwell wants to talk to me. Again." I didn't know whether or not to be concerned. I figured there was nothing she could do that was worse than assigning me decoration creation and setup.

Well, except for firing me.

So of course that became my number-one thought as I made my way to her office. This time I checked the seating area for any rogue parents, but it appeared we were alone.

"Please close the door and have a seat." This time she wasn't distracted. She was looking straight at me and I felt a little like how a mouse must feel just before a snake pounced and swallowed it whole.

I did as she asked and sank slowly into the chair. Her expression was so serious, so intense, that I knew this had to be bad news.

She pushed a stapled pile of papers toward me. "I would like to offer you a two-year contract, which is standard for what we extend to our first-year teachers."

"You want to offer me a contract? Now?" This was always done at the end of the school year. Always.

"You can read over it and return it later or sign it now if you wish. But you have my word that it is the same contract given to everyone who makes it past their probationary period."

"But . . . why?" I picked up the papers and started skimming through them. There was going to be a slight salary increase and a guaranteed job for at least the next two years. I wasn't seeing any hidden traps or things that wouldn't be to my benefit.

She leaned back in her chair, her arms folded. "Because if you sign it now you would have incredible leverage in case someone tried to dismiss you."

But wasn't she the only person who could dismiss me? And why would she fire me if she was offering me a contract first?

I tried to ask as much when she announced, "You are an excellent teacher and Millstone Academy will be lucky to have you stay on. I also will not let someone else try to dictate what hiring decisions I can and cannot make. You came highly recommended and I see that trust was not misplaced."

My mother. My mother was trying to get me fired. This was how she was going to make me regret walking out on her. By taking away a job that I loved and was good at. Just to punish me.

I leaned over and grabbed one of Ms. Gladwell's pens, and I signed the contract. Even if it might have some clause about forfeiting my eternal soul, I didn't care. It was gratifying to know the headmistress was on my side and that I had just made myself safe from my mother's attack.

Because who else could do this? Who else would do it? The two things I had going for me at the moment were that my parents were not donors to this school and Ms. Gladwell did not take kindly to being told what to do.

Once I'd finished signing it and handed it back, Ms. Gladwell also signed it and then stood, offering me her hand. "Congratulations on becoming an official full-time teacher here at Millstone Academy, Ms. Huntington."

I wanted to squeeze her hand tightly in thanks but instead shook it a normal amount.

When I got back to the gym, I saw Shay and Delia. But I realized that the first person I wanted to tell was Tyler. I hurried over to him and his smile when he saw me was like the sun breaking over the horizon.

"What happened with the headmistress?" he asked.

"She ended my probationary period and offered me a two-year contract!"

"Madison! That's fantastic!" He wrapped his arms around my waist, letting out a whooping noise as he pulled me up and then swung me around in a big hug.

I was laughing as he set me down. The string quartet began playing a slower version of "I'll Be Home For Christmas," and Tyler asked, his arms still around me, "This is our week, isn't it? We both got promotions at work!"

We both accidentally made out with each other; we were both now standing in the middle of a school gym with him holding me tight . . . yes, this was going very well so far. I settled on saying, "It is!"

He nodded toward the quartet. "It seems to me that you still owe me a dance. Are newly hired teachers allowed to dance?"

"That depends. Are roommates allowed to ask?"

"I say yes."

Then we were swaying gently to the music, even though I could feel almost every gaze in the room on us because the event hadn't even started yet and we were the only ones dancing. I didn't care who looked. It was probably a good thing that he'd collected on his dance here, in public, rather than in the privacy of our apartment, where I might be more apt to do something inappropriate. Like confess my undying love or try to make out with him.

Instead I listened to the music, trying to quell my raging heartbeat, my tingling skin. I thought about the lyrics and how I wouldn't be home for Christmas.

But maybe that was okay. Maybe I'd found a new home.

~

A few nights later, we went out to a Turkish restaurant for dinner. School had ended for the semester and winter break had begun. We were only a few days away from Christmas. We'd been chatting about our holiday plans when we discovered that neither one of us had any. He let slip that his mom hadn't even invited him home for Christmas. I told him mine hadn't, either.

The check came and he wouldn't let me pay for my half. Then again I didn't really put up much of a fight. After he handed the waitress his credit card, he said, "So our plans—I propose that we resolve to hang out during the break and eat too much junk food and watch too much reality television and then we'll get back to working on being cultured when our vacation is done. What do you say?"

"I'm definitely in."

Then he fist-bumped me. It was kind of humiliating to be fist-bumped by the guy you were in love with.

When we got home that night, Pigeon wasn't waiting for us in the foyer, which seemed odd.

"Do you hear that?" I asked. It sounded like whimpering.

Tyler nodded and we followed the sound. Pigeon was curled up in Tyler's bathroom. He called her name, but she didn't move. She didn't even lift her head.

Exchanging glances, we both rushed to her side and crouched down next to her.

"What's the matter, girl?" he asked, reaching for her. When he put his hand on her back, she yelped, loudly.

There was fear and despair in his eyes. I'd never seen Pigeon act this way, and apparently, neither had he.

"We have to take her to an animal hospital," he said. "Can you drive?"

I nodded while he carefully, so carefully, put his arms under Pigeon and lifted her up. She yelped again, but this was the only way to help her. I tried talking to her soothingly, but the whimpering only got louder. Hurrying out to the car, I opened the passenger door so he could get in and hold Pigeon on the way to the hospital.

He navigated me there, and I dropped him off in the front so I could find a place to park. After finding an empty spot, I ran toward the hospital, praying with each breath that she would be fine. I didn't know how Tyler would take it if something happened to Pigeon.

I didn't know how *I* would take it.

As I pulled open the doors, I saw Tyler and Pigeon in one of the examination rooms. She was lying on the counter, still crying and shaking. He was trying to calm her without petting her since touching her seemed to make it worse.

A nurse came into the room and asked what was going on. We tumbled over each other, trying to explain her symptoms and reactions.

The nurse nodded, listening. She tenderly touched Pigeon's back, and there was more yelping. "Let me go get the doctor."

She returned a couple of minutes later with the veterinarian in tow. He examined Pigeon, and came to a stop when she cried out again.

"Obviously she's in a lot of pain," the vet said, "and we're going to give her some pain medications so that we can run some more tests. This could be just about anything—a slipped disc, a pinched nerve, muscle pain. It'll take us a little while to check her out, do some blood work, maybe an X-ray. Given how late it is, why don't you leave her here and we will call you just as soon as we know what's going on?"

Neither one of us wanted to leave, but we weren't given the option to stay. I drove Tyler home with him speaking only to tell me which turn to take until I got to familiar territory.

We walked out of the garage, into the lobby, and into the elevator without talking. Part of me thought we should just go to bed, try to get some sleep. My hope was that she was fine, that this was something simple and she'd be okay. My fear was that something was really wrong with her and I didn't want to face what it would be like to lose her.

Tyler went into the living room and collapsed on the couch and I followed him. "Do you want to watch some TV while we wait? It will take our minds off things." It was the only way I could think to comfort him. Distract him.

He looked at me bleary eyed and for a moment I thought he would say no. Instead he just nodded and I picked up the remote.

Just as I got the TV turned on, his phone rang. He grabbed for it and I muted the television. Could it be the hospital calling us already?

"Uh-huh. I see. Send me the information." He hung up.

"Who was that?"

"Work. Some deal is potentially falling through out in California and they want me to get on a flight in a few hours to fix the situation. If something's wrong with Pigeon—"

"She'll be fine," I interrupted him. We had to stay positive.

"If something's really wrong, I won't go." He rubbed his face with his hands. "But I have to go. My whole job could be on the line."

"Like I said, she's going to be fine and we'll bring her home and I'll baby her until she feels better and then you'll be back home before we know it, right?"

He nodded.

"It does kind of suck, though, that they're making you come out the day before Christmas Eve."

"I'll be back in time for eggnog and presents," he promised.

That made me smile as I thought of the presents I'd gotten him. The first was a check for rent. I didn't know what he paid but I'd finally managed to smooth out my budget (in large part because I was finally able to stop replacing things) and I had enough to give him something. I felt very proud of it, that I could contribute and that he wouldn't have to take care of me. I figured we'd work out the actual amount after he opened it.

The second was a photo book I'd made from a website. I took that photo of him and Pigeon and got them some new background images: Buckingham Palace, the Leaning Tower of Pisa, the Grand Canyon. Things like that.

The last photo had a bunch of Pokémon images surrounding them. I didn't know which ones were his favorite, but I thought Tyler would get a kick out of it.

I had noticed a couple of presents with my name on them under the tree and it had taken all my willpower not to shake them or mess with them in any way. Okay, maybe I had a little. And one was heavy and the other was light and felt like clothes. But I could have been wrong!

"Turn the show on," he said, his head lolling against the back of the sofa. I nodded and we watched TV until an alarm sounded and he announced, "I have to go and get packed. A car's going to be here to pick me up soon."

I wanted to help him somehow. Maybe offer to assist him with his packing? But I knew there was nothing I could do. We probably wouldn't even hear anything until the hospital reopened officially at eight o'clock in the morning. And by then he'd be on his way to Los Angeles already.

As I washed countertops and swept floors just to keep my mind busy, he returned, wearing a suit and pulling his suitcase. He slipped his laptop into a bag and strapped it across his chest.

"Will you call me the second you know something about Pigeon?" I asked.

He nodded, weary. "I don't want to leave until—" His phone beeped. "My ride's here," he said.

"It will be okay," I told him.

Then his phone rang. The driver must have been impatient. Tyler answered and said, "Hello?"

His eyes went wide. "Yes? I appreciate you calling. So it was a slipped disc?" Then he put the phone on speaker so we could both hear.

The nurse's voice came through clearly and reassuringly. "We gave her pain medication and the doctor did a little manipulation of her spine, but she's going to be fine. We'll give you a prescription when you come to pick her up, but she should be back to her old self soon."

"Thank you!" I said, nearly ready to burst into tears I was so relieved.

"You can come pick her up in the morning," the nurse said.

Tyler echoed my thank-you, said goodbye, and then dropped the phone on the counter.

"Isn't that so great?" I asked. "I knew she was going to be okay!"

He didn't answer.

Instead, the next thing I knew, he had pulled me into his arms.

And then he was kissing me.

CHAPTER TWENTY-FOUR

At first there was just shock. Total shock that he was kissing me. It was like some kind of kiss explosion. One second he was saying goodbye on the phone and the next his mouth was on mine. I could feel his relief, but there was more. There was passion. There was joy. All those things being conveyed, and more.

He held me so tight that I should have felt suffocated; instead all I felt was delight at getting to touch him and hold him again. I loved the feel of his strength against me. His edges pressed against my softness, his corded muscles tightening around me to keep me close.

His mouth was a blur of action, moving so quickly I could barely keep up or breathe. But I didn't care. This was where I wanted to be. Kissing Tyler. Being held by him. Like no world existed outside of the circle of his embrace.

The electricity was still there, sparking and crackling as it filled up every part of me. But it was something more. Like the electrical storm had morphed into a firestorm. There was a blinding need and searing heat. My entire body felt like it was about to be engulfed in flames and I wanted to burn.

And I did. I burned and I burned until it was like my body had turned to ash, unbearably light, ready to float away if he didn't keep me grounded. Against him, against his lips.

This kiss wasn't pretending. It wasn't theoretical. He was kissing me because he wanted to. Because he was reaching out to someone who would understand, who had been feeling all the same pain and worry, and it was a way for him to connect.

For us to connect.

As his hands roamed, as he left trails of fire everywhere that he touched me, his kisses turned deeper. Wilder, fiercer, somehow even hotter.

I was in this little world that he had created, floating along in the darkness and the heat, my whole body throbbing with mindless want. He was scorching me from the inside out.

Then it wasn't just my lips that he planned on claiming. One of his hands moved up into my hair and the sensation of his fingers against my scalp sent shudders through me. He pulled back gently, exposing the line of my throat. Then his mouth moved against that delicate skin, skimming it and pressing intermittent kisses to it, so that I had to grab on to his shoulders just to stay upright.

Then he went for the bottom of my earlobe, onto the spot just behind my ear that drove me wild. Like he'd instinctively known exactly where to touch me to make me fall apart in his arms.

The kisses stopped. He was still holding me, but not kissing me. It was more than my brain could work out, muddled as it was. I blinked several times, trying to figure out what was going on. Then he looked at me. He looked at me with so much intensity, with so much want and need, that it took my breath away all over again.

He looked at me like he loved me.

"Madison?" His tone was low, growly, and sent little shivers through me. "Do you think we should stop?"

That took my brain a beat to process. What? Had his tongue slipped? Did he mean to say, *Come here and do that again*?

I shook my head. I didn't want to stop. "No."

Worried that he didn't believe me, I grabbed his face and dragged his mouth back to mine. I wanted to show him what I wanted. I also wanted him to feel the way I did, the way he made me feel. I wanted him to lose control, to be trapped under a spell of blazing torment.

And I was succeeding. He was frantic now, taking off his jacket, the strap of his laptop bag. I did my best to help him but my eyes were so unfocused that it was hard to see. This was taking too long and I needed his mouth on mine.

Unwilling to wait for him to start kissing me again, I reached out for his shirt, grabbing fistfuls of it as I pulled him to me.

His phone was ringing. We were both so caught up in what we were doing, what our kisses were creating, that I don't think we noticed at first. But it rang and it rang, persistent.

"Tyler." I muttered his name against his lips and he let out a soft groan of despair.

"I know, I hear it, too."

Then he released me, and it was like stepping into an ice bath. Everything seemed cold and cut off and shivery without him right next to me. I crossed my arms over my chest, trying to ward off the icy feeling. It took a second for my head to clear, my eyes to focus. I tried to calm my shallow breathing.

But the desperate need I had for him? To keep kissing him? That wasn't going anywhere.

"It's the driver," he said, looking upset as he ran his fingers through his hair. "I have to go."

I knew he did. So I just nodded, keeping myself away from him so that I wouldn't be tempted to try and change his mind. I had wanted to know what it would be like if he ever really kissed me and it was like . . . some out-of-body experience. Something beyond what I could fully comprehend. Like a roller coaster, jumping from a plane, climbing up a sheer rock face, finding designer shoes for eighty percent off, and Christmas morning, all rolled into one.

He put his coat back on and picked up his laptop bag. "Madison, about what just happened—"

"Don't," I said, stopping him. My heart sank in my chest. I wasn't going to let him ruin this by asking me to forget about it, because there's no way I could do that. "Don't ask me to pretend this didn't happen, because I won't."

"No." He looked surprised. "That's not what I was going to say."

Oh. "What were you going to say?"

"I . . ." His voice trailed off and he glanced down, almost like he was gathering up some inner strength before his gaze met mine again. The fire I saw there nearly knocked me off my feet. "I want to be with you. I want us. Together. Dating."

Now I had to be hallucinating. No way this was actually happening. "What?"

"You and me." He took a step closer, reaching out with his hand to hold the side of my face. "I want this." His thumb ran over my lips as he said the words and my lower abdomen tightened hard in response. My knees buckled. "And I want more."

His voice was growly and seductive. All I could do was stare at him as my pulse throbbed throughout my entire body.

"Do you want that, too?" For the first time he sounded a little unsure and I was struck by an urge to laugh hysterically.

Did I want that, too? More than I wanted my next breath. This was my chance to tell him . . . what? I couldn't admit that I was in love with him. He was saying he wanted us to get together, not that he had fallen for me. I couldn't jump us fifty steps ahead. We would just have to go slow.

He waited expectantly, and I had to say something. "I . . . I want . . ." Why couldn't I talk? It was like his kisses had muddled my brain's ability to function.

His phone buzzed again, reminding us both that he had a car waiting for him. His jaw tightened. "I have to go. My timing sucks. But please, think about it. Don't decide anything until I get back tomorrow and we can talk." Then his tone became serious, almost dark. "When I get back there are . . . some things we need to talk about."

Without another word or touch he was gone, leaving me to wonder what that meant.

Because . . . things? What kind of things? What had he been keeping from me? People couldn't just say stuff like that and leave you hanging because then you'd do nothing but stress and freak out when maybe all he wanted to tell me was that chicken parmesan was his favorite dinner.

And he wanted me to think about it?

Trust me, this was all I was going to be thinking about.

$\sim$

I'd brought Pigeon home and she seemed more like her old self, only a little more prone to napping, given her pain medications. I texted Tyler to let him know that everything was going well with her. He responded with a smiling emoji.

Then he said:

Can't wait to see you again.

It was like those smiling emojis had gone straight to my heart, filling me with absolute joy.

But before I could respond, he added:

Can't wait to kiss you again.

That sent thrills of excitement through me to the point that I had to sit on the couch because I felt a little faint.

I didn't know what to say back. I felt the same, obviously, but I hadn't told him that yet. It didn't seem right to do it in a text. He deserved to hear me say it, to tell him how very much I wanted us together.

I did still wonder about what he'd meant by *things we need to talk about*, because it was killing me not to know. I didn't ask him, though.

Instead, I did as so many women had before me—I called my girlfriends and discussed it with them.

After their excited shrieks over him saying that he wanted to be with me (including a very emphatic "I told you so!" from Shay), I asked them what they thought he'd meant by things he had to tell me. Of course neither one of them knew, either, but they had a lot of fun conjecturing.

"Maybe his new promotion means he'll have to move so you'll have to move?" Delia offered.

Shay said, "I'm sticking with he's totally in love with her and wants to tell her in person about his undying devotion."

While I appreciated her positive outlook, my internal pessimist had taken over and I had thoroughly convinced myself that he was going to say it all was a mistake and I'd have to move out and lose both him and Pigeon and my heart was going to shatter into a million pieces and I would never ever recover. "Whatever it is," I sighed, "I hate that I'm failing in love."

There was a pause. Delia asked, "Don't you mean falling in love?"

"No, the way I'm doing it, it's failing. Nothing seems to be going right. My mind is just all over the place and I can't quiet it down."

"You sound overcaffeinated to me," Shay said. "How many cups have you had today?"

"I don't know. Two? Eleven? I didn't sleep last night because of all this. My brain wouldn't turn off and now I'm exhausted and coffee is the only thing keeping me awake and somewhat coherent."

Our intercom buzzed and I told the girls to hang on. "Yes?"

"Miss Huntington, there's someone here to see you? She says her name is Oksana?"

I rolled my eyes so hard I almost saw my brain. Like Brad, apparently she didn't understand what *over* meant. "Tyler's not here. He's on a business trip. Tell her she'll have to come back later."

I thought that was the end of it, but then I heard Gerald's voice again. "She says she wants specifically to talk to you. Not Mr. Roth."

That was super weird. Some part of me thought of telling him to just send her away but the bigger part was strangely curious as to what she might say. Like I was about to be a part of a big confrontation in one of my favorite reality TV shows.

"Tell her I'll be right down."

I got back on my phone and told the girls what was happening and promised to call them after I talked to her. Shay offered to drive over and be my backup, but I told them it was unnecessary.

My heart beat a bit faster as I stepped off the elevator and into the lobby. Oksana was waiting there, looking gorgeous as ever, her arms crossed and her foot tapping. She had on a red leather jacket that my aunt would have loved. She was also smoking, even though I overheard Gerald telling her this was a nonsmoking building and to get rid of her cigarette.

When I got closer she finally did as she was asked, and put the cigarette out under her high heel.

"That day, in the sushi restaurant?" she said when I got close enough. "I knew you were there. I wanted you to see me kissing Ivan. I wanted you to tell Tyler so that he would be jealous."

Um, okay. Had she really stopped by to tell me that? *Merry Christmas, I know you saw me making out with somebody else and I wanted you to pass that information along?*

"I told him. He wasn't upset."

My response seemed to infuriate her. "I also know that you are in love with him," she continued, and I hoped I didn't look as shocked as

I felt. Was I that bad at hiding it? Had Tyler known all along? Was that what he wanted to talk to me about? "I could see it from the first time we met. It was pathetic. You are nothing but his maid."

"Roommaid, thank you very much!" As comebacks went, it wasn't great. I was sure to come up with a better one at around one o'clock in the morning when I replayed this incident for the hundredth time in my head. "And you came here just to insult me? I already have a mom for that. So I'll be going."

She reached out, grabbing my arm. "You do not know him. Not the way that I know him. He does not care about women. He uses them and moves on. You will be just another broken heart in a long line of broken hearts."

Was this sour grapes or was she trying to get in my head? Because if her goal was the second one, it was working a little. "That doesn't sound like Tyler to me."

"It is Tyler. He doesn't make commitments. You may think he is the hero, but he is not. He will do whatever he has to do to get what he wants. He is not the good guy. He is ambitious and can be ruthless."

I finally jerked my arm away, not wanting to hear any more. I had lived with Tyler, eaten dinner with him, gone out to restaurants and events with him, watched television with him, shared a dog with him, and slept across the hall from him. I'd kissed him and listened when he said he wanted to be with me. I felt like I knew him pretty well. I knew him well enough to be in love with him.

"I'm not going to listen to this," I told her. "You can see yourself out. I won't be coming down here to talk to you again."

She was shouting at me in what I assumed was Russian as I left the lobby. I wasn't going to let Oksana ruin what I knew to be true about Tyler. Although, a voice in my head whispered that maybe what she'd said had merit. Why else would she bother coming over here just to talk to me? Maybe she really had been trying to warn me.

Or had Tyler hurt her when she ended things and now she was lashing out? Trying to hurt and confuse me, someone who was, as far as she knew, his friend and roommate?

I couldn't see her angle or why she had made this kind of effort. It wasn't like Tyler was going to get back together with her after he heard what she'd said. So I had to assume that this was a mission sent solely to destroy me and the feelings I had for him.

Maybe I should have told her she'd failed.

I didn't believe he was capable of being a bad guy. I'd seen too much kindness and goodness in him. But the commitment thing? If that was her main hang-up? That could very well be true. Given his financial situation, maybe it was easier for him not to be serious with anyone because of how much he took care of his mother.

Would I be okay with that? But, how could our relationship not be committed and more serious if I was living in the same apartment with him? That could be a problem, too. We would be starting out from a more serious place.

When I got back up to my apartment, my phone was ringing. I'd left it on the counter when I went downstairs.

At first I assumed that it was Shay or Delia calling, trying to see what had happened with Oksana.

It was my oldest sister. I quickly answered.

"Hi, Violet. What's going on?" I wasn't going to assume that she needed anything. Maybe this was just a sisterly call and she was checking on my well-being.

That hope was dashed a second later when she said, "You know that favor you owe me? I'm cashing it in. I need you to come to Mom and Daddy's Christmas party tonight."

CHAPTER TWENTY-FIVE

"What?" I asked. This was more than a little alarming. It was also the very last thing I'd expected her to ask for. Come to my parents' annual, as they called it, Christmas Eve Eve party? They didn't have it on Christmas Eve because they were worried that if they did, people wouldn't come. That they would want to do silly things, like spend the evening with their families. So it was always the day before Christmas Eve and for many members of Houston society it was a tradition kept like any other Christmas tradition.

The party was an event for their company, family, and friends to show off their wealth and hopefully generate some goodwill by stuffing people with alcohol and food. It was the last place I wanted to be, especially since I knew Brad and his family would be there. Was this another lame attempt on my mother's part to get me to reconcile with him?

"Why do you need me to go?" I did consider the fact that she might just be lying to me if our mom was manipulating her.

She let out a big breath. "Because I'm going to tell our parents that I'm not marrying Howard and that I'm in love with Santiago."

My head jerked back, almost as if she'd been able to smack me through her phone. "You're going to what? Do you want to die just before Christmas?" Or possibly send my parents to the hospital after they had dual heart attacks?

"It's time. I have to tell them before things go any further. I know Howard's planning on proposing tonight. Mother's going to make a big show out of it. I have to stop it, and I need you there with me. If you want to be."

"Of course I will be! Whatever you need. Only, I don't have a dress to wear." This event was always black tie.

"I can send over one of your dresses from your room. Or I could get one of my personal shoppers to pull some gowns for you and send them over."

The idea of a new dress sounded intriguing, and would technically be no cost to me (since I knew Violet would cover it), but I wanted to stop being indebted to people. I couldn't claim to be standing on my own two feet if my sister was buying me ball gowns.

"Maybe the dark-green velvet that we got in Milan two years ago?" I asked. "That would work for a holiday party. And I'll borrow some jewelry if you have some extras lying around."

"Done!" Violet said, and I could hear real happiness in her voice. "I can't believe I'm doing this!"

"I can't believe you're doing it, either. Look at you being a rebel. I'm proud of you."

"Thanks. I'll see you tonight."

I hung up and then called Shay to let her know what had happened with Oksana and where I would be for the rest of the evening.

"Call me when it's over. I would offer to go with you, but I don't want to. Even though the temptation of observing the apex predator in her natural habitat is intriguing. So I'm going to need a full reporting of how things go with your family," she said. "I'll wait up. And good luck!"

My next call was to our dog walker, asking her if she'd come by tonight and dog sit. She said she'd be happy to do it. I knew that was overkill, that Pigeon would be okay, but I hated the idea of leaving her alone while I went to this thing. Especially because I didn't know how long I'd be gone. Would Violet tell them right away? Or would she wait a few hours? Figuring it might take her some time to screw up her courage, I decided to make sure that a recovering Pigeon was looked after.

I texted Tyler.

> I have a last minute family thing tonight. I got Kailen to come over and watch Pigeon. She's doing really well!

He responded:

> Okay. I'm about to fly back to Texas, have some work stuff when I get home. I'll be home late. Is it okay if we talk then?

With my heart in my throat, I messaged him back:

> Yes.

My dress arrived a couple of hours later, and Violet had included a pair of black high heels to wear with it, along with diamond earrings the size of small ice cubes and a diamond choker that I thought belonged to my grandmother. This wasn't jewelry I'd ever had access to before, just Violet and my mother (something Vanessa complained about endlessly, but things tended to go missing after she wore them). I figured this was probably Violet's way of signaling to my parents that she had at least one person on her side.

I also made a mental note to return them before I left for the evening so that I wouldn't be accused of stealing them.

A few hours later, as I got ready, it felt like I was putting on actual armor, readying myself to go into battle. I wasn't getting dressed up because of their expectations; I was doing it for me and Violet. I needed to know that what I was wearing would be flawless.

Then everything seemed to be happening at once. The dog sitter arrived and then Tyler texted me he was in Houston heading in to work, saying he'd missed me and was counting down the minutes until he could see me again, and Julio was there to pick me up. I brought Kailen up to date on Pigeon's situation, showing her where the dog food was, responded to Tyler that I was just leaving and would be back in a few hours, saying I'd missed him, too, and then went down to meet Julio.

When I got to the mansion, the doors were open as guests trickled inside. Even though I was at their house, I felt giddy and buzzed. Tyler wanted to be with me. He wanted to kiss me. Not even my mom could kill this feeling.

All the same, I was glad to be surrounded by people, as my mother would lean toward not making a scene that could embarrass her or my father.

Although it made me wonder again if Violet was somehow setting me up. If my mother wanted me here solely to show their business associates and friends a united front. We always had to appear to be one big happy family to the outside world.

There was a sign by the door welcoming everyone to the Huntington Victorian Christmas, where we would be edified and uplifted by the decorations and entertainment. I tried not to snort. Nobody was leaving this party smarter or better off. Just hungover and regretting their life decisions.

Coughlin took my coat with a nod of his head as I walked toward the ballroom.

For a second I thought I saw Frederica—there was a woman with her hair color wearing a bright-red dress going into the room. But why would she be here? Were she and my mom on speaking terms again? It was so hard to keep track of when they were friends and when they weren't.

But if Frederica was here, then that might be good for me. It took very little to make her get into a fight with my mother and all Mom's hateful energy might be focused on her sister and not on me.

When I got into the ballroom, I saw that it was my aunt. I waved to her, but she walked off in the opposite direction. As if she hadn't seen me when I knew she had.

What was that about? I thought about following her but surveyed the decor instead. There were thick garlands, the old-fashioned lampposts set up in the corners with wreaths on them, curtains of twinkling lights hanging down from the ceiling. The orchestra wore Victorian outfits, complete with bonnets and hats, and I wondered how long they'd be able to keep them on before they got too hot.

As I was looking around I saw Brad, standing with his parents. I squared my shoulders, preparing a whole speech in my mind for what I'd say when he came over. Reiterating that we were through and were never getting married.

But all he did was raise his glass to me, with one of those knowing looks on his face that made me want to punch him.

Vanessa was the person who approached me. "You have a lot of nerve showing up here."

"Violet asked me to," I told her, grabbing a flute of champagne from a passing waiter. If I was going to have to deal with my sister and my mother, I would need the liquid assist.

"Interesting."

"Whatever. Are you just here to torture me?"

"About how you were a fool to walk away from Brad and now you get to suffer our parents' wrath? I'm always happy to fill in."

I sighed. "Sounds about right. You want me to be unhappy like you, right? You don't have to be, you know. You could even run for Senate instead of your husband. We both know you'd do a much better job. It would give you something else to focus on besides me and my problems. It's pretty great when you stop letting everyone else dictate your life and you get to make your own choices."

"That's the price I pay for the life I want." She shrugged, but I could see that my words had affected her. That she was thinking about what I had said. I'd meant it—I actually thought Vanessa would be a much better politician than she would a politician's wife.

"You don't have to be married to . . ."—I almost said *an idiot* but thought better of it—"Gilbert to have the life you want."

She studied me, like I was a piece of art she was considering buying. "Remember what you said. The thing about making your own choices. And nice earrings."

What kind of weird mind manipulation was that supposed to be? I waited for her to say more, but she just gave me a catlike grin and walked away. But she didn't go far.

I was thinking about demanding that she explain herself but Violet found me first. She grabbed me by the arm and pulled me away from the crowd of people to my left.

When she was certain we were far enough from everybody else, she whispered, "I can't do it. I can't tell them."

"You can. I'm here to help you and support you."

She shook her head, and I could see the tears in her eyes. "No. I thought it would be easier during the party with all these people here. That they couldn't make a scene. But . . . what if they do? What if they fire me? Right here, right now? In front of everyone?"

I grabbed her hands. "We already know what you'll do. You will find a new job. And I'm proof that you can survive without them."

"Are you?"

My mother.

Turning around, I noted that she had on a pink Chanel gown covered in crystals that resembled tiny snowflakes. I wondered where my father was.

"Madison, we didn't know you would be here tonight." Her voice was sickly sweet sounding and I knew something bad was about to happen. That she was lying and had in fact known I would be at the party. Which meant she'd figured out a way to hurt me.

"Violet invited me." I made big eyes at Violet, hoping that maybe my sister would take the opening I'd just offered her. Instead she looked down at the floor, unwilling to make eye contact.

Then she mumbled, "Excuse me," and left me there alone with my mom.

So much for supporting each other.

"And have you had the chance to say hello to many people? Did you talk with Frederica?" my mom asked.

"I saw she was here but no, I didn't talk to her." More bizarre questions. I wondered if Violet was okay and whether I should go check on her.

"I've found her advice so sound," she said with a smile. "Haven't you?"

"What is happening right now?" This was heading into alternate dimension territory.

Vanessa had made her way over to us, and she stood next to my mother. She didn't speak and it was her silence that was most disconcerting.

My mother started to do enough talking for them both. "Did you really think you just lucked into your current life? That your uncanny 'survival' skills are what saved you? Your indomitable strength? That you've really stood on your own two feet?"

Why did her words fill me with dread? "I have stood on my own two feet. I've had to be stronger than I knew I could be. I am strong."

My mother let out a fake tinkling laugh. "Darling, how would you know? You've never been strong. You've had two moments of defiance. That's not strength. Even now you're being cared for. Spoiled."

"What . . . what do you mean?"

"Your job? Who do you think recommended that you be hired?"

Shay had put in a good word for me. As soon as I thought it, I knew that wasn't the only possibility. Given how competitive the school was, I had to admit that my mother and father would know enough influential people to pull some strings. It was a possibility I hadn't even considered.

And they obviously did know some powerful people at Millstone Academy, as evidenced by the fact that they had just tried to get me fired.

"Or what about your car? Where did you buy it? From the dealership that your aunt recommended? Your aunt, who was in need of money? Who is here tonight as my guest, as we've repaired our so-often-fractured relationship? Who would do anything for her dearest sister? And tell me, did you buy the car from the manager at a reduced price?"

"No . . ." My voice sounded shaky and I tried to shore up my reserves, but I felt sicker and sicker by the moment. "I negotiated that price. On my own."

She laughed again. "How naive."

Had they really been involved with that, too? Why? To show me that they were still in control of my life? After I thought I'd taken over the reins? I knew they wanted my gratitude. They wanted me on my knees, thanking them from the depths of my soul that they were wise enough to keep controlling my life. The job I had, the car I drove. I thought they had all been my decisions and my mother was telling me I was wrong.

My chest constricted and I found it difficult to keep sucking in air. I wasn't going to let them keep doing this to me. I'd had enough. "Look, I don't know what you're all up to but I'm not going to stand here and—"

"Here's your father. And speaking of meeting people here at the party, you absolutely must meet his guest. One of the up-and-coming stars at Weston Wilshire. Madison, I believe you know Tyler Roth?"

CHAPTER TWENTY-SIX

I couldn't process what was happening. My dad was there, in a tux.

And so was Tyler.

They were together. And Tyler worked for my father's company? Why hadn't he told me? An unsteady pulse started throbbing against my right temple.

"What's going on?" I asked.

"Madison?" Tyler sounded confused. "What are you doing here?"

My mother was in her element. "And then we come to the matter of your apartment. Frederica was more than happy to show you the worst possible places to stay so that when an opportunity became available with one of our most valued employees, well, we liked the comfort of knowing that you'd be looked after."

The apartment? Pigeon?

Tyler?

They'd had a hand in all that? Was I actually in control of any part of my life? I'd walked into all their traps, trusting and unknowing.

Naive, as my mother had said. She had a cold, calculating grin on her face. Like a viper who'd been lying in wait for the perfect time to strike.

And she'd found it.

But Tyler? How could he have agreed to be part of this? My heart wrenched painfully.

"Why?" I asked him.

He opened his mouth to speak, but my mother was faster. "Why else? For the promotion we gave him."

A ringing started in my ears as blood rushed into my heart, making it beat faster and faster until I felt like my chest was going to explode. All that time, when I was trusting him and trying to respect him and his rules and be his friend, all that time he'd been deceiving me?

For that stupid promotion?

That he had lied to me, tricked me, was bad enough. That he'd made me think he might have feelings for me and wanted us to be in a relationship was terrible. But that he'd allied himself with my mother?

That was a betrayal I would never be able to get over.

She'd won. My mother had promised to make me regret my choices, and she had. She had ruined everything in my life that meant anything to me.

It was all lies.

I grabbed my skirts and I ran. I heard Tyler calling my name, but I ignored him. I had to get out. Get away from all the people in this room who thought they knew better than me. That I was too stupid to make my own decisions. That they needed to be in control of me, watching over me, deciding how I spent my time and who with.

He caught up to me in the front hall, reaching for my wrist. "Madison, wait. I didn't know the Huntingtons were your parents."

I didn't know whether to laugh or cry. "It's okay. You can stop lying to me now. I know everything."

"I'm telling you, it's the truth. None of what she told you back there is real."

"Which part? That my desperate aunt arranged all this for money? Tricking me by taking me to horrible apartments I couldn't bear to live in so that your place would seem like paradise? Or that you were willing to put me up in your place for free so that you could get your precious promotion? Did you have a good laugh with my mother over making me clean when I had no idea what I was doing? Was pretending to want me and kissing me part of the deal, too? So you could make sure I wouldn't move out?"

"No! I kissed you . . . because . . ." He ran his fingers through his hair, showing me his frustration. "Because I was falling in love with you. I'm in love with you. And I shouldn't have kissed you, because you had a boyfriend that you've been with for eight years. The first time the two of you had just broken up and I was such a hypocrite to make a move, especially after I instituted that stupid rule that we couldn't be together."

My breaking heart wanted to mend, to rejoice that he loved me, that he had been trying to be a gentleman and not make a move on someone he thought was vulnerable. Problem was, I didn't believe him. I was so truly sick of being lied to and manipulated and, seriously, Tyler would choose this very moment to confess his undying love? "Did my dad put you up to that part? The rule? Because that sounds like him."

"How could you think me capable of any of this?"

Now it was Oksana's words that filled my head. That Tyler was ruthless and ambitious. That he wasn't the good guy or the hero of my story. That I knew if this was Brad who'd been caught in the lie, he'd be doing the same exact things Tyler was trying to do right now. Distract me with protests of love. Claim he hadn't known what was happening. Deny everything he'd done.

"Look." Now he sounded desperate. "I told you about my promotion. From the beginning. We celebrated it. Why would I do that if I'd gotten it in exchange for hurting you? If I were trying to trick you, I wouldn't have said a word about it."

How did he expect me to believe that? How was I supposed to see him as anything but another lackey willing to do anything my parents wanted in order to achieve his goals? "Or you did that to throw me off the scent. How did you never tell me where you worked?"

"It wasn't intentional! Sometimes those things don't come up. Like you never once said who your parents were. You never said their names."

Was that true? I couldn't remember. "You know my last name!"

"You aren't the only family named Huntington!" His voice softened. "I didn't make the connection. You're just Madison to me. My Madison."

Again I felt my weak heart waver as my breath caught, but I wasn't going to be taken in. Not again.

As if he sensed my resolve slipping, he said, "I should have told you that I loved you when I first realized it."

Was this part of the plan? Where he'd only meant to lie to me about living in his apartment but, whoops, accidentally fell for me? Which, again, would be to his benefit?

I could only imagine how much bigger and better his career would be if he were with me. Because that's how things worked in my family. If Violet ever did tell my parents about her personal trainer, Tyler might just end up the new Weston Wilshire CEO.

Or he would if I were by his side. Coughlin came to the front, carrying my coat. Tyler reached out, as if he wanted to help me, but I backed up. I didn't want him to touch me.

I didn't want him near me.

"I don't believe you," I told him. "But if you do care about me at all, don't follow me or try to contact me."

My lungs started to constrict as I put on my coat and stepped outside. Hot, unshed tears blinded my vision but somehow I found Julio and asked him to drive me to Shay's apartment, giving him the address. I rolled up the dividing window between the driver's seat and the back. I needed the privacy.

When we pulled away from the house it was then that I finally allowed the sobs to break free and shake my entire frame. I cried so hard I worried I might vomit.

My mother had ruined everything. Tainted every memory I had of the things I'd accomplished.

And all my memories of Tyler.

The car dealership? That was where our friendship had started. Had my mother forced him to go with me?

I ran through all my interactions with Tyler in my mind, wondering what I'd missed. The signs that he was my parents' employee this entire time. Were they all laughing at me? At how easily they'd continued to manipulate and control my life without me even knowing it?

Julio got me to Shay's and I somehow managed to climb the four flights of stairs to her apartment. I knocked on her door, hoping she was still up. I was about to call her when the door opened and she took in my mascara-stained appearance.

"What happened?"

She led me over to the couch and had me sit down. I started crying all over again and it took a while before I could stop and actually speak. I told her everything that had gone on that night, ending with Tyler's betrayal. She stayed uncharacteristically silent as she listened, periodically handing me tissues so that I could dab at my eyes and blow my nose.

"I'm going to quit the academy," I announced, unnecessarily dramatic.

"Why would you quit? You just signed a two-year contract."

"Because now that I know my parents are responsible for getting me my job, how can I stay there? They ruined it. I didn't earn it on my own."

Shay shook her head. "I recommended you, too. Maybe it was a combination of both things, or neither one. It doesn't really matter. You're the one who interviewed. You earned that job. You got a contract because you're good at what you do. Who cares how you got in the door? Now that you're here, stay and prove Ms. Gladwell was right to have faith in you."

"I guess you're going to tell me not to return my car, either."

"Well, you can't return cars. You could sell it, but you'll lose money. So I think you're stuck with it, to be honest. And again, even if your parents are the ones who put that in motion, you're the one making payments on it. It's your car. Who cares how you got it in the first place?"

"Now are you going to say the same thing about Tyler? Who cares how it started, only that we've fallen in love with each other?"

She didn't reply.

If she wasn't going to speak, I still had some more complaining to do. "I did tell you and Delia, that night at the bar that I had a type. Men who suck up to my father. The streak continues."

"Hmm," was the only sound she made in response.

"What does that mean?" I asked between sniffles, because I was starting to get annoyed.

"Nothing. I'm on your side."

Why had she felt the need to clarify that? "Which actually means you're on my side *but . . .*"

She reached over to grab my hand. "I'm on your side but what if Tyler was telling the truth? I wouldn't put it past your mom to orchestrate this whole thing and leave Tyler in the dark. I've seen her handiwork before."

Shay hadn't been there. She didn't get it. I shook my head. "I know what my mother's capable of. I also know that the things she told me were true. Why would she lie now?"

"To hurt you more? Since she was already plunging in the knife, she decided to twist it a little? Is it at all possible he didn't know?" she asked gently.

"How could he not? Wasn't it common sense?"

"That he didn't immediately link you, somebody he'd never met, to the owner of a company he worked for? Because you guys are the only people in all of Texas named Huntington?"

I was starting to get a little angry. "He knew I used to be rich and my last name."

"You were asking him to connect a lot of dots with no numbers attached to them," she said, pausing. "You were introduced to him through Frederica, who has a different last name than your parents."

"So again, we're back to I should just forgive him in case I've forgotten whether or not I specifically said my parents' or my sisters' names?"

Why did some part of me want her to say yes?

"That's not what I'm saying," she told me. "I'm saying you may not have all the facts and that I think you should find out whether or not he actually betrayed you before you write him off. Make a decision based on facts, not on feelings. And whatever you decide, I'm behind you a hundred percent."

She got up and grabbed sheets, a pillow, and a blanket for me. She also offered me some clothes to change into. I thought I wouldn't be able to fall asleep, but I passed out as soon as I lay down.

The next morning Shay woke me up with a cup of coffee.

"Good morning."

"Morning," I mumbled, reaching for the mug. It was Christmas Eve and I felt the opposite of festive.

"I'm going to my mom's today and tomorrow. You are coming with me."

No way. "I don't want to crash your family celebration again. I don't want to bring everybody down, either." When I saw that she was going to protest, I said, "To be honest, I don't really want to be around that much happiness right now. I think it would be good for me to have a break and think."

She kept telling me to come with her, and I kept declining. Eventually, when it was time for her to go, she hugged me and made me promise that I'd call her if I changed my mind.

I wouldn't.

I found an old and slightly stale box of Lucky Charms in her pantry, and it was what I had for my Christmas Eve dinner.

Thinking about Tyler was the last thing I wanted to do, but with absolute silence and nothing else to distract me, I found it difficult not to.

Was this why he pulled away after he kissed me? The night we found out Pigeon would be okay? Because he wasn't a total sociopath and felt guilty for using me to get his promotion? I remembered the night he'd gotten it, when he talked about how he'd done things he hadn't wanted to in order to get it. Did that include me?

Maybe he'd fallen for me by accident. That he'd only meant to keep me around and had caught feelings for me, despite himself. Did that change things for me?

Wasn't this very situation the "things" that we had to talk about? It was what made the most sense. That he had to confess his involvement in my mom's scheme before we could move forward.

But . . . what if Shay was right? And Tyler wasn't to blame for this? What if he'd been used by my parents just like I had?

It wasn't like I had been blameless in this mess. I'd spent a long time covering up things I didn't want him to know. Did I even have the right to be mad at him if he did lie? He'd forgiven me so easily for lying to him. Shouldn't I do the same?

At the time I'd confessed my past misdeeds, he'd said that desperation could drive people to do crazy things. Was that why he'd done it? Had desperation driven him to do something crazy?

But as I thought about it between my third and fourth bowls of cereal, and maybe I was rationalizing, the two situations felt different to me. He hadn't told me harmless white lies. He had been using me. Tricking me to get a promotion. He'd been another person in my life trying to manipulate me to get what they wanted.

I'd never meant to hurt anyone. And Tyler had set out to hurt me.

It definitely wasn't the same.

But knowing that didn't stop the hollow ache inside me that missed him.

~

Shay got back after celebrating the holidays with her family and found me pretty much the same as she'd left me. Sitting on the couch, intermittently crying, eating cereal, and watching television.

Over the next week or so she did her best to cheer me up, but I wouldn't leave the apartment. There was nothing outside worth getting dressed for. She sometimes watched TV with me; sometimes Delia came over and they were just there for me, like I needed them to be.

Each morning I woke up, I hoped things would get a little easier. But they didn't. I worried constantly about Pigeon, and I almost texted Tyler a dozen different times just to make sure she was okay. To make sure that he was okay. Even though I was furious with him, even though he'd hurt me, I missed him fiercely. Not knowing how either one of them was doing was painful. My heart literally ached for both of them.

Delia and Shay begged me to come out with them on New Year's Eve, because given how the calendar had fallen this year, in two days' time we'd be back at work. They figured it would be my last chance to celebrate and forget my troubles, but I declined. I was in no mood to party and my two best friends deserved to have a good time.

There was a knock at Shay's door just before midnight and I wondered if they were drunk and had forgotten their keys. And why they were home before the ball dropped.

I got up to answer it and was shocked by who was standing out in the hallway.

It was Violet.

CHAPTER TWENTY-SEVEN

Before I could say anything, she came into the apartment and sat down on the couch. "Do you have any idea how hard it was to find you?"

Not understanding what was going on, I shut the door and followed her to the sofa. I sat facing her. "No?"

"You haven't been answering your phone. You weren't at your apartment. You haven't been there in over a week."

"Did you talk to—" I wanted to ask her if she had spoken to Tyler and how he sounded, but I couldn't bring myself to finish the sentence.

She must have been able to interpret my meaning from my expression, because she said, "He sounds miserable."

Gulping, I nodded. I didn't know whether that information made me feel better or worse. I landed on worse. I didn't want him to be in pain. Even if I was mad at him.

"The servants love you too much. I finally had to bribe Julio to get him to tell me where you were, and that was only after I promised that I was going to help you, not hurt you."

"Help me? How?"

"Vanessa couldn't wait to fill me in on everything that happened with you at the party. First, you need to know that I had no idea what was going to happen. I really did invite you there just for my benefit.

They kept their plans from me. And I gave them a heads-up about half an hour before the party started because I was hoping that if I warned them you would be there, they wouldn't make a scene. Although Mom had on her evil grin when I told her, so I probably should have known. I'm so sorry for what happened."

That twisted part of my brain, the one always on the lookout for pain, warned me that maybe my mother had sent her. To make sure the damage was complete.

I chose to believe my sister, who had gone out of her way to find me and apologize for something she hadn't even done. "Thank you."

"Tyler had nothing to do with what Mom did."

The news shocked me, temporarily robbing me of my ability to breathe. "How could you possibly know that?"

"Bribing people is extremely effective," she said, setting her purse down on the floor. "And my first stop was Frederica. Who very quickly owned up to the fact that she'd told our parents you were looking for a place to live and about meeting Tyler at a company dinner and how he was looking for a roommate. They decided to match you two up with neither one of you being the wiser. Frederica was just your caring aunt and, as far as Tyler knew, some nice lady he'd met at a party. You know how important appearances are to Mom and Daddy. They couldn't have anyone discovering that you were living in some one-bedroom apartment on somebody's couch."

That part made sense. It would have eternally shamed them if any of their friends had found out that I'd moved into one of those terrible places my aunt had shown me. "But why would Frederica do any of this?"

"Like Mom mentioned, Frederica was low on funds, and she and our mother came up with this lovely plan, putting aside their normal hostility."

"So, for money. And to control me."

Violet shrugged. "Maybe it was some way for Mom to hold on to you. To show you that she loves you in her own bizarre way. By helping you find a place to live, a car to drive, a good job. Maybe, initially, she thought that it would make you trust her more if she could show you what a good job she'd done running your life."

My sister was far more forgiving a person than I was. That was the problem with my parents. They didn't just want my trust; they demanded it—along with total obedience. And it made it so that I didn't want to trust anybody.

Especially not the people who deserved it.

Like Violet.

Or Tyler.

And now, according to my sister, he had been nothing but trustworthy. That realization made me feel like I'd been punched in the gut, and I wanted to fall apart into a million pieces. He'd been trying to tell me the truth and I'd been ugly and dismissive.

I'd behaved like my mother.

And that made me feel like the absolute worst.

"Why would she set me up with Tyler? When she so desperately wanted me to marry Brad?"

"Oh no." Violet shook her head. "Frederica told Mom that Tyler was way out of your league and would never date you."

I didn't know how to feel about that information. "That's kind of insulting."

"She also thought it would light a fire under Brad, you living with someone so attractive. That it would motivate him to finally propose."

I couldn't help but let out a rueful laugh. "And then I screwed up all their plans by falling in love with Tyler."

She reached for my hand, her eyes sympathetic. "You love him?"

Her kindness was almost my undoing. I nodded, ignoring the giant lump in my throat. "I do."

"So, Mom trying to control where you lived turned into you finding the man you love and turning away from the man she chose for you. I'm pretty sure that's the textbook definition of ironic."

I laughed again, wiping away my tears. There was still something I didn't quite understand. "Mom had no idea how I felt about Tyler. He doesn't even know. So why would she throw Tyler under the bus? How could she know that framing him would hurt me?"

"According to our aunt, who may not be the best person to rely on, she told Mom that she suspected you had a crush on Tyler. And then Mom saw you at an art exhibit and assumed you were a couple because of the way you were looking at each other. Some woman was there that you both know and spoke to you that night? I forget her name. But later on she told Mom that you and Tyler were boyfriend and girlfriend."

Mrs. Adams. She'd assumed we were together and we hadn't corrected her, and that was what she'd told my mother. I sat there in raging silence, not knowing what to do. I wanted to hit something. Or someone.

Violet added, "It sounds like Mom made an educated guess on what would hurt you most, and ended up being correct."

She'd been more than correct. She'd hit her target with a deadly accuracy. "Why didn't they actually do it?" I asked. "Bring Tyler in on it, offer him the promotion?" There were too many variables to the situation, and it would have made more sense to have him be a part of it. Because things could go haywire, like me falling for him.

"Frederica said something about how he has a reputation for being really honest and they didn't think he would do it. So they tricked him into it, too."

That made everything worse. My own parents had known that Tyler would never be involved in a situation like this, while I'd immediately decided he was guilty.

He was never going to trust me again.

"You should call him," Violet offered. I nodded, but there was no way I could do that yet. I needed to process this and figure out what to say. How I could apologize and make this up to him.

After a few seconds of us both sitting there in silence, she asked, "Is it okay that I told you?"

"Yes! I'm glad you did. I just don't know what to do next and I don't know how to stop feeling sad and angry."

Dealing with emotions had never been our family's strong suit, so it didn't surprise me that Violet's way of fixing it was to say, "I could tell you something happy. Would that help?"

"Sure."

"Not long after you left I told Mom and Daddy that I wasn't going to marry Howard and that I was in love with Santiago."

"How did they take it?"

"About as well as you'd expect," she admitted. "It certainly knocked our mother off her smug high horse."

I had to admit, that did give me a pang of satisfaction. That my mother hadn't been able to glory in my downfall for long.

She kept talking. "Daddy did fire me, but I've had four job offers in the last few days. And that's during the holidays! Santiago thinks I should wait and see what else comes in once everybody's back to work."

"He's right. And that is great news. I'm really happy for you."

"Thank you!" She was practically glowing, excited for her future with a man she loved. I deeply envied her and wondered if it was even possible for me to get that back or if I'd been so awful to him that he couldn't ever forgive me.

"But," she said, "all that work stuff is going to have to wait. Santiago wants me to fly to Puerto Rico to meet his family. I think he might be gearing up to ask me to marry him. The one problem is Daddy has all my money and I don't have access to my air miles or the private jet. I don't know what we're going to do to get there."

"Fly coach," I told her, shaking my head. She was in for a very big surprise, and she had managed to make me smile and feel slightly better. It was like the old saying—you could lead a horse to the airport, but you couldn't make her fly commercial.

We chatted for a while longer, mostly about her excitement about possibly getting engaged to Santiago. She mentioned overhearing Vanessa and Gilbert arguing about her being the one to run for senator, and I had to admit that it surprised me that she might actually do it. But I was glad because I knew it would be good for her. Then it was really, really late and Violet told me she'd call as soon as he asked, and to both of our surprise, we hugged.

"Travel safely! And good luck and a preemptive congratulations!" I said, walking her to the door. I hoped flying coach wouldn't put her off airline travel for life.

When I shut the door, I was swamped by thoughts of Tyler, thoughts I'd been able to keep at bay while my sister was there. How could I have ever doubted him? When the entire time I'd known him, he'd always been honest with me. With everyone. He never wanted to fudge or tell a half truth about anything. And I had actually believed that he'd spent all these weeks lying to me? Using me?

Now I felt incredibly dumb. Part of me wanted to run to him and beg for his forgiveness, but the other part thought I didn't deserve to just waltz back into his life and say, "Whoops, sorry, my bad." Thanks to all those dysfunctional years in my family and a lying, cheating boyfriend, I was seriously lacking in my interpersonal communication skills. I didn't know how to talk to Tyler or how to apologize. I'd accused him of something pretty awful and refused to believe him when he told me the truth.

I'd compared him in my mind to Brad, which was totally unfair.

I hadn't even given Tyler a chance. I'd just cut him out of my life. The way that my parents had cut me out of theirs.

It was wrong.

But even knowing all that, I wasn't ready to face him yet. More accurately, I wasn't really ready to face how untrusting and awful I'd been toward him.

My mother had wanted me to think the worst of him and I had.

That was not the person I wanted to be.

Regardless of who I wanted to be, I currently felt a bit like a hermit/coward. Shay had told me that I could stay as long as I needed to, but I didn't want to go back to staying on her couch. I needed to move forward. I didn't tell her what Violet had told me, because I had to work through it and figure out what my next step would be. I would have to start looking for my own apartment, now that I knew my aunt had deliberately steered me away from decent places that I could have afforded. I decided my next step was to go back to the apartment and get my clothes and my car and my toiletries.

So I waited until the day after New Year's Day, knowing that Tyler would be at work, and went at noon to his place.

Gerald didn't stop me, just waved, and I felt a sigh of relief that he hadn't been told not to let me up.

When I got upstairs, Pigeon was waiting for me, her tail happily wagging. Seeing her broke my heart all over again. I was so happy that she was okay and back to her old self, but I was going to be leaving her once more. I crouched down to pet her and tell her what a good girl she was.

"Madison?"

I straightened back up. Tyler was here. Surprised as I was, I drank in the sight of him. His hair was ruffled and there were dark bags under his eyes. As if he hadn't slept.

He was still the most beautiful thing I'd ever seen.

"I'm sorry." My words were little more than a whisper. "I thought you'd be at work."

He walked into the living room, his arms folded, and went to stand by the couch. "That would be a little strange, considering I don't have a job anymore."

"What? You quit?"

"Right after you walked away at the party. No matter what your mother says, I didn't know. I never would have been involved with some scheme like that. I never would have hurt you that way. And for them to lie and claim that I was? That's not someone I want to be working for. So I quit."

He'd quit his job for me. My throat started to ache as my eyes welled up. "But what about your mom?" He needed that job to take care of her.

"I called her and told her things had to change. That I wasn't going to be in investments any longer and was going to one of those boot camps for coding and, as a result, would be making a fraction of what I'm making now. Her lifestyle's going to have to change pretty radically. She wasn't happy about it."

"That's not hard to imagine." I was so proud of him for standing up for himself, for following his dreams. For not letting his mother take advantage of him any longer.

We stood there, neither one of us sure what to say. I pointed at the Christmas tree. "You didn't open your presents."

"It wasn't Christmas without you." He said it in a way that tore my heart up all over again. "Do you want to open them now?"

"Okay."

Not sure where this was going or what I should be doing, I sat on the floor next to the tree. He sat with me and Pigeon came to settle herself between us. "This is the one I got for Pigeon." I handed it to him.

He showed it to her, but she yawned her disinterest. So he opened it, carefully, as if he didn't want to rip it. "A pigeon?" he asked in delight.

"A girly pink pigeon. With a bow. I thought she might like it."

Tyler handed it to her and she put it between her paws, laying her head on top of it. "I'll take that as a yes," he said.

I handed him the photo book next. He opened it and looked at the title. It was the same hashtag he used in his Instagram posts, #ohtheplacesyoullgo. He gave me a look of confusion as he began to turn pages. He laughed when he saw the pictures, flipping through each carefully until he got to the final one. He grinned with delight when he saw the Pokémon-filled one.

"I thought when you finally get to take Pigeon to all these places, you might like to catch some Pokémon while you're there," I said when he stayed silent.

He nodded, clearing his throat. "I love it."

It was so close to *I love you* that for a second I couldn't breathe. I forced myself to start sucking in oxygen and handed him the envelope. When he pulled out the check, he furrowed his eyebrows at me. "What's this?"

"It was what I was able to save up this month thanks to your budgeting advice. I wanted to start paying rent."

"Does that mean—" Then he shook his head, as if he'd caught himself before he could say more. Instead he picked up the lighter package and handed it to me. "Here."

I opened it up and it was a purple T-shirt that said Team Tyson on it. "Thank you?"

He let out a chuckle, understanding that I didn't get it. "When we put up the tree, we decided we made a great team? *Tyson* is our names put together. Tyler and Madison."

Oh. That sent little pink arrows into my heart. It was both thoughtful and adorable. "Thank you."

Then he handed me the heavier package, and after I tore off the paper, I found a label maker. Just like the one Delia had. The one I'd offhandedly mentioned wanting. I never would have thought he'd even noticed, let alone made some mental note and then bought me one. "I love it. I can't believe you remembered."

"Of course I did. You're important to me. You, not your family. I don't care who your parents are. I hope you know that."

"I do. My mom, she's vicious, you know? She knew exactly what to say and do to get me to doubt you. And I did. And I'm so sorry for that."

He reached out and grabbed my hands and I nearly cried out from how wonderful it felt to be touching him again.

I wanted him to have the full picture of where I'd been coming from. "Not that it's an excuse, but I had also talked to Oksana that morning."

"Oksana?"

I nodded. "She stopped by specifically to see me. She said all these terrible things about you. That you weren't a good guy and were ruthless and ambitious, and it stuck in my head."

"So when your mother told you the same thing . . ."

"It was easy to believe. And I've been lied to so many times I just couldn't bear the thought that you would lie to me, too."

"Oksana said what she did because I told her things were completely over with us and that I was starting to have feelings for someone else. It probably wasn't hard for her to fill in the blanks."

"I'm sorry. I never should have doubted you," I apologized. "Then you said we had things to talk about and my mind just went to a bad place."

He leaned his forehead against mine and I was again struck with that feeling, that relief mixed with love and the recognition that this was where I belonged. He was my home.

"Here's the thing I wanted to talk to you about. I should have been more honest with you," he said. "I wanted to tell you how much I loved coming home to you every day. That I found myself heading home early even though I should have stayed at the office. At some point you became more important to me than my job. I wanted to be with you, all the time. I couldn't admit it out loud, but I knew that I was falling for you."

"Oh." That was the absolute sweetest thing ever and I didn't know what else to say.

"Because from the very beginning you made me feel invincible. Like I could do anything I set my mind to. You believed in me in a way no one else had in a long time. I had to pretend in so many parts of my life, like I was playing some role. But I never felt that way when I was with you. I was always just me, and I loved that. And I also loved that you were bad at things like crafting and cleaning but you did them anyway and always gave it your best."

"Hey!" I protested, basking in his warm laughter as it washed over my face. He pulled back, letting me look into his gorgeous blue eyes.

"That night when I came home early and you tried to crack my skull open?" When I didn't respond, he clarified, "The first time we hugged."

Oh, I hadn't forgotten. "I remember."

"I wanted you that night." His words sent heated barbs of excitement through me. "And I felt like a hypocrite and a bad person. I had that rule, and here I was, ready to throw it aside without even talking it over with you first. Plus, you had a boyfriend."

"No, I didn't."

"I didn't know that then. Just like the first time we kissed, I'd just found out that you'd ended things with him. I didn't kiss you to help you out. I kissed you because I had wanted to kiss you for a very long time. I felt like the biggest jerk and I was worried that I was taking advantage of you, that you might have been vulnerable given that you'd just gotten out of an eight-year relationship."

He'd already said as much before, but it didn't hurt to hear it again. To listen to the things he thought were important to share. "No. We'd ended a long time before that and I was totally over him."

"I didn't know that."

"You didn't ask," I reminded him.

"No, I didn't. And it was a mistake, not asking. I felt awful about making such a big deal over us staying just friends but then kissing you. The next morning you said you didn't want to date anyone, and I took that as my cue to try and move on."

"I was only saying what I thought you wanted to hear. I said I didn't want to date anyone else because I was in love with you!"

His face lit up in a goofy grin. "You love me?"

"Yes. And I have for a long time."

"You've never said it before."

"Really? Because I think about it constantly. I just really wanted to respect your boundaries because no one seemed to ever respect mine."

"I'm such an idiot," he groaned. "I never should have had that rule. We wouldn't have wasted so much time. Because since you've been gone, I've realized just how much . . . Pigeon misses you."

"Just Pidge?" I teased, loving that I could be like this with him. That we were us again.

"She won't leave your room. She needs you. I need you. I'm lost without you. I was content in my life before I met you, but I can't go back to how things used to be. There's only being with you and missing you. The only life I want is one with you in it."

"I want that, too," I said. "But I purposely came over here today, thinking you'd be gone. Because I was afraid that after what I did, what I said, things would be over and you'd never want to see me again."

"Why would you think that?" His hands tightened around mine.

"Most of the people I've loved stopped loving me after I made mistakes. And I didn't want that to happen with you, because being with you is when I feel most like me. Like I'm the person I always wanted to be. As if I get to see myself through your eyes. And you are such an amazing person and I love everything about you and I feel so lucky to get to be with you." My voice started quivering as my emotions began to overwhelm me.

"You didn't make mistakes by making the choices that you did. And it's on them for ending things, because you are one of the most lovable people I know."

"I am?"

He kissed my forehead. "You are so good and kind and smart and funny and brave and I adore you."

"Just adore?"

Taking one of my hands, he put it against his chest, over his heart. "I love you in the worst way possible. With everything that I am."

I couldn't stop my tears, but this time they were happy ones. With his free hand he reached up to wipe them away.

"You still love me even if I was maybe a little flexible with the truth in the past?"

"Madison, I don't think you understand. I know you. I know who you are and what you want and I love everything about you, good and bad. Not to mention that now I know who your parents are, the lying is understandable, given that you didn't have great role models."

That made me laugh, and it felt amazing to laugh again. "I will do my best to be completely honest going forward."

"Me too." He took in a deep breath. "I didn't like my life growing up, so I hid it. I got the right job, the right clothes, leased the right apartment, dated a certain type of girl. I hid behind all of it. Nobody ever got to see the real me. Until you. When I'm with you, I never feel like I'm hiding. You see me. You're the only person I've ever been able to open up to. I'm always going to be honest with you. I'm always going to love you."

His words were like sparkling fireworks setting off inside me. "And you understand that I have a lot of baggage."

"Good thing I work out," he said. He paused a beat before adding, "Because I'm strong and I can carry it—"

"Yeah, yeah, I got it." I grinned at his stupid joke and was excited to think about the fact that I was going to spend a long time grinning at dumb things he said.

"I'm going to have to get a cheaper apartment when the lease is up," he said. "Which is good, because we're only going to need one room."

"Are you asking me to move in with you?"

"What I want is for you to marry me. But we can talk about it when you're ready."

I loved him so, so, so much. I'd marry him today if he wanted. "You don't talk about it. You ask."

"I will. But for now, come here." His voice was low and rough, like he was having the same onslaught of loving feelings that I was.

He pulled me into his arms, holding me tight against his chest, and I nestled against his shoulder. I breathed the smell of him in.

I sighed. "Orb weavers."

"Did you just say *orb weavers*?" he repeated, laughter peppering his voice.

"They put out this pheromone that makes moths fly to their deaths, and Delia asked us what that scent would be for us. This, you, you're that scent. You smell like freedom. Possibilities."

"Funny," he said. "I was just thinking that you smelled like all of my tomorrows. My future. My wife."

"That's closer. Next time, make it a question."

The next time, he did.

AUTHOR'S NOTE

Thank you for reading my story! I hope you liked getting to know Tyler and Madison and enjoyed them falling in love as much as I did. If you'd like to find out when I've written something new, make sure you sign up for my newsletter at www.sariahwilson.com, where I most definitely will not spam you. (I'm happy when I send out a newsletter once a month!)

And if you feel so inclined, I'd love for you to leave a review on Amazon, on Goodreads, with your hairdresser's cousin's roommate's blog, via a skywriter, in graffiti on the side of a bookstore, on the back of your electric bill, or any other place you want. I would be so grateful. Thanks!

ACKNOWLEDGMENTS

For everyone who is reading this—thank you. Thank you for your support, for your kind words, and for loving my characters as much as I do! You are the reason I get to keep putting out books.

Thank you to Alison Dasho—thank you for all the amazing opportunities and the support and for your encouragement, wisdom, and expertise. I'm so grateful that I get to work with you and the entire Montlake team. I know what a rare honor that is, and I'll never take it for granted. A special thank-you to Charlotte Herscher, who is part therapist, part friend, and all developmental editor. You always help me make my stories so much stronger, even if I may temporarily resist your suggestions. I'm still trying to track down those narcotics for next time.

Thanks to all the copy editors and proofreaders who went over this manuscript with a fine-tooth comb (including Lauren, James, and Kellie). A special thanks to Philip Pascuzzo for the totally adorable cover.

Thank you to the best agent ever, Sarah Younger of the Nancy Yost Literary Agency, for making me feel like I'm your only client, and for being my partner in making my professional dreams come true.

For my children—by the time this book comes out, two of you will be away at college, and I'm afraid it will feel like half my heart is missing.

And Kevin, for yesterday, for now, for forever.

ABOUT THE AUTHOR

Sariah Wilson has never jumped out of an airplane, has never climbed Mount Everest, and is not a former CIA operative. She has, however, been madly, passionately in love with her soul mate and is a fervent believer in happily ever afters—which is why she writes romance. She grew up in Southern California, graduated from Brigham Young University (go Cougars!) with a semi-useless degree in history, and is the oldest of nine (yes, nine) children. She currently lives with the aforementioned soul mate and their four children in Utah, along with two cats named Pixel and Callie, who do not get along. (The cats, not the children. Although the children sometimes have their issues, too.) For more information, visit her website at www.SariahWilson.com.

Made in the USA
Las Vegas, NV
28 January 2022